DANCING UNDER
THE MOON

CELIA ANDERSON

Boldwood

First published in 2016 as *Moondancing*. This edition published in Great Britain in 2025 by Boldwood Books Ltd.

Cover Design by Rachel Lawston

Cover Illustration: Rachel Lawston

A CIP catalogue record for this book is available from the British Library.

Paperback ISBN 978-1-83678-196-7

Large Print ISBN 978-1-83678-197-4

Hardback ISBN 978-1-83678-195-0

Ebook ISBN 978-1-83678-198-1

Kindle ISBN 978-1-83678-199-8

Audio CD ISBN 978-1-83678-190-5

MP3 CD ISBN 978-1-83678-191-2

Digital audio download ISBN 978-1-83678-193-6

This book is printed on certified sustainable paper. Boldwood Books is dedicated to putting sustainability at the heart of our business. For more information please visit https://www.boldwoodbooks.com/about-us/sustainability/

Boldwood Books Ltd, 23 Bowerdean Street, London, SW6 3TN

www.boldwoodbooks.com

In memory of my favourite teacher; the magnificent Mr Bunting

'But who's going to do our lunch if Mum's staying in bed?' asks Max.

'If people need stuff putting in boxes, they'll have to do it themselves for once,' says Jake through gritted teeth, as he tries to make toast, unload the dishwasher, find clean socks for Hattie's netball match and avoid the small pile of cat sick by the table leg. He sighs and mops up the squelchy mess on the floor before Theo spreads it around the kitchen with her big boots.

It's only the third day of term so the proper foolproof system for school mornings hasn't kicked in yet, and even the two kittens look offended, meowing around Theo's feet as she rifles through her school bag for her lost homework.

Jake feels as if he's dropped into some alien, much less relaxing world. His early-morning routine usually involves sitting at the kitchen table drinking strong coffee and keeping some kind of order while Molly dashes around serving up milky tea, bacon sandwiches and muesli to their four children. As she cling-films sandwiches, throws yoghurts and chocolate biscuits into plastic bags and sorts out last-minute crises, she talks him through the day ahead. She likes him to know what's going on.

Theo still hasn't found her homework. Jake and Molly's eldest daughter is reasonably chilled as a rule, but today she's in a filthy mood. Her form tutor has given a final warning that if anyone else comes to school with purple streaks in their hair, he'll make them wear his grey woolly hat to lessons. Theo's managed to cover the offending bit of her fringe with black poster paint, having run out of dye, but she knows if it rains things could go badly wrong.

Jake can hear Theo muttering as she abandons the homework search and opens a tin of food for the yowling kittens, gashing her finger in the process and bleeding all over Sam's newly made tuna sandwiches. She spits out all the rudest words she knows, and so does Sam, which makes Hattie run round the table screaming, 'He said the "F" word, Dad, and she said "Bugger"!'

Jake's patience, never his strong point, runs out. 'At your age,' he thunders, 'me and my little brother did all the chores for our mum before breakfast, went to school without moaning and then came back and did our paper-rounds. We weren't spoiled like you lot – you're all an absolute disgrace.'

Theo pulls herself up to her full five feet four inches. She hasn't been allowed to have a paper round due to Molly's fear of possible rapists and muggers on the loose. It's a peaceful village as a rule, but there's a first for everything.

'And presumably you all lived in a paper bag in the middle of the road?' she asks. Jake knows when he's beaten.

Max is the only one who's not bothered by all this. He's quietly feeding Coco Pops to the kittens, who like them much better than bloodstained Whiskas. Jake ruffles his small son's hair. It must be great being four and a half. Big School's huge fun, in Max's eyes. After only three days of it he's already settled and happy. He loves the sand pit, he's friends with everyone, and he thinks his teacher, Mrs Slater, is the funniest, loveliest person in the world. If only the other three felt the same about education.

Glancing at the kitchen clock, Jake bellows at everyone to hurry up, and runs upstairs two at a time to check on his wife. He's not surprised to find Molly still curled up under the duvet, eyes tightly shut, the window opened wide to let in the sweet morning air. Tears of self-pity and frustration are trickling into her pillow.

Jake can't ever remember Molly getting so blind drunk before, even when they were teenagers experimenting with cider from the corner shop. Tipsy, yes. Slightly merry now and again at a party, even wobbly on her feet sometimes and a bit giggly. But last night, she'd staggered in from the pub after a night out with her three best friends, cackling like a lunatic and singing something about wind beneath her wings.

What was all that about? Jake had just been building up to seeing if she was up for a bit of a cuddle when she'd lurched off down the corridor and thrown up in the bath. It was a long night. It's a wonder all four kids didn't wake up. Luckily, their huge Victorian semi is fixed up so Theo, Sam and Hattie can have the loft conversion to themselves. Max, in his box room on the first floor, is quite able to sleep through a tornado or a herd of elephants stampeding through his bedroom.

'Can I get you anything?' Jake says, loudly. Molly shakes her head without opening her eyes.

'Do you want me to phone work for you to say you won't be in, Moll?'

'No, I can't miss today. They'd kill me. It's the playgroup cake sale.'

The thought of food is clearly too much for Molly, and she flings back the duvet and hurtles into the bathroom. Jake listens to the hideous noises, rolls his eyes at his reflection in the wardrobe mirror and goes downstairs to muster the troops. The words 'only yourself to blame' roll around his head, but on reflection, he decides not to say them right now.

2

Driving along the narrow country lanes into town, Jake's anger develops into a huge black cloud of self-pity. Why did Molly have to go off the rails on a school night when they've both got a hard day at work to get through?

He sighs heavily, feeling the snatched bowl of Weetabix beginning to churn in his stomach. Being a foreman at the brewery is a steady job, even if it's not that exciting, but he needs to be alert to do it properly. It's not his dream job – not even close – but it pays the mortgage. Last night's broken sleep was as bad as the early days with teething babies. Jake doesn't need this. He loves Molly and his four kids, his home, his allotment and his prize-winning leeks, in that order, usually. He likes to cook, if somebody else has done the shopping and if he can use his home-grown vegetables.

He looks after his pride and joy carefully – an ageing Range Rover, temperamental but solid. At weekends, he gives a hand with the cleaning, if he's not at work or on the allotment. In all his thirty-nine years he's never really wanted more than a quiet life. Is he demanding? Jake thinks not, on the whole.

The September morning sunshine is breaking through the mist, but Jake's mood darkens even more as he drives along the winding lanes to Hopton. The early rays warm the freshly cut grass along the verge, the evocative smell bringing unwelcome memories of a time, years ago, when he lay in the wild meadow at the edge of the sports field, trying to persuade Molly to let him see her new bra.

'Honestly, Moll, you can't get pregnant just by taking off your PE shirt,' he'd said hopefully. Molly's aertex PE shirt was all that lay between Jake and the wonderful lace and wire construction that kept her chest in order, but there was no way she was letting him do more than stroke the bare skin of her back.

'Look, it's all right for you, no one calls *you* a slag if you let them feel your... you-know-whats...'

'But I haven't got any you-know-whats.'

'Don't be pedantic.'

'How can I be pedantic, I don't know what it means? Anyway, I only want to give them a bit of a rub – over your bra, not even under it.' He'd shuddered at the wonderful thought of actually being allowed *underneath* a girl's bra.

Jake sighs as a sharp pang of nostalgia for such simple times brings a lump to his throat. The radio plays Eva Cassidy – a heartbreaking song about leaving in autumn, leaves turning, and all manner of other sad stuff. Can the day get any worse?

Swinging round a blind bend and squelching through three steaming cow pats, he screeches to a halt, narrowly missing the little red Mini that's slewed across the road and half embedded in the hedge, with pieces of gate scattered around it.

He leaps down from his car, desperate to vent his fury on anyone who dares to stop him on a morning like this. As he shoves his way through the small huddle of onlookers, he sees the focus of their amusement. Molly's best friend Kate is standing in the middle of the lane, slim as a reed, hands on hips. Her black boots are staggeringly high, her skirt and matching jacket are figure hugging in the extreme, and her short hair is standing up on end as if she's been dragging her fingers through it angrily, which she probably has.

Jake guesses Kate's language must be verging on the obscene because even the farmer is blushing. Redheads are said to be feisty but this one is in a league of her own. The sight of Jake is all it takes to make her flip completely.

'I don't know what *you're* doing here gawping at me, Jake White, but you can do something useful for once, you great long piece of piss – tell these sexist cretins that no driver, woman or not, can avoid a herd of cows if some silly bugger leaves his gate open!'

* * *

As he drives Kate to work – her car's a total write-off, like the farm gate – Jake once again thinks wistfully of their school days when he used to help Kate to tuck her skirt in her knickers so that she could climb trees faster than his mates. Flicking him a sultry sideways glance under her lashes, she selects a poison-dart.

'Did Molly enjoy herself last night when she came out for Wednesday Wine Night with the girls, then? Home in time to get your cocoa and read you a bedtime story, was she?'

He ignores her, driving in icy silence, while a vision of Molly drinking red wine and laughing with her friends floats into his head. After a while he relents.

'So, what did you ladies get up to last night? I bet you gave

the locals something to ogle, didn't you? Were you lot drinking
at the only decent pub in the village, Kate, or don't they serve
hen parties in there? A gang of screeching women?'

She blinks, and for a second he thinks he's gone too far, but
then she grins.

'Good-looking hen parties are welcome anywhere, Jake, but
we were hardly in that sort of league; just us four and not a
cowboy hat or a fluorescent sex toy between us. I'm not a tart,
but I know how to enjoy myself, which is more than you do, you
boring old sod. When was the last time you gave your wife a
good time and took her clubbing? No, don't strain yourself
trying to remember. Rod Stewart's drawing his pension now!'

Jake frowns. He hopes that Molly hasn't told her friends
about the way he likes to entertain her with his dance moves in
the bedroom to the soundtrack of 'Do Ya Think I'm Sexy?'

'Going out isn't easy these days. Babysitters take some
arranging.'

'Not that you'd know much about sorting childcare – from
what I can see, Molly's always done the necessary grovelling to
the kids' grandparents when she needs a bit of help with the
school run and so on, hasn't she?'

'Well, I suppose so, but there'd be no need if she'd listen to
me. She still doesn't trust Sam or Theo to look after anyone but
themselves for more than half an hour at a time, but I reckon
they're big enough to cope now if we wanted to go out for a
quick pint or two. Molly likes being at home in the evenings
anyway.'

'Does she?'

'You know she does – she's a typical... what do you call
'em...? Earth mother, that's it. She's just like my own mum. My
dad always used to say, "We've never had a cross word, have we,
Daisy? We're as happy as pigs in muck, aren't we, pet?"'

'And what did your mum say to that? I always thought Daisy had a bit of spirit. Maybe she'd have liked to go out sometimes?'

Jake's shoulders slump as he gives up the struggle. Is there any point in this conversation? His dad's long dead, his mum will never talk about the past, and Molly is fast becoming a mystery to him. Kate glances across at Jake and seems to realise the battle's over.

He supposes she's disappointed; a good spat would probably have livened her day up no end. Molly's told him that Kate is always looking for excitement and diversions to keep her going through the long hours of auditing, staff tantrums and paperwork. To be honest, he knows that's true, being a recent convert to the world of Instagram and TikTok. He's found out a lot from those sites, although he's still more comfortable with his old friend Facebook. Kate seems to spend quite a bit of time updating her social media. The classy furniture store that Kate manages must be a dull place to spend the working day, even if the discount's good.

Kate starts to undo her seatbelt. 'You can drop me here if you don't mind, Jake; I'll go and see Bill at the garage about a hire car – he owes me a favour after last night!'

Giving him her best lewd wink, she swings out of the car, slamming the door behind her. Jake hates his car doors being treated with disrespect, and Kate knows that very well. As she wiggles her way down the street, her heels tap out a menacing rhythm and Jake can't help looking admiringly at the muscles rippling in her calves – that treadmill in her garage is obviously doing the trick. He wouldn't have known about that if it hadn't been for the comments on Facebook.

Kate glances back over her shoulder and grins as she sees Jake watching. He feels his face flame as he pulls away from the kerb, rubbing a hand over his eyes as he drives carefully down the High Street, past the dry cleaner, the greengrocer and the butcher's shop. Jake doesn't notice Molly's other friend Poppy waving to him as she leaves the bus stop, wrapped in her usual vast, multi-coloured collection of clothing. Poppy's expression is thoughtful as she enters the steamy Cherry Tree Café for her morning shift.

3

Kate carries on down the street, planning the day ahead. Thank God for work and social media is all she can say. She'd go insane without some sort of responsibility and focus in her life, and the online chatting is the icing on the cake when time drags.

This is a small town, with a mentality to go with it, she thinks bitterly. The vast brewery provides most of the jobs around here, and everybody knows everybody's business, or so it seems. You can't get away with much before someone starts to talk. It's a good idea to keep your head down as much as possible, but being discreet has never been Kate's strong point.

The town is fairly quiet now term's started, with just a few retired couples pottering about, heading for the Thursday market and the precinct. There are always a lot of summer visitors to the new nature reserve near Hopton. They bring their tents and caravans, and they seem to like the old-fashioned cheese shop and the canal with its visitors' moorings and the mining museum in the old Baptist chapel. The bespoke furniture shop where Kate works is the coolest place for miles –

everything else is out of the ark. She's used to the slow pace of Hopton life, but sometimes it drives her crazy.

Kate's husband Steve is a good bloke but he's so very sensible, and all he wants to do these days is coach rugby and drink real ale. The girls are growing up and they don't really need her now. Her son Mason spends all his time on his PS5 or on the football field. Kate could disappear for days on end and no one would even notice she'd gone. She often wonders if she should try it sometime.

Molly doesn't realise how lucky she is, thinks Kate. She's got that great big cosy house and all those kids who really like her and still need her there, even if she moans about them taking her for granted. She lives in the prettiest part of the village – well, come to think of it, Mayfield's all pretty now the pit's closed and they've landscaped everywhere. She gets on with her parents and her mother-in-law. And she's even got Jake too. Just because she's got curves and a cleavage and that massive tangle of dark curly hair, and she's so bloody nice, she gets it all.

Kate knows Jake can be a bit irritating, what with his temper and his leeks and everything, but he's still pretty damn fanciable with his spiky, unpredictable hair and his long gangling body. He's not changed much since school really. Last Christmas she'd almost got to kiss him under the mistletoe at the brewery Christmas party – Jake and Steve work in the same section, both foremen, but Steve usually works nights – and Jake was just standing there looking lost. There was a reasonable band playing that night, and they'd just launched into their Elton John medley.

Kate could hear the intro to 'Sacrifice' – she'd always loved the words to that one, and she started to sidle across the room. Jake obviously hadn't even noticed the mistletoe but Kate could see some of the women from the packing line nudging each other and sniggering. She was just going to slip up behind him and make a big joke of it, but grab a quick kiss at the same time, when one of them suddenly shouted, 'What's up, Boss? Waitin' for the woman of yer dreams to whisk you off yer feet?' and pointed to the huge bunch of fake greenery hanging over his head.

He'd jumped as if he'd been shot, and blushed like a twelve-year-old when he saw Kate approaching. They had grinned at each other, and all the women whooped with laughter, but then Molly had turned up to see where Jake had got to, and Steve had suddenly appeared to ask his wife to dance. Bloody hell, the first time he'd done that in ten years and it had to be at the wrong moment. Kate downed way too much vodka after that and didn't see Jake again until they met at the door. When no one was looking he pulled a tiny sprig of plastic mistletoe out of his pocket and slipped it into her hand, closing her fingers round it. The next time she saw him they were back to the usual sniping and teasing, business as usual. She's still got the mistletoe though – she keeps it in her bag in the secret side pocket.

As she nears the furniture store, Kate suddenly needs coffee very badly. She checks her watch – still twenty minutes to spare. Turning on her heel, she hurries back to the café. Poppy knows just how Kate likes her first coffee of the day; strong and black, with three sweeteners. Kate heads for the warmth of the Cherry Tree Café. This is no time for getting to work early.

Settling into a corner table, Kate gets out her phone. Poppy's busy so she's got a few minutes on her own. Checking that no one's looking, she gets the plastic mistletoe out, arranges it on the table between the shiny red salt and pepper mills, and takes a quick photo. She presses *send* and hears the satisfying little noise as the picture sets off into the ether. Let's see what ripples that sets in motion, she thinks, leaning back and reaching for the menu. This might even be a fruit compote day.

4

Molly wonders if she'll ever be the same again. This is probably the worst hangover in the history of the universe. Those painkillers were a big mistake at three o'clock this morning – she'd risked a pint of water with them and hoped it would cure her while she slept, but everything went pear-shaped after that and her stomach feels as if something has died a horrible death in it.

At four o'clock she'd decided to get up and eat something bland, thinking that if she went back to sleep afterwards, her digestive system would right itself by morning. Bad idea. Marmite on toast seemed like a good choice at the time but five minutes later it didn't look so great. That's not the worst bit though. Even more worrying is the nagging feeling of guilt. A vague memory of someone asking her if she stills sings these days, and she can remember the start of the impromptu karaoke session and finishing a spirited rendition of 'Wind Beneath My Wings' with Kate, but after that, things are a bit hazy.

She makes it to work at the playgroup, wobbling in on her bike, green in the face and with two minutes to spare. When the morning is finally over, Molly pushes her bike along the road and abandons it outside the Cherry Tree Café to drink milky coffee and to try to numb her thumping head with a handful of Poppy's homeopathic pills.

Jill and Kate are having an early lunch together and lovely, voluptuous Poppy is on her break, demolishing a huge, bacon-filled baguette. Molly groans at the sight of food. Shouldn't she be past the age of going out, getting drunk, and having hang-overs? She ought to be respectable by now, or that's what her mum says, anyway. Mum can talk – no one can shift the whisky like she can, even now she's in her seventies. Oh, bad move... mustn't think about whisky.

Although Mayfield is only a small village, Hopton is much larger. Unfortunately for Molly though, Hopton's got very few pubs that cater for anyone above the age of twenty-five and most people decide to travel the two miles to one of Mayfield's coun-try-style Olde English inns.

There's the Square and Spanner opposite Molly and Jake's house, but not many people go there because your feet stick to the carpet and they only do microwaved dinners, and then there's the Boathouse, next to the canal, where it seems Molly's incredible intake of Shiraz was noticed last night. Lots of people moor there for a night or two, and the food's brilliant. Molly remembers the celery and red pepper soup – another bad move, beads of sweat pop out on her forehead. She reaches for Poppy's glass of water and gulps half of it down quickly.

The really worrying thing is how fast news travels around here. No less than five people during the course of this morning have asked Molly if she's feeling better, fully recovered, still in good voice, ready with an act for the Christmas concert, and if she knows Mr Jennings very well?

Molly shudders as she remembers the hellish morning.

Three hours avoiding bending down is tricky when you're tying someone's laces or mopping up spilt orange juice, and it's not easy avoiding being on your own with the nosier helpers. There are three of the ladies working in the playgroup who hunt in a pack, and if they get you cornered, you're done for. They don't need thumbscrews, they just wear you down and you end up telling them everything they wanted to know and more for luck.

Finishing her last mouthful of warm bread, Poppy pats Molly's arm reassuringly. 'Stop worrying, sweetie. You haven't let rip for ages – so what if you did go a bit too far? All the endless child-rearing and riding that old bike must take it out of you. Cut yourself some slack.'

'Let rip? What do you mean, Poppy? What did I do, for goodness' sake?'

'Look, Moll – life's for living. A few drinks, a bit of a dance... where's the harm in that? You can't get a lot of fun out of cycling to work and clearing up after everybody, and you've been saying for ages you've let your music slide lately,' Kate chips in, sniffing at Poppy's choice of second course – a clotted cream scone with extra jam.

Why isn't anybody else feeling sick, thinks Molly? *They were drinking too, surely?*

'But I can't remember anything after we finished that second bottle,' she wails, 'and what's wrong with using my bike? It's the only exercise I get apart from dragging the kids down the road to school.'

Poppy pours herself another cup of tea, adds a generous couple of sugars and burps contentedly. She's never been inspired to take up cycling. Molly's tried to persuade her once or twice, but just the thought of Poppy's body in those clinging clothes always makes its owner laugh like a drain. Molly has told her time after time that she doesn't need to dress as if she's in the Tour de France, but Poppy says her curves are even curvier than Molly's and they would never tolerate such torture. She's got a point, thinks Molly. Poppy's chest alone is enough to send her over the handlebars.

Poppy says she used to be slim, but the others are a bit doubtful about that. They've all asked her to show them an old photo, but she says they all got lost because she's moved house so many times. Anyway, Poppy is beautiful, with her bright blue eyes, and that huge mop of auburn hair curling down her back. She's got soft, freckled skin, so fair that even half an hour in the sun turns her into a lobster.

Poppy pats Molly's arm again. It feels kind of patronising this morning though, not mumsy, like Molly's guessing she wants it to be. Poppy doesn't really do maternal anyway – she always seems allergic to small children, although she puts up with those belonging to her friends, and she's godmother to Molly's brood – they met her when Molly was having Sam and the friendship just went from there.

Poppy treats Molly a bit like an endangered species; a strange breed of woman who loves pregnancy and childbirth, and finger painting and bedtime stories. She says she just doesn't get it.

'By all means carry on riding your bike, love, but leave some room for other pleasures.'

'Yes, Molly,' said Jill, 'why don't you do what you've been threatening to do and join an orchestra again? You've got the clarinet or the flute you could take up – you can't have forgotten how to play? It seems a waste of all your talents somehow.'

'I wasn't thinking of those sorts of things. Drinking red wine's good for you; doesn't it stop you having heart attacks, or something?' Poppy asks vaguely. 'And eating's good for you too. Here, have a bit of baguette.'

Molly waves the bread away, feeling her stomach lurch, and Poppy sighs – she worships food; buying it, cooking it, and best of all eating it are her chief reasons for living. In fact, Molly met Poppy when they both enrolled on a French Cookery course at the local college. Molly still thought garlic purée in a tube and a few tubs of spices were all you needed to make a meal special, but the crunch came when she made an experimental quiche with a thick layer of the purée on the bottom, another layer dotted over the top, and with rather a lot of garam masala in the middle. Even Jake refused to have a second piece, and he said it was a week before any of the women would come near him at work. So when the advert appeared in the local paper, Molly knew that a cookery course was just what was needed to make her more sophisticated, and to set her up for her new life as a mum.

So, Poppy and Molly have their big love of cooking in common, but just lately Molly's not felt so much like joining in their usual orgies of shopping, slicing, frying and drinking. Poppy is disgusted. She suspects Molly's trying, furtively, to *lose weight*, which is as bad as devil worship in her book. And it's true that Molly thinks her spare tyre's hideous, but it isn't just that. These days it's hard to get in the mood for all that foodie nurturing stuff. Poppy keeps on nagging her though, and even today, with Molly in this state, she's trying to lure her friend to her flat to eat.

'Come round tonight, Moll – in fact, all of you come over, if you like? I'll make us a Thai curry, and we'll tell you what you did last night if you play your cards right!'

'Sorry; it's open evening at school. You know – they like us to meet the teachers before the kids get into too many bad habits. The others might be free?'

'I'll come,' Kate smiles and gets out her phone to tap in a reminder.

'Oh, I'm really sorry too, Poppy, but I've got my church fellowship group,' says Jill, with what sounds a lot like relief, 'and we're just getting to a really good discussion point on loving thy neighbour. I don't want to miss it because I really think that horrible old man next door has been putting bleach or creosote or something on our conifers again, and I keep having dreams where I'm chasing him with a machete.'

Although it's blindingly obvious that she is glad to be out of Poppy's post-mortem, Jill seems worried about Molly too. They've been friends since they met in the doctors' waiting room ten years previously. The conversation that day started as Molly lowered herself onto the hard plastic chair with a wince. She'd glanced at the small, pale person next to her. The woman was grinning sympathetically.

'Will there ever be a time when I can sit down without swearing, do you think?' Molly had asked.

'And will my nipples ever stop bleeding?' countered Jill, sighing.

'And will I ever quit being knackered?'

'And will my jeans ever do up?'

'And how long will this breastfeeding lark go on for – I'm dying for fizzy pop, lager and pickled onions.'

'Will my boobs ever stop squirting milk when I laugh?'

'And will I ever have sex again?'

They'd looked at each other, and said together, 'What's sex?'

When Jill gave up her job to stay at home to bring up her two boys, Molly had suggested that she might try childminding. After a shaky start involving a small, angry girl who bit anything that moved, Jill met Kate.

Kate was at the end of her tether. The local day nursery had told her that her eldest daughter, Claudie, cried so much that they couldn't cope with her, and that baby Sophie, whose nappy rash was so severe that she couldn't sleep unless rocked for hours on end, was an even bigger problem. After a week of soul searching, Kate had come to the desperate conclusion that her career would have to be put on hold and at this point had discovered that, although taking the pill, she was pregnant again. Molly had popped in unexpectedly for a cup of coffee and was horrified to see smart, well-organised Kate still in her nightie, with matted hair and a pregnancy testing kit on the table in front of her.

'Kate, is that vodka in your glass? It's only ten o'clock!' Molly had said, sniffing the inch of liquid in the tumbler.

Kate put her head down on the table in some leftover Weetabix and cried as if her heart would break. Molly hugged her, kicked a large pile of sticky baby clothing under the table and removed half a cold sausage from the chair that she was about to sit on.

'Look, nothing's as bad as that. What? Pregnant again? Ah, right... well, maybe it's time you accepted that you need to go back to work... *hang on*, Kate, I know you can't go yet. Okay, calm down now, I meant when the baby's born.' Molly picked up the screaming Sophie, began to unblock the sink with her spare hand, and told Kate about Jill.

'Honestly, she's wonderful – she loves being with children, she likes painting and making biscuits, she doesn't charge much, and you need a break.' Kate wiped her sticky face on a damp dishcloth and sniffed more hopefully.

'Would she take all three though, Moll? They are bloody horrible kids. Well, no, they're not that bad, the new one might even be a boy...'

'Kate! It's whether it's healthy that matters, not if it's a boy or girl.'

'I know, I know, it's just, I am *so bored with little frilly dresses*!'

'I'm sure she'd take them all, boys or girls. Now, give me that vodka bottle, and put the kettle on.'

Molly wrote down Jill's phone number, gave Sophie her bottle and sent whining Claudie out to the neglected garden to play with Sam, who cheered her up immediately by showing her his willy. And after several stressful months, Kate had her own little boy. Jill took care of them all.

She's like a little elf, only 5'2" tall, with pale hair in the same style that she has always worn it; looped behind her rather large ears. She wears red-rimmed glasses, and has a sort of earnest, peering look when she's talking to you, that kind of makes you want to tell her everything. She loves Patchouli oil, and dresses in long Indian cotton skirts with fringes and small bells and mirrors, or faded, patched dungarees. Her husband Roger says she's stuck in a time warp, but then, who is he to talk? He called their dog 'Mr Tambourine Man'. Jill has quite recently discovered God. Molly can tell she's worried about her – she keeps asking Molly to come to church with her – but how can she tell either Jill or God what's wrong if she doesn't know what the matter is herself?

Kate and Poppy screamed with laughter last night as Molly got drunker and wilder, but Jill was quiet. Although the rest of them shimmied with gay abandon into the car park, Molly vaguely remembers that Jill stayed behind, watching. That same expression is on her face today, come to think of it.

'How well *do* you know Robin Jennings, anyway, Molly?' she says.

Molly decides to cut her losses and go home. It'll soon be time to collect Hattie and Max from school. This day doesn't seem to be getting any better. She has a sudden desperate need to see her mum. Why can't Peggy be the sort of grandma who retires early and spends her time knitting for her grandchildren and waiting for the end of the school day so that she can pick them up, feed them nourishing soup and make cakes until their mum rolls up for a cup of tea and a scone?

She grimaces. It's a dream, that's all. She knows there's no chance of Peggy retiring. Her dad has never been the sort of man to pay into a pension fund, and the village shop that they run would soon close if her mum wasn't there to run the show. Geoff's a great dad and grandpa in lots of ways, but motivated he isn't. If he can find a way to avoid hard work, he will. It's a wonder Peggy hasn't strangled him before now but marriage is a funny thing, and Molly knows you can never see inside someone else's life. Her own is proof of that.

5

Daisy sits in her kitchen at the end of the cul-de-sac of retirement bungalows, warden controlled for extra security. She doesn't need a warden – that sounds as if she's in a mental asylum, or a prison. She's not mad, or even bad – she's Daisy White, and proud of it, loving mum of Jake and Matthew, widow of Reginald, affectionate mother-in-law of Molly, enthusiastic granny and longtime backbone of Mayfield Methodist Chapel. Her hair is as white as her name, styled into a rigid arrangement of smooth, glossy curls. A weekly visit from her hairdresser keeps it in shape, a little luxury that Daisy has allowed herself since Reginald died; what's a widow's pension for, if not to keep up appearances?

Neat, tidy and amply upholstered in her wrap-around pinafore, Daisy opens a packet of crisps and cuts a lump of the cheddar. Her Reginald would turn in his grave (or his urn, if we're being strictly accurate – he's still on the mantelpiece) if he could see her now, as she tips light ale into her glass and flings the empty bottle into the recycling box where it lands with a satisfying clunk. But why should she cook meat and two veg just for herself when this is exactly what she fancies? She leans over and puts the cheese back in the fridge. Better save some for another day.

That's the nice thing about these bungalows, you can reach everything in the kitchen as you sit at the table. Daisy can even see what's going on in the street from here. It's much better than the terraced house where she brought up her boys. Reginald would never have moved from there – he'd always said that if he left Colliery Row it would be feet first in a box – but Daisy loves it here. She thinks for a moment about her dear departed bloke. She misses him... some of the time. Some people, including their youngest son, used to say that he was a stubborn, bigoted man, but what Daisy always says is, Reginald never forgot to be kind to anyone in trouble. He was happy if he could divide his days between the allotment, his three shifts down the pit, the pub, and his family. They often didn't see Big Reg awake for days on end.

During his last illness, Reg suddenly began to talk to her, for the first time ever. He worked his way through his hopes for the boys, his misgivings about their under-ambitious Jake and his fears that Matt might be going to be 'one of them gays'. Being gay was Reginald's idea of evil. He had never trusted the influence of Jake's best friend at school.

Shaun had always been the first in the dressing-up box when he came round to play, and spent a large part of his time wearing Daisy's high heels and old feather boa, which Matt found most acceptable. Daisy had tried to reassure her husband, saying that lots of little boys liked to dress up and pretend, but his suspicions were confirmed when Shaun left school at sixteen and went to drama college, specialising in all that was camp and glittery.

Luckily for Reginald's blood pressure, Shaun moved to

Brighton, which as far as Daisy could gather was the best place for him. Reginald was convinced that being gay was catching, and would never leave Shaun alone with either Jake or Matt in case it somehow rubbed off. She wishes Shaun would just leave her boys alone. It was even worse when Matt moved to Brighton too, and Daisy knows Shaun's still close to Molly as well as her sons. At least Matt's in Portugal for a month or two now, on loan to his office over there. Maybe he'll meet a nice foreign girl and have some babies. He just needs the love of a good woman, Daisy's sure.

Reginald was also worried that God would turn him away from heaven for being a grumpy old heathen. He talked to her at last about all these things, and of his undying love for Daisy, his soulmate and the love of his life. He'd whispered, 'Daisy, love, when I first saw your blue eyes, I thought a little bit of the sky had come down into Mayfield. I've loved you since that moment, pet. Stay and hold my hand now; it won't be for much longer...'

Daisy had wanted to scream, 'Why did you have to wait so long? I've been desperate for you to tell me about your feelings ever since I married you, you stubborn devil!'

Well, she talks to him all the time now, in his little urn. The boys reckon it's weird, but she is going to sprinkle his ashes properly, one of these days. She just hasn't decided where yet. Sometimes she thinks he'd like to be in the churchyard with his mum and dad and his old mates, then sometimes she changes her mind and thinks he'd like a bit of sea air. But then he loved the allotments, and the canal, and the hill and... oh, it's just too tricky.

Now, sitting in this peaceful kitchen surrounded by blue-and-white china, the warm breeze blowing in through the open door jingling the bead curtain that Molly bought for her last

Mother's Day, Daisy is completely happy. There is nothing to do on this sunny afternoon but to potter in her tiny garden and maybe make some new curtains for the kitchen window from the blue and yellow chintz she bought in Worthingtons' sale last week.

There's no dinner and pudding to cook, no dusting or polishing to finish before teatime, nothing to do but please herself until she goes to the Ladies' group at the Chapel in Mayfield. Since she moved to Hopton, Daisy has missed her friends in the village, but Sarah Slater's always ready to give her a lift to and from Mayfield when necessary – she keeps Daisy up to speed on what's happening, who's seeing who, who's not speaking to who, and all that. And even though Daisy is twenty years the elder, Sarah never makes her feel it. She also never tells Daisy anything about Molly and Jake even though she's next door, and Daisy really respects Sarah for that. Maybe she knows the damage gossip can do. There are not many people in Mayfield who remember Sarah's husband, but Daisy does. She's not going to forget Kenneth Slater in a hurry.

She sighs happily, downs her beer, then pushes the empty glass behind a plant pot as she sees Jake's car stop outside. She takes a quick glance at the urn to see if his dad's looking as Jake slams the car door. The gate clangs and seconds later he bursts into the kitchen, taking up all the space until he folds his long body into the only other chair. Daisy stands up and goes over to put her hands on his bony shoulders. She wishes he'd eat more – there's no meat on him at all. Reading her mind, he looks up.

'Any chance of a sandwich?' he says, attempting a smile. He doesn't fool his old mum and as she looks down at her much-loved, exasperating boy, Daisy's blood runs cold. He's definitely looking old today, and his skin's got a funny, yellowy look about it. A sharp jab of panic makes her want to sit down, but she bustles round putting the kettle on and making him a cheese and pickle roll. Maybe he's ill; his dad started just the same, by looking shattered every day. Perhaps he's come to break the news to her gently.

'Not feeling very well today, my duck?'

'Oh, I'm okay, Mum.'

Daisy sees Jake trying for a reassuring grin, but his mouth doesn't cooperate, and the lopsided result convinces her that he's in the last stages of a wasting disease, and has only come round to tell her what song he wants playing at his funeral. Her mind races ahead – she hopes it's not 'My Way'. They had to have that for Reginald; bloody awful song. But what's she thinking of? How can she possibly bear it if her son is ill? Her heart will crack in two. She puts a hand up to her chest.

Seeing Daisy's horrified expression, Jake seems to realise that he'll have to do better than 'okay'. As he starts a stumbling account of the last couple of days, he hesitates so many times that Daisy finds it very difficult to decide what his problem is, but it doesn't seem to be terminal, thank the Lord. At least he's not facing 'the final curtain...' Although now she's got that stupid song running through her head, it'll be stuck there all day.

There's only one thing for it. Usually Daisy makes a point of not interfering in her children's lives, no matter what sort of mess they're getting themselves into. But this is more serious, and it seems that it's high time for Daisy to make a phone call to her daughter-in-law. Molly must be able to throw some light on Jake's funny mood, surely?

6

It seems like a lifetime since Peggy got up this morning. Her throat's as dry as the Sahara in a heatwave and her feet are aching, but lunchtime in a village shop, especially Mullholland's, is a very bad time to need a cup of tea and a breather. For the last hour there's been a constant stream of customers desperate for sandwiches, pork pie, lemonade, lager and her homemade Eccles cakes. They're an unhealthy lot round here – the wholemeal salad cobs are still virtually untouched but all the pasties have long since gone.

She peers out of the front window between the adverts for oven chips and lard. That skinny boy is still there. He's sitting on the bench on the green right outside the open door of the shop; he seems to be really enjoying his pastie, his can of Coke and the patch of warm sunshine. He gulps the last of his drink down, and burps – she hears him even through the toughened glass – then wipes his mouth on his sleeve. He hasn't gone unnoticed out there. The villagers aren't only anti-healthy food, they don't like originality either. They must be used to such sights on the TV, but the residents of Mayfield are just not used to seeing blue spiky hair and eyebrow, nose, lip and tongue studs in the flesh, and that chain from nose to ear looks... well... painful to say the least. Surely all that punk business is out of date now? He looks like some sort of refugee from the days of the Sex Pistols.

Peggy wonders if Molly knows anything about the lad. She decides to ring her daughter as soon as she gets time, whenever that might be. Molly usually has her ear to the ground when it comes to village gossip.

The boy seems quite happy just watching the steady flow of locals as they dash in and out of the shop. He has what you might call an inscrutable gaze (oh yes, Peggy Mullholland can use big words with the rest of 'em), which has unnerved some of the customers and antagonised others. He eats contentedly, slurping his second can, burping loudly again. 'Narrow-minded gits,' she mutters, standing on tiptoe to see better as another villager stops and looks at him in amazement. The boy scratches his crotch and begins to roll a tight little cigarette, wasting no precious tobacco as he brushes away his crumbs and settles himself sideways on the bench with his dirty old boots propped on the armrest. His eyes are closed now, and the shadows under them are blue-black in the bright sunlight.

Shaking herself, Peggy gets back behind the counter ready for the next onslaught, and wonders, not for the first time, where the bloody hell Geoff has gone. She's running this place on her own, most of the time. 'I'll be there in a minute, love'; 'Just popping out to water the gladioli, back in a tick'; 'Won't be a second, if I don't open this post, we might miss finding out about winning our dream holiday', etc. His whole life's a flaming dream holiday, it seems to his wife.

The dog-eared card in the window asking: 'Part-time helper wanted. Are you responsible and hard working? We need you!'

has been no help at all. The few youngsters in the village prefer to travel to Hopton for their jobs; at least there's something to do in the lunchbreak there.

These days, Peggy often finds herself feeling that there must be more to life than this. She wonders if she's really too old to start again somewhere else. They could shut the shop, sell up, buy a little bungalow like Daisy's, maybe? But what would they live on?

She still looks good – better from behind these days but not bad considering she had four babies in quick succession. Three under-fives; that was a job and a half but she loved every minute, and she never got weary in those days, or not until they lost Maria. It's impossible to forget Maria – she's right there in Peggy's heart, and that's where she belongs. But she picked herself up again, made herself carry on, and always tried to make the best of her looks. She's not very tall, but she's skinny, and strong as a pit pony and she knows she's got a great pair of legs on her, everyone says so, even now she'll never see seventy again.

Peggy's hair is scooped up on top today and even though there's plenty of grey in it, she doesn't feel old and she definitely hasn't let herself go – her earrings are gold hoops, the real deal too; she always tells Molly never to stint on the jewellery. Quality shows, not like that muck Molly wears from the market, all glitz and false glamour.

She looks around to nag at Geoff, but he's still nowhere to be seen and Peggy realises that once again he must have 'seized the moment', as he likes to put it, and sneaked out to the garden for a quick smoke and a look at his geraniums. Does she really have to do everything around here? Couldn't he even hang around long enough to get them both a sandwich and a cuppa? Nipping to the back of the shop and peering through the French windows, she catches sight of her beloved with his Panama hat tipped over his face, snoring gently on a lounger.

'How dare you?' she mutters to herself with blinding fury. 'You're a feckin' lazy old devil, sure you are.' As the red mist descends even further, Peggy grabs her bag, and heads for the front door, flipping the catch just as Alice Delaney's top-of-the-range people carrier draws to a halt outside. Peggy can't stand Alice. She'll be here performing one of her supportive drop-ins, or in other words, challenging Peggy to see if the only local shop can keep up with what the villagers really want.

'You can stuff your flaming fresh coriander, you snobby cow, so you can,' Peggy hisses, snatching her car keys from the hook and speeding out of the back door. She passes her sleeping husband and can't resist thumbing her nose, in a gesture she hasn't used since she was in the playground at school.

'See how *you* like pleasing her ladyship,' she whispers, through gritted teeth. He sleeps on... for now. Crossing herself quickly, she picks up speed; like Elvis, Peggy has left the building.

7

'Mr Jennings, Mr Jennings! Quick, Ashley's got his best marble stuck up Josh's nose again... we can see it, but we can't get it out. Eurgh, it's all slippery. It's gross.'

The village school playground is full of squealing children, milling around the boy on the floor. Rob Jennings trudges over, trying to decide which of his emergency tools is right for this job. He knows he should ring Josh's mum to take him to A&E but last time it happened, she made such a fuss about missing a really important board meeting and waiting for four hours to see a doctor that he's seriously thinking of just having a go at it himself.

It must be nearly time to blow the whistle – where's that bloody dinner lady anyway? Ma Baker's never anywhere to be seen when marbles and noses come together. She's probably round the back of the school having a crafty fag. She doesn't hold with all those NO SMOKING signs everywhere.

'It's all right, Mr Jennings, Peter's got it out with his pencil but now the rubber's gone off the end of it, and a bit of the pointy part. They've gone right in, and Josh says he's probably got lead poisoning.'

Rob begins to explain about the changes that have taken place in the manufacture of pencils since Victorian times, then gives up and heads back towards the office. Sod the board meeting – he's not risking being sued for losing his tweezers up there. He sees the dinner lady lurking in the shadows by the fence.

'Mrs B! You're in charge – it's an emergency!' he shouts, to the delight of the reception class. They all immediately become ambulances and paramedics, loudly charging round the huddled figure of Josh, who begins to howl in a big way.

In the tiny office-cum-staffroom, the only other teachers, Sarah Slater and Ffion McCarthy, are eating their sandwiches and discussing the never-ending problem of teaching too many children of too wide an age range in too small a space. Sarah teaches the entire infant group of twenty-two children from reception to year two in a leaky Portacabin with mould in the toilets. Goodness knows what will happen if she decides to take early retirement – she's the coordinator for most of the subjects and the only one who can fix the boiler.

Ffion is only twenty-six, still at the stage where she needs lots of encouragement with managing her seven- and eight-year-olds, and Rob's older ones are bursting out of their little room. Ffion looks up as Rob comes in, and waves her sandwich excitedly, dropping bits of tomato, borlotti beans and lettuce into the computer keyboard. She's very jolly, with wide blue eyes and blonde curls – the children love Ffion, and don't notice that she occasionally has terrible wind from all the beans.

'Er... Rob, we were just thinking, what if we had a sponsored sleepover this term, for the new classroom fund? They could all bring a sleeping bag and we could have tents, and barbecue sausages, and have stories around the campfire and...'

'Mmmm, great idea, but I can't help thinking that Health and Safety will pour cold water on it – only need one stray spark and some parent will sue, you know how it is, sorry, love.'

Ffion looks crestfallen and Sarah shoots Rob a look of disapproval. She is desperate for a new classroom. The reason for the overcrowding is a good one but that doesn't really help Sarah. The school is suddenly doing well after years of stagnation, and now Rob just doesn't know where to put everybody. The previous head managed to single-handedly bring the place to its knees before he arrived. He's heard how she insisted on free movement around classrooms, the minimum of discipline, and the encouragement of 'a healthy level of noise and laughter to encourage the developing characters of our young people'.

Unfortunately, this scheme resulted in a bit too much free expression in some cases, culminating in a rather nasty court case. The parents of the children in question were eventually persuaded to withdraw charges of assault, and the windows were soon repaired, but the final nail was hammered into his predecessor's coffin that day. She left, in a flurry of doctor's notes and Valium, to pursue her other hobby: cross-stitch pictures of cats.

The school secretary/chief midday supervisor – the formidable Ma Baker – stayed behind so as not to let the side down, but is finding Rob's new rule heavy going. He's not very understanding when she disappears to do her shopping during the morning, or when she needs a slightly later start than usual due to her Bill's shift pattern, or when she smokes outside the boiler room, or when she frightens the reception children by taking her teeth out for a joke when they bring her the dinner register.

However often she explains that the previous head never minded, and never expected such a ridiculously early start (8.30 a.m., for heaven's sake!) she and Rob still don't see eye to eye. Rob thinks Ma B only stayed because she believes that a good secretary keeps a school going. She's right, to be honest – it's her definition of 'good' that's shaky. Also, at her age, jobs for under-qualified part-time secretaries and dinner ladies are a bit thin on the ground. It isn't even fair to say, as with Ffion, that the children love her – children instinctively pick out the adults who don't like them, and the Mayfield infants and juniors keep well out of Ma B's way if possible.

Rob takes off his glasses and rubs his tired eyes. His stomach knots as he remembers, for the umpteenth time today, the disastrous way he spent yesterday evening. Glancing out of the window as the whistle for the end of lunchtime blows, he sees Max dash into view, followed by Hattie, and he's back in his ridiculous dreamworld; a teenager again. The dream has even got a seventies backing track like one of those adverts for compilation CDs around Father's Day. At the moment, the song going round and round in his head is the really cheesy 'When Will I See You Again?' which must have been playing on the jukebox at some point last night.

He'd gone into the nicest of the village pubs on the spur of the moment, on his way back from a walk to blow the day's cobwebs away and to put off the moment when he'd have to go home to Lydia. As he'd stood at the bar, chatting to the landlord and trying to make his half of bitter last as long as possible, Rob had found himself watching the group of them – Molly and her friends. Not in a weird way, it was just that they seemed to be having so much fun.

After a bit, they started to include him in their conversation, and he'd recklessly ordered another drink for himself plus one for each of the ladies and accepted their invitation to join them. So it had seemed rude not to let Kate buy him a pint back, and the impromptu karaoke that the landlord had organised had been so funny that he'd not been able to tear himself away, even though he'd known that there would be hell to pay. And what a voice that woman's got. His phone had bleeped several times after he'd let Lydia know he'd been held up, but after the first two he'd switched it off.

Later, Molly had gone over to the jukebox and put on what she'd said was her favourite dancing song, 'Needle in a Haystack', pulling him to his feet to join her as they all whirled around the tiny dancefloor, egged on by the locals and a few fascinated visitors who'd wandered in from the canal.

The crazy dancing had eventually spun them through the open back door into the smokers' yard, and Molly's soft cloud of dark hair seemed to be sparking and fizzing as she cannoned into the wall. To Rob, it was like a scene from a romantic movie – *Brief Encounter* with extra hormones and electricity. A full moon shone down, lighting up the tiny paved area. A harvest moon, he remembered thinking, loving the way the moonlight caught the glints of dark blue in Molly's mass of black curls. The others melted away tactfully, leaving Molly and Rob staring at each other in the semi-darkness of the tiny garden. The music from the bar was still audible but the tempo had changed.

Rob held out a hand. 'Dance with me? This is a slow one – it's more my style.'

Molly hesitated for barely a second before moving into the circle of his arms. The twinkling white fairy lights strung around the garden were reflected in her eyes as she looked up at him, their bodies close now, an irresistible warmth spreading between them. Rob's left hand, seeming to move of its own accord, slid up from her waist to touch Molly's bare shoulder.

'What are you doing? Stop it immediately!' he told the hand.

Molly giggled. 'Do you always talk to parts of your body?' she'd asked.

'No,' he'd croaked. 'Or only when they seem to be out of control, anyway. Look, there they go again.'

This time he'd put both hands on her shoulders and turned her round to face him. Molly had looked back, eyes widening. Rob could see every freckle on her nose and each long black eyelash. She was wearing sparkly eyeshadow and some had landed on her cheek, making her look vulnerable, like a teenager trying too hard. She made a token effort to pull away.

'It's no use flashing those big brown eyes at me, Mr Jennings – I'm not one of your Young Mums fan club!' she grinned. 'And did you know you've got felt tip on your chin?' She licked her finger and reached out towards his face. He'd moved at the last minute and kissed her fingertip, catching hold of her hand and moving down to kiss the inside of her wrist.

If the door from the pub hadn't crashed open, letting out one of the more drunken locals, God only knows what would have happened. Rob, in the cold light of day, is relieved and frustrated in equal measures. It's definitely not part of his career plan to seduce one of the mothers in a pub yard. How could he have been so stupid? The two of them had leapt apart as if they'd been burned, which in some ways, they had. Rob is still burning. The memory of Molly's soft, scented skin is tantalising. How can you resist a woman who smells like vanilla and lemons?

* * *

At the end of the school day, as the grubby children file out of the door and burst into freedom, Rob suddenly finds it necessary to have a breath of fresh air and to walk across to... to look at the boiler house.

He checks his reflection in the glass of the office window and wonders what Molly really thinks of him in his weekday uniform of baggy linen jacket, waistcoat and slightly over-long trousers. His sandy hair's going a bit grey now but it's cut really short so you can't tell it's receding and he still feels young, especially today. He's even managed a bit of designer stubble. Some of the parents have been heard to say he looks a lot like Chris Evans.

Rob can see Molly out of the corner of his eye now; as usual, she's wearing a touch of red which makes her easy to spot. Sometimes it's only a scarf – other days she goes the whole hog in a scarlet sweater or red jeans. Is it wishful thinking or does Molly make an instinctive move in his direction? He begins to weave his way through parents and children to hover by her side. She's on the edge of a group of mums, and he blushes as he recognises a couple of the ones Molly was probably referring to when she mentioned his fan club.

'Afternoon, ladies,' he says, trying to include them all in his smile. He stuffs his hands deep in his pockets to hide the tremors of remembered lust.

A tiny dimple appears in Molly's right cheek. She takes a deep breath and looks up at him. She's quite tall, but Rob is easily 6'4" so she has to crane her neck a bit to speak to him.

'Hello, Mr Jennings, ready for the open evening tonight?'

'Ready as I'll ever be – I think the whole village will be out in force tonight!' She's so beautiful – he wants to grab her and take her away somewhere. He wonders fleetingly if she'd meet him one night. No, she wouldn't. Anyway, he can't. He must think of Lydia... bloody Lydia... bloody, bloody Lydia.

'You'll be ready for bed by the end of that lot!'

'Oh, all part of the job, Mrs White.'

How pompous can you get? That's blown it for sure. And what does she mean, ready for bed?

'Well, I'd better get these horrors home. It'll be just me tonight – Jake's on a late shift.'

'Never mind, half a cake is better than no pudding!'

What did he just say? What a prat! Is she flirting? No, she can't be. She's gone all red.

'Yes, well, see you later, Mr Jennings.'

Molly walks away – she seems to be having trouble rounding up her children, but she doesn't look back. They move in opposite directions at speed, both cannoning into other parents as they rush to escape. Rob completely forgets his earlier thoughts about looking for the strange boy that someone reported to be hanging around the village and school lately. He hurries into the office and flips through the card file with the emergency contact numbers and email addresses in it.

Five minutes later, overwhelmed with guilt at forgetting his important task so easily, he rushes back outside, but the playground is deserted, all but for a lone infant with Sarah waiting for a very late parent.

'Erm, Mrs Slater, I don't suppose you've seen anyone unfamiliar out there today, have you? A youngish teenage lad? Thin, with blue hair? Piercings?'

Sarah blinks at him, obviously thinking he's gone mad. 'Blue hair? In Mayfield?'

'I know it seems weird, but the phone call earlier definitely described him like that.'

'Has this boy been causing a problem then?'

'Well, no, I don't think so. But you know how people are around here. They get suspicious if anything unusual happens. I was just checking.'

'Right. Oh, here's your dad, Henry. Off you go.' Sarah is distracted by the new arrival and Rob, after a token scout around the premises, heads back to the office. He's got a call to make.

8

Nick, hunkered down behind the school shed, hears all this and laughs to himself. *Has this boy been causing a problem?* That's funny. Not yet, but I soon will, he thinks. Just because you notice me when I want to be seen doesn't mean I can't disappear whenever it suits me.

Nick's been watching Molly and her family for about a week now, ever since he and his brother Kris went their separate ways. He's heard quite a lot of interesting stuff just lately. He's beginning to get quite a good picture of how the land lies with Molly.

Last night, he'd been sitting under the tree near her kitchen window as Molly got ready to leave for her night out. The shouting had made him flinch – he'd thought he'd picked on a happy couple here, but there are deep waters, it seems. Nick heard the skinny geezer shouting, 'What have you done with my seed catalogue? Molly? You've thrown it out, haven't you? Oh, sod the lot of you – I'm going to the allotment...' and she yelled right back, 'That's just typical of you, Jake – running away. Well, you can't this time because you need to be here with your kids.

It's my night out with the girls. Had you forgotten?' Then she'd slammed out of the door.

The playground's quiet now. He peeps out from behind the shed to see if the coast's clear and sees Rob Jennings disappearing back inside. So that's what's going on, is it? Molly and the school's boss... hmmm. Good job he left the shop for a bit and came down here for a nose around. He'd thought Molly would be here, somehow. Mums with kids are the easiest to track; they're so predictable.

That headmaster – what a tit! He looks like he's got more charity shop gear than Nick has. And the women, flapping their stupid eyelashes and acting like he's something special. Does Molly really fancy a tosser like that? But Nick's thinking on his feet here. If she really gets off on that sort of flirting, she must be tired of her old man. And if she gets rid of him, she'll have space for a new one in her life. An older son – to keep an eye out for her, not like that Sam, who only looks after himself. Once that's sorted, maybe Kris will come back. They'll be together again at last. Twins shouldn't be apart. It hurts too much.

As he slopes off towards the village shop again, Nick kicks a stone along and thinks about families. His own parents used to do rows, big time, that is when he had the full set of parents, which wasn't for long. That's probably what drove his mum away, although his dad said it was because they were such horrible kids.

They all got farmed out after she left, with any silly bugger who'd have them, but Kris and Nick always managed to stay together. He doesn't see the others much, but twins are different. They should always look out for each other. It's weird being here without Kris but they had to split up when they dreamed up the bet. He won't be far away though – he didn't fool Nick with his, 'See you sometime.'

Nick and Kris are identical, or at least, they were once. Their mum liked David Bowie – a lot. Kris says both their faces look like Bowie's when he was being Aladdin Sane: high cheekbones, hollow eyes, spiky hair and stuff. One thing Nick does remember is that his mum had a copy of the old album with the pale-faced Bowie on the front and she used to paint a stripe down her face just like he did and dance in the garden. Well, what passed for a garden. And it was probably a streetlight that helped her to see what she was doing, come to think of it, but she always called it 'moondancing'.

His mum seemed to fall over a lot in those days – she was a lot like Bowie too, all angles and sharp edges. She said she was one of those people who bruise easily. She loved drinking red wine, and singing along to 'The Prettiest Star' and dressing up in crazy clothes. She should have been more careful. Clumsy, she was, and kind of crazy. Shelley was about nine when Dad took over looking after the family. He only managed it for three weeks before he called in Social Services. Kris and Nick were six and Oliver was just a baby. The poor little sod can't remember Mum at all, and Shelley doesn't want to.

Nick rattles the small amount of loose change in his pocket as he walks. Not much money left now. It must be time for Plan B to swing into action. Plan A's just about done. He sniffs the air. Someone's having a bonfire and the smell of the trees is all around him. It's great here. He knows they're going to like it, him and Kris. They need a proper mum of their own now. They'd be okay if they had a new mum to love them and cook for them and keep their clothes nice and stuff. People might say it's too late for all that, now they're nineteen, but Nick doesn't care what anyone else thinks. He's going to make it happen. Because, you know what? If they don't find her soon, he doesn't think either of them will make twenty, somehow.

Oh yes, things definitely need to change around here. In the meantime, he'd better hurry up and get back to the shop. He reckons someone there's going to need him very soon.

9

The trees look wonderful in their new autumn colours as Molly ambles homewards with her children, and a red-gold carpet of leaves is already forming along the path to their house. Molly loves all shades of red, but she's too preoccupied to pick up leaves or take photos today – the children kick them around automatically as they walk along, lost in their own thoughts.

Molly's trying hard to keep her mind off the recent playground encounter with Rob Jennings, but her cheeks are still glowing. Trying to distract herself, she thinks about that boy. She didn't see him at school today, but he was hanging around yesterday and she's sure he was outside her mum and dad's shop earlier. Maybe she should mention him to Rob. Her face flames again and she turns to hurry the kids up. They don't look at all happy today. Max hops on and off the pavement, humming a mournful little tune, and Hattie has a face like thunder.

They pass the old Methodist chapel with its red bricks and tall concrete steps, and Molly is suddenly reminded of her mother-in-law, Daisy. She looked a bit tired last time Molly saw her; now when could that have been? It isn't the same just talking to her on the phone and it seems ages since they sat down together for a proper natter. Must make an effort to ring or pop in, thinks Molly. She misses Daisy now she's in town. Mind you, she can't really share this current worry.

Molly smiles grimly. She can just hear herself. 'Oh, by the way, Daisy, I'm thinking of having an affair. Your son is driving me insane and the new headmaster is gorgeous. What do you think?'

She really needs someone to talk to though. Maybe Kate would listen? They've been friends since they started school but even so, Molly doesn't feel as if she knows Kate all that well. She's so prickly sometimes, and she's very anti-Jake for some reason. Molly can't think what her husband's ever done to Kate. Or maybe it's the opposite, and Kate fancies him rotten? There was the mistletoe night, after all. Jake always makes out that he finds Kate annoying but Molly's beginning to wonder if it's a case of protesting too much. Poppy would be a good one to talk to, but Molly has a feeling her advice would be just to go for it – her philosophy is along the lines of 'if it feels good, do it'.

Jill would definitely tell Molly to put Satan behind her and go forward in faith to strengthen her marriage. Those that God hath joined together, and all that. Molly sighs. Life seems to be passing her by, somehow. She likes living in Mayfield on the whole, close to the family and near her oldest friends. She gets on well with her parents, most of the time. So what's wrong with her? Why is she feeling so discontented with her lot?

She gives herself a shake and tries again to hurry the children up but as she plunges her hands into the pockets of her denim jacket to find the door key, she feels her phone vibrate. The ringtone is usually switched off because she gets so irritated with it when she's busy, but she can never quite bring herself to turn the phone off completely in case there's a major crisis; Jake

finds this habit intensely annoying, almost as if the phone was a
third party in their relationship.

Molly digs out the phone and the key at the same time and
sees she has a message. Pressing keys to view it, she's stunned to
see the terse words displayed:

> You are driving me crazy.

Her cheeks, only just back to normal, redden again as Hattie
tries to peer over her shoulder.

'Who is it, Mum? Is it Theo? Does she want some more
money again? Mum? You're not listening! Show me!'

Molly quickly thrusts the phone back into her pocket. The
number is unfamiliar, but it must be him. Now what? This game
is getting out of hand. Jake hardly ever texts her. When they got
together mobile phones weren't an option when you wanted to
chat someone up. Molly just got a silver and gold Valentine's
card with a crumpled note in it, saying:

> *Meet me behind the bike shedz on Wensday at harf 5 cuz I
> fancy you.*

It had 'Jake 4 Molly' written all over it in red biro, and
'S.W.A.L.K.' on the envelope. Molly went to the bike sheds but
he wasn't there – she was gutted. Then she saw his mates in a
huddle laughing at her and ran all the way home crying her
eyes out.

Molly heard later that Jake had found out what his mates
had done and played hell with the one who wrote the letter.
She'd been touched that he'd cared enough to do that. Afterwards he owned up that he'd just hated the thought of someone
using his name, but either way, Jake and Molly had ended up in

a really big smooch at the next disco and that was it really. He was her first proper boyfriend, even though by then she'd been sixteen.

So this is how it's done nowadays, she thinks with a shiver. It starts with a simple text. Although it's probably much more complicated than that. Molly isn't all that clear about how her older children communicate. Boy meets girl, boy WhatsApps girl, girl Snapchats boy, boy responds, end of story? They look at each other's Instagram and other profiles and connect; they're in love. Much easier than the old way. But she can't help thinking you could get yourself in too deep before you've even done the first kiss stuff. It's too easy. She could say what she likes on this little screen and get an instant answer.

All she has to do is write something light and flirty, press the button, and, hey presto, she's on the way to back-seat lust and long meaningful moments in isolated places. At least, that's how she imagines it – they could hardly meet at Molly's house and she's sure Rob's wife wouldn't leave her comfy sofa for long enough for them to borrow it.

Come to think of it, the neighbours would have a field day at the sight of Rob and Molly creeping into his select cul-de-sac carrying bottles of champagne and erotic finger food. His street is the smartest in Mayfield – all massive new executive-style dwellings with multiple en suites and triple garages. All the houses are circled round a 'village green' – manicured, with a whimsical wishing well in the centre – so none of Rob's neighbours can miss much that goes on. The rest of the village is more spread out, and mostly on one long road, but Molly's house is right opposite the least smart of the two pubs, and gets a lot of traffic past it. Also, Sarah Slater is next door, of course. If Molly was going to have an affair (which she's not, she tells herself sternly), she's in the worst possible situation to plan one.

Not that it matters, because she's definitely not going to reply to his message.

'Can I use your phone when we get home, Mum? I want to play that game Theo showed me,' says Hattie.

'Maybe, but I need it for a bit,' Molly answers hastily, trying to delete the message quickly. Her fingers fumble and she puts it back in her pocket for later.

'Hurry up, Mum, I need a wee, and it's coming!' whimpers Max, so they scurry homewards. It's never a good idea to make Max wait.

Safely home, Max and Hattie disappear into the garden with some Kit Kats and a couple of apples to keep them happy. Molly makes a very strong pot of tea and gets out the ginger nuts because her stomach suddenly feels hollow, and she urgently needs calories. At least her hangover's been driven away by all this excitement. Just at the moment when the first biscuit is mid-dunk, her tricky eldest daughter texts. She usually does this as briefly as possible, but today she has a lot to say.

10

Theo has decided to call in on her grandpa on the way home from school. She often does that, partly to get a supply of chocolate, but mainly because he's by far her favourite person. Molly filled that slot when Theo was younger, but lately her mum does Theo's head in – on and on with this continuous stream of nosy questions about school and nagging about the way she apparently doesn't pull her weight around the house or do enough homework. She doesn't seem to understand anything about her eldest daughter. What's the point of homework? Theo's leaving school as soon as she's old enough anyway. When is she supposed to see her friends if she's always doing stupid poxy homework?

Grandpa Geoff never criticises, he never complains and he thinks Theo is the most beautiful girl in the world. *He* doesn't like hard work either, and he hates to be nagged. He's really good at being somewhere else when anyone needs him to do anything, especially if it's Gran.

Theo wanders along the dusty lane, glancing into the windows of the houses as she nears the shop. She's fairly satisfied with her appearance today – the purple in her hair shows up well in the sunlight (she washed the paint out in the toilets), and her legs don't look as chunky as usual in thick black tights and biker boots, with her skirt hitched up right to the limits of stupid school uniform rules.

The boots are not strictly uniform but the bosses at school have pretty much given up on nagging about footwear these days. Parents won't buy sensible shoes if the kids refuse to wear them. Theo's thinking of having an eyebrow ring, but is it worth the grief that she'll no doubt get from her mum and dad? What about a tongue stud? No – way too basic now. Whatever she chooses, she knows there'll be trouble, and after the row last night, she feels a bit delicate. She hates it when her mum snaps at her dad and then it slides into a full-blown slanging match. They should grow up a bit. She supposes they think that she and the others can't hear them if they're all upstairs, but sound carries even in an old house.

Theo stops dead in her tracks, then hastily pulls herself together and studiously ignores the sight of the blue-haired boy on *her* bench. Flinging open the shop door, she prays for a poker face – must try to look cool. *Who the hell is that? God, he is just, just... Where's he come from?* The shop is, annoyingly, full of people.

'Hi, Grandpa,' she yells, as the bell pings cheerfully again and again. The door slams shut behind her, rattling the glass – Gran has been asking him for months to fit one of those things on the door to make it shut slowly but he hasn't quite got round to it yet.

'Hello, my little pudding,' says Grandpa, not looking at her. Something's not right. He looks ruffled... almost cross. His ginger and grey hair is all anyhow and even his eyebrows are standing on end. There's a queue of customers waiting, and some of them seem a bit impatient.

Quickly, Theo slides behind the counter and begins to serve, muttering, 'Where's Gran?' out of the side of her mouth.

Grandpa hesitates, weighing humbugs for old Mrs Lavender. When she's out of earshot, he mumbles, 'Gone.'

'Gone? Gone where? Shopping? WI?' Theo realises that Gran would never go off to do either of these things at teatime, when the shop is full of schoolchildren (who often need reminding that they should pay for their sweets) and pensioners who want to chat, and grumble about the prices the shop is charging.

'Just gone,' says Grandpa, trying to check on the three boys behind the magazine rack and simultaneously serve four giggling girls who are trying to look a lot older than they are.

'When?' Theo is beginning to feel slightly concerned. This is getting weirder by the minute.

'Well, I was just grabbing five minutes' shut eye, and I heard your gran's old Rover start up. Next thing, flaming Alice De-flaming-Laney was bashing on the door, and I had to come in and sort out some fancy fufu, or toofu stuff she'd ordered – foreign muck!'

'Vegetarian, not foreign, Grandpa.'

'Same thing. Anyway, she's gone.'

'Who, Alice?' Theo was getting confused.

'*No – your gran!*'

'Okay, Gramps, keep your hair on. I'll go and make us a nice cuppa as soon as we get rid of this lot, shall I?'

The shop is emptying now, and they sell the last dregs of the pick'n'mix to a little boy with a cold who has a large heap of pennies and shows no sign of doing anything about the state of his nose. Gran would have wiped it with one hand and helped him to count his money with the other. Grandpa, however, is getting grumpy.

Why hasn't Theo seen Grandpa in this mood before, she wonders? He's usually ready for a chat at this time of day, and he'll sit and listen to her news for ages while she puts the kettle on and makes tea and gets out the chocolate biscuits, never asking questions like Mum does, always siding with his granddaughter against the world. They both raise their eyes wearily as the door slams again, but it's only her brother Sam this time.

'What's up, folks?' he asks airily. 'Someone died?'

For the first time, Theo wonders if Gran is okay. Surely nothing bad could happen to a tough little lady who regularly wins glamorous granny competitions, and likes to indulge in hobbies such as scuba diving and line-dancing? Surely someone who says she can boogie her granddaughters under the table must be indestructible?

'Has Gran gone out?' asks Sam, puzzled. 'You two fallen out or something, Gramp?'

Could that be it? Do old people fall out? What would be the point?

'You didn't, did you, Gramp?' Theo asks incredulously. 'Where has she gone, anyway?'

But Grandpa just shrugs. 'She's been a bit fed up about having no help in the shop,' he eventually mumbles, looking at the floor.

Theo and Sam exchange glances. Neither one of them is keen on working in the shop. It's really not the sort of thing your friends should see you doing. Okay for half an hour, and to go home when you've had enough, but definitely not for a real job.

The doorbell jangles again, shattering the uncomfortable silence that has fallen, and all three jump as the strange boy with the blue hair wanders lazily through the door, blinking as his eyes struggle to adjust from the brilliance of the sunshine outside.

'Saw the notice on the door that says you need an assistant,' he says, so quietly that Theo has to lean forwards to hear him. 'I'm probably just what you need to get this place sorted. What's the pay, anyway?' He pushes his grubby hands deep into the pockets of his baggy, faded jeans, and looks Grandpa up and down.

'What? Oh, the job. I don't know... I mean I, we don't usually... erm...' stammers Grandpa with what looks like deep embarrassment.

He should just tell the boy to bugger off. Theo will if Grandpa doesn't. Or Sam will, by the look of the way her brother's squared his shoulders.

'I can add up, take away, clean the floors – anything you need, I can do it,' says the boy. 'What you gonna do if you don't get some help – your old lady's obviously done a bunk and this pair ain't gonna get their hands mucky, are they? Are you?'

He looks at Theo properly for the first time, and she blushes and begins to tidy the counter. Cheek! Who does he think he is? There's a pause, during which she just knows the bloody boy's eyes are on her red face. He's laughing at her. But, and here's another weird thing, she can smell his fear, which is strange, because he looks so cool. The silence gets more and more uncomfortable.

'Better come through to the back, lad,' says Grandpa, shrugging helplessly at them. 'The kids will hold the fort, won't you? We need some help, that's for sure – perhaps you came just at the right time, eh?'

The boy smiles – he gives a funny little old-fashioned bow to Theo, tips an imaginary hat to Sam, and saunters into the back room with Grandpa.

'Kids? He can't... we've got to stop him... he can't just...' Sam stops, winded.

But somehow, Theo has stopped being angry and has begun to feel all strange and fizzy inside, like the night before Christmas. She wrinkles her nose. The unfamiliar smell of the boy's sweat is tantalising. Something's going to happen now, she's sure of it.

11

Texting backwards and forwards with Theo soon gets way too complicated, so Molly rings her for a proper update. After ten minutes of listening to her daughter gabble, she puts the phone down and frowns. Her mum has walked out without a word, or a note, or a list of instructions for the rest of them to follow? Not Peggy, surely? Nothing like this has never happened before.

Molly's kneejerk reaction is a wave of jealousy so strong it takes her breath away. She wishes she'd thought of the idea first. She can't see why they're all panicking – Mum's probably only gone into Leicester to do a bit of window shopping. That's always been her escape when life gets her down. Funny that Dad seems worried though, and even weirder that the blue-haired boy has appeared at the shop. Molly frowns. She definitely needs to find out more about him, but for now she's got other priorities.

After half an hour upstairs, she's at last ready to go out for parents' evening. There's no trace of hangover left, but she doesn't feel like her usual self at all. In fact, what she really feels like is a tossed salad. Her lip gloss is, well... a bit too glossy really, like olive oil on fat slices of red pepper. Her hair's all light and fluffy with scrunch spray (curly endive, or maybe that frilly red lettuce?) and her freshly showered body smells of posh lemon verbena bath oil.

She's wearing her best bra, she's moisturised everywhere, her crimson silky shirt is floating nicely over the bulgy bits round her waist, and she's still got tanned legs from the summer holiday in Norfolk. She slaps some 'extra summer glow' cream on them, and looks down at her feet; sparkly sandals, with kitten heels, for God's sake. Even Molly's toenails are newly painted, gleaming like stained glass – three coats of 'Damson Dream'.

All this for a school open evening? Molly's deeply embarrassed by how keen she is to see Rob Jennings again, and to... well... kind of impress him with what he's missing. Because that's all it is. That's definitely all it is. She's only playing, there's no harm in it, and anyway, she knows that she's not the only mum to go to these lengths before a school appointment. She wonders if it's just because the school mums don't see all that many men as a rule? Most of them are either at home all day or at work with a gang of other women. They never even catch a glimpse of a fit bloke. Or maybe with Rob, it's his lovely smile and his kind brown eyes, or... maybe the way he keeps blinking through those little glasses? Or perhaps it's because he seems so tall; he towers over them all in the playground and makes them feel more feminine, maybe?

Molly tells herself she's being ridiculous now. What in heaven's name is she doing? Has she no shame? The man's married too, for pity's sake... although his wife's a right moaner by all accounts. Marriage is marriage though. She should know better. But he sent that text to Molly, not any of those skinny younger yummy mummies. She actually heard them calling themselves that last week – pathetic.

She gets her phone out of her bag where she buried it and looks at the message again, seriously tempted to reply. After a moment, on a sudden impulse, she goes over to the laptop open on the kitchen worktop and clicks to connect to Gmail. There are a few agonising seconds, during which time she manages to convince herself that there will be nothing to find, then her emails are displayed in glorious blue and white. Two new messages. Her fingers have clicked again before she's had time to get her hopes up; she reads the first one quickly.

Hi, Molly (or I suppose I should say 'Mrs White?')
Sorry about the text – I don't know what I was thinking of. Well, I do, actually, but that makes it even worse. Anyway, I know you are a happily married mum with a very busy life, and in my job, I should be pleased to see that, as it's quite unusual…
So, I won't text you again. That is, unless you want me to. I'm sending this quickly before I chicken out.
Rob Jennings
xx

The next message is much shorter:

Molly – that was totally out of order, I'm so sorry. Blame a midlife crisis, or something!
Rob x

Yes! Molly punches the air, then sits down before her legs give way completely. Her heart is pounding scarily and she's tingling all over. So she didn't imagine it – he felt the same. After a few deep breaths, she clicks on the reply button.

Hello Rob

This is all very new to me – mums of four don't normally inspire passionate texts and emails, or if they do, they probably keep it to themselves? I don't object to it at all, but of course, as you say, I'm happily married so in the words of the late, great and sadly missed George Harrison, 'Handle me with care!'

Molly x

She checks it through rapidly – spelling mistakes would never do in this situation. It must be chatty, friendly and casual. She presses send. Wow! What a mad thing to do on the verge of her forties, with huge responsibilities as a parent and as a wife, daughter, employee, member of the PTA and good Catholic girl too. Seconds later, a wave of horror washes over her – where has she sent that message? Has it gone to his school address? Or worse still, home?

Shaking so much her fingers slip off the keys, she checks and double checks. The name at the top is Rob Jennings, but it's part of the school email address. Does that mean it's private? Surely it must be – he wouldn't have risked Molly replying if it could have got into the wrong hands, or been seen by the wrong eyes. She takes a few deep breaths, swaying between scrubbing off her war paint and slapping on a bit more, but then seizes her bag and rushes out of the door. Any virtuous thoughts have gone right out of Molly's head. It's time for some fun.

'Back in a couple of hours, Sam!' she yells. 'Get the little ones in their jimmies, love, and don't forget to take the dog for a walk.'

There is no answer, but she knows the children have heard because Alexa's volume shoots up several decibels and Max and Hattie begin to play their special jumping game on the bed. *Thump, bang, pound, crash, thump.* She makes a dash for the door, just as the phone begins to ring, but decides to let one of the others answer it. She's got more important things to think about.

12

Sitting behind his mahogany desk, Rob's worked his way conscientiously if a bit mindlessly through most of the long queue of parents. His office smells of stale coffee and dust, and he'd love to be outdoors, walking up the hill to the viewpoint, where the statue of the miner makes a long shadow, and the canal winds away into the distance. But this is his penance for the text and emails. There's been no reply to either, so she must be very annoyed. What has he done? How stupid can you get?

His fingers are itching to refresh the Gmail screen just one more time – as each parent leaves, he tries to craftily click to see if there's an answer, but they follow each other so quickly that there's no opportunity at all. He can't help sighing, then he has to quickly turn the sigh into a cough as the current visitors to the tiny office look at him with disapproval. This is not officially a parents' evening – it was meant to be a showcase night for the school, and a chance to talk about plans for the coming term – but most of the mums and dads are taking the opportunity to interrogate the teaching staff, and to grumble about any area that doesn't meet their standards.

Adjectives like 'helpful, thoughtful, individual, independent and well-motivated' trip from Rob's lips, and the satisfied parents preen. Fortunately, the list of words that began 'obnoxious, irritating, violent, aggressive and disruptive' are not needed, as Sharnie and Shane's parents haven't bothered to turn up, and River and Storm's mum and dad haven't been able to be in the same building together since their vitriolic custody battle.

Rob can't resist a glance at his watch as Alice and Rupert Delaney wade through their list of questions about Quentin's performance. It has taken far too long to discuss the six-year-old twins already; Jasmine and Camilla are both unusually sensitive, apparently, and have 'so much to give'. Their parents are recommending that the development of their older children must be nurtured and informed by up-to-date literature, enabling them to release both their individual and collective potential. Rob wonders if that was from the *Guardian* Education Supplement? It sounds vaguely familiar. Quentin (a small, damp-palmed boy of five, with no friends) seems to need even more support.

'Well, this has been extremely informative – you know how we appreciate parents who work alongside us to develop and encourage young minds. I know Mrs Slater also would like the chance to chat with you both.'

Silently apologising to Sarah, Rob ushers them out of the office, slides back inside and finally manages to check his emails – at last, one new message! He reads it three times, then leaps to his feet. Bursting into the corridor, he runs slap bang into Molly who is lurking right outside the door, and seems to be fighting a serious fit of giggles.

'Well, Mrs White, please come this way.'

Oh, please come any way you like.

'Thank you, Mr Jennings, I hope I haven't kept you waiting, but I had to see Sarah, and I could hear you were busy, and...'

'No, no, that's fine. I'll just close the door so we won't be disturbed.'

Blissful thought. He wants to touch her so badly. He really mustn't. She smells wonderful.

'Erm, why are you sitting on your hands?'

'Oh, I'm sorry, it's just that these seats get uncomfortable after an hour or two.'

Doesn't she know that if he didn't sit on them, they'd start to tear off her clothes? He must look as if he's got piles.

They gaze at each other for several endless seconds.

'Please, Molly – can I email you again?' The words are out before Rob can stop them but she looks delighted.

'Well, okay then, if you're sure you want to?'

'I don't normally go in for this sort of thing, you know,' Rob mumbles. He stands up, and so does Molly. Moving clumsily round the desk, he gently pulls her towards him and kisses her. Her lips are warm and she tastes wonderful but she's rather sticky. They both pull back sharply as shouting begins outside. Oh, so River and Storm's mum and dad came after all, thinks Rob, with the small part of his brain that's still able to focus on his real world.

There's a loud crash in the corridor, and Molly blurts out, 'Look, Rob, we really can't do this – it's stupid. We're both married, there's a fight going on outside your office, and I think someone's just broken a window.'

Rob listens to the uproar outside his office and thinks it's probably time to call the police. At least he knows a good glazier, thanks to previous experience. As he reaches for the phone, Molly slips away.

13

Walking quickly down the corridor, narrowly avoiding cannoning into a couple of people who seem to be having some sort of brawl, Molly tries to stop hyperventilating. Now she's done it. That was a really, really stupid thing to do. She feels sick and dizzy and her lip gloss is probably all over her chin. But, bloody hell, what an amazing kiss.

The shivers of after-shock are still making her catch her breath. It's an effort to place one foot in front of the other at first, but as Molly gets closer and closer to home, the doubts begin to creep in. This is a crazy thing to get into. Flirting... with the married headteacher of the school where two of her children spend their days? Risking her marriage, even if Jake does seem to find her boring these days? The nearer to facing Jake she gets, the more certain Molly becomes that she can't do this. She can't deal with a future of deception, lies about where she's going, all the uncertainty. She wants to, though. Oh, how she wants to.

Molly gives up being sensible just for a moment or two and slips into a fabulous daydream. She's floating down the street on the opposite side to the village shop when she sees the blue-haired boy out of the corner of her eye, standing by the open door. He's talking to someone just inside.

She pauses, undecided. The last thing she needs now is an interrogation from her dad. She wants to be on a plane flying to Rio, with Rob next to her ordering them both a huge drink. Then they'd get a taxi to their fabulously expensive hotel, or perhaps a horse and cart to their beach-side villa, or... but she's going to have to stop and check if her mum's appeared and what that boy's doing there.

'Hi, Dad – what's the latest on Mum? Is she back and getting your dinner ready?' Molly calls.

The boy turns to face her, not quite meeting her eyes, and Molly's dad steps forward. Geoff is a handsome man. At seventy-two he's a bit younger than his feisty wife – tall and stocky, with no sign yet of his greying sandy hair getting any less curly or bountiful. His glasses have slipped down onto the end of his nose and he takes them off as he sees his daughter.

'Molly! I've been ringing you. She's still not back. Where do you think she is?'

Molly crosses the lane to join them. The boy looks at the floor.

'Hello,' she says to him, 'I don't think we've met, have we?'

'Oh, this is Nick,' says Geoff, patting the boy's shoulder, 'and he's applied for the job in the shop. With the mess I'm in at the moment, I snapped his hand off.'

'Really? You want to work in a village shop? Are you staying round here then?'

Molly tries not to make her voice sharp but the words sound as if she can't imagine why anyone would offer to do such a thing. She wants to ask her dad more about why Mum might have gone off in a temper but she's not going to air their dirty linen in front of this strange, blank-eyed individual. He must be the one who the mums have been discussing, and she's not surprised. There's something unsettling about his stillness as he considers Molly's question.

'I don't mind where I work, to be honest,' he says. 'Just glad of a job right now.'

'And Nick's going to stay in the spare room for a couple of days while he gets himself sorted,' says Geoff. 'He's even offered to cook supper for us. Well, your mum's not here, is she? And I don't know how to do it.'

Molly is lost for words. Today is going from bad to worse. The hangover, the memories of last night, the stupid, dangerous flirtation, her mum taking off without a word, and now this unknown boy walking into her dad's life. She glances at her watch, remembering that she's left Sam on his own for more than half an hour with his brother and sisters for the first time. It was either that or miss parents' evening. She'd better get back. But is her dad safe? And where the hell is Mum?

As if reading her mind, the boy smiles at her. His face is completely different when he's not looking secretive – wide blue eyes two shades lighter than his hair, cheekbones to die for and a dimple that appears unexpectedly. Oh, hang on – only one of his eyes is blue; the other's green. It gives him an elvish look somehow. He looks clean enough, even if his clothes are shabby and on the weird side.

'We'll be fine, love,' says Geoff. 'She's bound to be home soon – I'll ring you as soon as she gets in.'

'Right, well, I need to get back. Jake's still at work and Sam...'

'Loosen up, pet. Sam's a big lad. He'll have no trouble minding the nippers. Just give him a chance to grow up, eh?'

'Hmmm. I hope you're right. Yes, ring me. Don't forget.'

Molly reaches up to kiss her dad's stubbly cheek and raises a hand in farewell. The boy waves back, and before Molly is far down the road, Geoff and Nick are inside the shop. She hears the door clang but her thoughts are already flying ahead to what she'll find at home and whether Rob Jennings will be in touch again. Half of her hopes desperately that he won't. The other half feels very differently.

* * *

The phone rings just after eleven o'clock and Molly's nerves are in such a state by this time that she snatches it up and shouts, 'No, I can't, honestly, I can't!'

'Molly?' says Dad.

'Oh, sorry Dad, I thought it was... erm... Theo mucking about, or something.'

'Right, well, I was just thinking – when was the last time you saw your mum, Molly?'

'I saw her Monday lunchtime, why?'

'I was just wondering, that's all. Did she seem strange in any way on Monday?'

His voice has an anxious tone that Molly's never heard before. Geoff is normally the epitome of laid-back manhood. Molly attempts to focus properly on a subject other than herself, her annoying husband who isn't home yet and her possible future misdeeds. Light dawns. 'Is Mum still not there?'

'Bingo! I can really see why you passed all those exams now. No, of course she's not here! Why would I be ringing you at this godforsaken time if she was back? Haven't you been worried?'

'Well, of course I have.' And she has; it's just that her mind's so full of Rob that everything else is struggling to fit in. Not to mention that the kids, although perfectly behaved for Sam, have been truly horrible since she got home. 'I'm sorry, Dad, so, where is she then?'

Molly hears Geoff take another deep breath before losing his temper completely and carries on hastily, 'Oh, I see, she's missing.' She realises, belatedly, what she's just said. 'Hang on, Mum's missing?' A sound emerges from the phone that could pass for a sob. 'Dad? Are you okay?'

'No, I'm not okay actually, Molly. Your mother has disappeared without trace, I've got no idea why' – he coughs – 'and a strange boy has moved in with me.' He seems to be covering the receiver as he says, 'Sorry, Nick, not that you're strange, of course.'

'Dad, what on earth is going on? Right, tell me about this properly. I've heard it from Theo but she doesn't always get her facts straight. When did Mum go? What's happening?' Molly babbles. She can hear her voice verging on hysteria – it's been a very odd day so far.

'Oh, for goodness' sake, love, pull yourself together – let me speak to Jake, perhaps I can get some sense out of him.'

Molly looks at the clock – it's 11.15 p.m. Jake finishes work at 9.45.

'He's not here. I... I don't know where he is.'

'Oh, brilliant. Well, I'm phoning the police. Your mum's not answering her mobile and she's never been out this long or this late before without organising it days in advance. She always leaves my dinner ready. And she hasn't taken a coat. I'll call you when I've spoken to them.'

The line goes dead and Molly finally begins to wonder where her husband could be.

14

Molly goes over to peer out of the big bay window. She can see the lights on in her next-door neighbour's house – Sarah Slater usually does her marking late into the evening, and as she opens the window to lean out for a better view, Molly can just hear the sound of a Mozart piano concerto.

Jake normally wheel spins onto the drive in a shower of gravel at ten o'clock when he's on the afternoon shift, ravenously hungry and grumpy as hell. Molly's been so preoccupied with checking for non-existent emails that she hasn't given much thought to her husband. Now she really can't decide who to worry about first. Neither her mum nor Jake have ever given cause for concern like this and to give them their due, they're both painstakingly punctual.

Come to think of it, Jake and Peggy aren't the only ones acting right out of character today – Molly's dad doesn't usually ask strangers to come and live with him either. Fortunately the children are all in bed and asleep now. Molly couldn't have stood the weight of their worry too. At least puzzling and fretting about Jake and her mum's whereabouts keeps her away from the computer for a while, although the thought of Rob still makes her stomach flutter alarmingly.

She hasn't felt like this about any man for years – possibly never. Jake and Molly have known each other all their lives, so even when they first got together at the school disco, it was never this wild and exciting. They were so very young to decide on a life partner – they didn't know what we were getting into. Molly remembers not wanting anyone else to have him, but she wasn't filled with this prickly energy, as if her life is about to spin out of control.

When Geoff and his accompanying police officer arrive at the door, Molly's heart freezes and her legs suddenly refuse to move, but they have only come to add her statement to her dad's.

'When did you last see your mother? How did she seem? Was she depressed in any way?' stutters the young constable, flushing to the roots of his hair as he tries not to stare at Molly's cleavage. Pulling her dressing gown tighter, Molly tries to look as if she's in control of the situation. She longs to howl that her mother is never depressed. It is not in her nature to be anything other than efficient, cheerful, controlled and managing.

'Do you have any idea at all where your mother could have gone?' he says finally.

Glancing out of the window in what is rapidly becoming a reflex action, Molly replies that she can only suppose that her mother felt like taking a break from her responsibilities – what woman wouldn't, for heaven's sake? The silence that greets this comment drags her attention away from the dark driveway to her father's grim face.

'Let's ask Jake what he thinks, love,' he pleads, clearly desperate for some male solidarity. 'He must be back from work by now. Has he gone to bed already?'

Pulling the blanket from the sofa around her cold shoulders, Molly shakes her head.

Much later, dressed in her most enormous pyjamas, Molly hugs a hot water bottle to her chest. She can never get warm in bed without Jake. The young police officer seemed stunned that Geoff and Molly have both been careless enough to mislay a spouse. He was more interested in Peggy's disappearance, being a lone female out in the night. Jake, seemingly, must be able to care for himself. But where is he? Like Peggy, Jake isn't answering his phone. Molly has rung three of his workmates, all who say he left work at the normal time and didn't mention going for a beer or anything.

She's still holding back from ringing her mother-in-law, Daisy. It would panic her terribly to get a call at this time of night, and surely if Jake had had to go round to his mum's in an emergency he'd have got a message to her by now? After half an hour of alternately trying Jake's mobile and getting up to look out of the window, Molly rings the local hospitals. Nothing. His clothes all seem to be in the wardrobe and no cases are missing. Has he left her? Guilt washes over Molly in great, bitter waves, but how could Jake have found out about Rob? And anyway, nothing's happened. Has he left her for some other reason then?

Molly's thoughts veer back to her mum, lively, edgy, full of fun and ribald backchat. They argue more than they agree these days, but she helped Molly to juggle kids and work when the grandchildren were small, and still ran the shop and tried to get Geoff motivated to build an extension so they could add a dry cleaning business and a catering service to their thriving business. He never did it.

Molly thinks of how her dad looked tonight, and her heart aches for him. She knows he loves Peggy, but he's disappointed her so many times over the years. The shop looks seedy; it really needs a coat of paint. And he never put the double glazing in that he promised to sort out so the putty's cracking all round the edges of the windows. Mum must have felt frustrated and angry more times than everyone realised. She used to be quite house proud when her children were younger but Molly's noticed she's a lot less interested in keeping everywhere pristine now. And her parents are both getting older. They can't have much energy for major renovations these days even if her dad had the motivation.

Molly's brother and sister haven't lived around here for some time – they sensibly moved out as soon as they could. Pete said Mum never stopped nagging him and their dad to get things done and Sandy and her mum were just too alike, so they both got cross with Geoff for the same things. Molly's starting to see how Pete felt now but she knows she's the same with Sam and Theo. She just wants them to achieve something, not sit around like Dad. He's an old charmer, she knows that, but he's just so lazy; everything's done at snail's pace, if at all.

Molly's mind flits from Peggy to Jake. Has she nagged him too? *He* definitely isn't lazy. He says he appreciates what he's got, and likes a simple life, but Molly realises now that she's probably always wanted more than that. A whole lot more. Jake's a bag of pent-up energy at times. She just hasn't worked out what it is *he* wants yet.

* * *

After a long, sleepless night, during which Molly phones various surprised friends, including Shaun in Brighton and even Matt (who doesn't pick up the call) and eventually the police, who are dismissive, she acts completely out of character and goes to early Mass in Hopton. She leaves a note by Sam's pillow in case the others wake before she gets back but she knows they won't unless there's an earthquake, or a visit from outer space – and then not necessarily. Now Jake's not here, she's got no choice but to trust her firstborn. He'll not mind – Sam will be glad she's finally seeing him as grown-up enough to be in charge.

The Church of Our Lady of Perpetual Succour is at the end of the shopping precinct – new and stark, with geometric, primary-coloured stained-glass windows and an irregular red roof. Molly misses the old place, but half of it fell down some years ago during a freak storm and the other half wasn't worth saving. The statues are lovely though – Our Lady must have been keeping her eyes open that night.

Molly goes through the motions automatically, making the responses in a monotone. She normally hates to hear the regulars doing that – she can't help wondering if they ever hear the monstrous things they're promising or asking for.

Back at home, spiritually spring-cleaned, Molly finds the house in silence. Part of her had expected to see Jake's car outside and to find him in the kitchen, frying bacon and making a huge mess. Of course, he isn't. Somehow, during the night she's convinced herself that Jake's left her after hearing rumours of her infidelity (if a furtive look or two, some hot-ish emails and a delicious kiss can be described in that way).

After over twenty calls last night, Molly has had to accept that no one knows where her husband has gone. Her first thought was that Jake had somehow bumped into his best friend Shaun and gone on a bender with him, but Shaun's still living in loved-up bliss in Brighton with his lover, Simon. Shaun is the most spontaneous person Molly has ever met and she and Jake have both missed his mad phone calls at random times of day and night with invitations to go on picnics, to parties, on a coach trip to Blackpool, and so on. Even hearing his voice on the phone makes Molly feel better for a minute or two, but he has no clues to give her.

Molly has phoned her dad nearly as many times as Jake's friends too – there's still no sign of her mum. Her eyes ache from lack of sleep and too many tears, and her head is thumping alarmingly. She puts away her contact lenses, slips on an old pair of prescription glasses and quickly rings the playgroup to report another terrible migraine (that much is true anyway).

The school rush is worse than ever. The kids are easily convinced that their dad has gone into work early but all of them seem hellbent on being as awkward as possible. Molly ends up screaming at them like a fishwife, hustling Sam and Theo out of the house at the speed of light, and then bustling the little ones down the lane so fast that their feet hardly touch the ground.

She avoids the gaggle of mums at the gate, dishes out swift kisses and marches off towards home – and Jake still isn't there. Finally, she switches on the answering machine, and heads for sanity. This isn't going to be easy.

15

Sitting in Daisy's warm kitchen, gratefully inhaling the comforting smell of fresh toast, Molly tries hard to smile at her plump, reassuring mother-in-law. Daisy doesn't seem particularly surprised or worried about the disappearance of her son or of her old friend.

'Come on, love, chin up and have a nice cup of tea. I was just on my way to see you, funnily enough – you know what they say about great minds thinking alike,' she says briskly, sipping a mug of the bright orange tea that they both love, and looking across at the mantelpiece. 'I bet your mum's just having a little break somewhere, and our Jake has been acting very oddly lately – he probably just needs to think, on his own, doesn't he, Reginald?'

Molly looks at her in mild alarm, and she flushes.

'But where the hell have they gone?' Molly bangs hard on the table and slops tea into the sugar bowl. 'People don't just go off for a break or a think without telling their families – we could all do that if we felt like it, Daisy.'

'Well, perhaps we should, Moll, my love. Maybe the world would be a better place if we all had a bit more space.'

'More space? What about the kids? What about... about... oh, work and stuff? Mothers and fathers can't just take off when they feel like it – the world would fall apart, not be a better place!'

'Well, perhaps you're right, ducky. I know I've felt like taking off more times than I could tell you.' Daisy pours more tea, now even brighter orange. Molly shudders; even she can't drink it quite so stewed, but then she registers what her mother-in-law's just said.

'*You* have? When?'

Daisy just smiles sadly.

'So why didn't you, Daisy, eh? Why didn't you just leave the whole boiling lot of them and go? I'll tell you why: you're not irresponsible, that's why! You care about your family, not like...'

Molly finally begins to cry – great heaving sobs that shake her from head to foot and make her mouth go square and ugly.

'Where are they? Where's Mum and where's bloody Jake?' she wails, unable to stop. 'I want them here!'

Daisy cradles her steaming mug in both hands and watches Molly falling apart, moving only far enough to pass the kitchen roll. When the sobs die down a bit, she shakes her head in the old familiar gesture that causes her glasses to slip down to the end of her nose. She can look at Molly properly now over the top of them. What she sees makes her get up heavily and move around the table to hold her in a tight hug. Molly leans on Daisy. She feels solid and substantial; Molly can tell she's wearing her corsets. They stay like this for some time, the gentle creaking of ancient elastic making Molly feel secure at last. She thinks how much she loves Daisy – Jake always says they are very much alike.

'But you won't do anything silly, will you, Moll?' asks Daisy, patting her on the back a couple more times and moving back to her own chair.

'How do you mean?'

'I don't know, love; you seem as if you're not sure what you want.' Daisy puts the kettle on again. In her eyes, you can never have too much tea.

'I... erm... well...'

Daisy looks at Molly with an intensity that is frightening. 'Molly, Jake loves you. You must know that, my pigeon?' The endearment nearly finishes Molly off; no one but Daisy ever calls her that.

'I guess so. Yes, of course he does.'

'So it'll all come right in the end. My friend Rob always says that you get what you work for, and you work for what you get in this life, whatever that means.'

'Rob? Who do you mean?' Molly knows she's blushing but she has absolutely no control over her burning cheeks.

'Oh, you know, love, Rob Jennings? The headmaster at the school? Him and me have been mates for ages. Nice bloke, but of course, you know him, don't you?'

'I... er... we talk at school sometimes but I wouldn't say I know him very well really.' Molly stands up to put her mug in the sink, desperate to get her back to Daisy.

'Oh, I talk to him a lot. He comes to our chapel with the kiddies and we often have a little chat while Sarah sorts the littlies out. Nice chap, but he doesn't know how to run his marriage, I reckon. Men like that let women walk all over 'em. Give me a proper old-fashioned chap any day. The man should be boss in a marriage.'

The two women look at each other for a long moment. The clock ticks slowly.

'Come off it, Daisy. You were always in charge!'

'No, my love. If I had to do it all again, I might be, but even so, I'd have no respect for a man who let me take the reins completely, that's one thing I know for sure.'

* * *

Later the same morning, Molly is walking up to Forest Point, trying to clear her head, looking down on the village and the sleepy canal and imagining all the people going about their business unaware that her life is in bits. Not that most of them would care even if they knew. She can see the track stretching ahead to the visitor centre and the far car park, and notices that the young trees are getting well settled and even have small heaps of golden leaves mounting up around their fragile trunks.

This place was part of the coal mine when Molly was a child; she and her brother and sister were banned from coming here in case they fell into a mineshaft or got crushed by the heavy machinery. The pits are long gone, and the landscape was desolate for years before some inspired councillor took up the cause and made this a nature area with bike tracks, a lake, playgrounds and educational features. It's pretty good – the family have all had fun here. When Max was a toddler, he fell in the water and Sam had to jump in and fish him out. It was a boiling hot day and Molly dried their clothes on a gorse bush while Sam paddled in his boxers with Max on his shoulders.

Molly trips on a rutty patch and nearly falls as her phone vibrates. Her hands are shaking so much she can't press the right buttons – it's an unfamiliar number. She manages to stammer out a wobbly, 'Hello?' It's the nice young policeman; her mum's car has been found abandoned just over the hill from here, very near to the woods where she and Geoff did their most passionate courting. The police are trying not to seem alarmed now – the area is a regular meeting place for drug dealers after the hours of darkness, and nowadays only very brave or desperate courting couples dare to drive up the rough track to park beside the flooded quarry.

Molly runs back down the path, gasping and sobbing at the same time – she must get to her dad quickly and break the news. When she gets to the shop, the police have beaten her to it and are waiting in the police car for her to join them for the short drive to the old quarry entrance; they arrive just as the frogmen begin the grisly task of dragging the lake. They didn't need to come – there was never any doubt about whose car it was – but somehow, they can't quite believe that Peggy would ever leave her beautiful old black Rover.

'I don't know what they're looking in there for; Peg can't swim,' said Dad, blinking as a cool September breeze blows off the choppy surface of the reservoir.

'Oh, Dad, you know very well why they're looking. They think she's topped herself.'

'If they only knew our Peg, they'd realise she'd never, ever do that. She hates people who give up on themselves – she'd be more likely to finish me off than do herself in!'

Molly's logical brain agrees with him but her heart feels as if it's been put in a mangle. They stand shoulder to shoulder, gazing after the divers, until the sergeant tries to move them on.

'You two need to be at home by the phone in case she rings,' he says stoutly, stepping back a pace as Dad fixes him with a look of deep misery and anger.

'And you should be getting off your backside and finding my wife, young man!' Grabbing Molly's arm, he hurtles towards the police car that's still waiting in the rutty car park. She throws a last look over her shoulder at the bobbing heads in the wind-ruffled water. Why would Peggy abandon her car? And why here?

16

Molly cleans the house very thoroughly that afternoon, in between checking on Geoff, the shop and the unblinking answerphone. She gets rid of cat hairs, feeds the wildly mewing kittens, picks heaps of privet for Hattie's stick insects and even washes out the cloudy, smelly fishtank. She avoids her laptop, even going so far as to unplug it forcefully. The house has never been so well polished and scrubbed before, and she feels slightly better for the earlier chat with Our Lady – the parish priest was also most gratified.

It's been quite a while since Father Michael's seen Molly, or indeed any of the family, with the exception of her mum, of course. Father will be distressed to hear about the disappearance of one of his most faithful parishioners – Peggy can always be relied upon to pad out the congregation, make her responses in a clear Irish brogue (which reminds him so strongly of his mother in Dublin) and slip him an excellent bottle of the hard stuff on feast days. She's also on first-name terms with the Bishop.

Father Michael noticed that Molly didn't come up for communion, but was eager to get back to his breakfast, so probably forgot to follow this up. Molly fully expects he'll call when he hears the news, although he will no doubt make sure his visit coincides with the hour when the sun is approaching the yardarm.

Later in the day, Molly fetches the younger two from school, and the older children wander home soon afterwards. There's no avoiding the issue now – she has to break the news of the two absentees. After a frantic session of questions that she can't answer, they give up and spend the next part of the evening wandering in and out looking forlorn, occasionally beginning to argue but, in the main, quiet and subdued. It has been a very strange day.

Molly worries and rages alternately, still unsure about Jake's reason for taking off in such a hurry. She's terribly afraid that he might have had an accident, or even a blackout of some sort, although he's never had any problems like that before. She rings him again, but his phone goes straight to voicemail now – probably flat. It's a wonder he's even got it with him, but of course it makes no difference if he isn't answering it. Jake hates technology, and only agreed to have the phone because his brother wanted to be able to text him the stupid jokes they both love.

Peggy is just the same, although Dad loves to use his mobile, sending regular texts to Sam and Theo, often at the most inconvenient moments. Where on earth could Mum be? Molly chews her already massacred nails, peels both kittens from her leggings where they've attached themselves with needle-sharp claws and rings Poppy, Jill and Kate to ask their opinions. Poppy and Jill are supportive but Kate's voicemail is on and her recorded message sounds even more terse than usual.

Geoff rings to say that he and Nick have eventually opened up the shop, eaten lunch together, and that he is trying not to panic. He tells Molly that his pipe is never going to be unlit today and that Nick has smoked a lot too and seems deep in thought. Theo seems interested in this fact, but the mention of Nick's name causes Sam to slam up to his room with a loud 'Huh!'

Jill and Poppy appear at teatime, armed with three bottles of supermarket plonk and an enormous shepherd's pie. They have already been to see Geoff to ask if he'll come for dinner, but he refuses to leave his post by the phone. Poppy grabs Molly's blue-and-white-striped butcher's apron and pours herself a glass of wine before she slides the dish into the hot oven, throws chopped cabbage into the biggest pan to boil, and begins to create her special gravy. This involves quite a lot of garlic, beef stock and red wine, with gravy granules to make it thick. Poppy will add the water from the vegetables later, and the result will be awe-inspiring. The children have been known to drink it straight from the jug if there's any left.

Today, everyone watches her bustling around the kitchen with less than the usual enthusiasm. She stirs, tastes, adds various pinches of this and that – a dash of chilli flakes, a shake of celery salt – and Jill lays the table, patting Max and Hattie on their heads, which annoys them no end. Eventually, everyone is sitting around the kitchen table, picking at the food. It smells wonderful but Molly feels queasy. Only Poppy seems really hungry.

'So, where do you think Dad's gone to?' asks Hattie, her brow furrowed in puzzlement.

'I expect he's... um... gone to see one of his friends,' answers Jill. Theo raises her eyebrows and Max looks mutinous.

'But he doesn't go to see his friends. He comes home to see us,' says Max. 'Uncle Shaun's still at the seaside so he might go and see him, I s'pose.' He sniffs and tries to swallow a big mouthful of pie, but it makes him splutter.

'He's not there this time,' Molly answers, giving Max a quick hug.

'Well, everyone likes a change now and again,' says Poppy brightly. There is a silence, as Poppy and Jill try not to look at Molly.

'And what about Gran? Did she fancy a change too?' mutters Sam.

'Look, I don't know where they are, but they had better get back here, and soon!' Molly says, jumping up from the table and beginning to clear plates, crashing far more than is necessary. 'And you lot should be in bed, anyway.'

Poppy gets up and puts an arm around her shaking shoulders. 'Sit down, love. I'll do that in a minute.'

'No, I've got to do something, let's have some coffee – there's some brandy somewhere, I think...'

'Great idea, put the kettle on, someone.' Sam scowls, but after a glance at his mum, slouches over to the sink and fills the kettle. Theo begins to take mugs out of the cupboard, flicking her hair about angrily. Hattie and Max slide down from their chairs and slink off towards the living room, thinking that they might as well take this opportunity to play on the PS5; it isn't usually allowed after seven o'clock. The three women eventually sit down at the table with a cafetiere of coffee and the brandy bottle.

'Mum, your phone just beeped! Do you think it could be Dad or Gran?' shouts Theo from the hallway.

'Oh, erm, hang on, I'll get it,' Molly mumbles.

'It's okay, I'll read it for you, I'll just...'

'No! I'll do it, leave it alone!'

Theo drops the phone onto the table in amazement.

'Keep your hair on, Mum. Who are you expecting to text you – Brad Pitt?'

There is a silence that seems to go on forever. Molly reaches for the offending phone, turning away slightly to read the message. She can feel her face getting hot.

'Go on then, who is it? Let's have a look!' says Theo, reaching over.

'Oh, it's just one of those advert thingies, I get them all the time. Anyway, your dad's left his phone at home, as usual,' Molly bluffs. Poppy and Jill studiously avoid each other's eyes, and Poppy pours brandy with a flourish.

'Come on, drink up, Moll. If ever you needed a brandy, this is the time. I bet one or the other of them will phone any time now. And no news has got to be good news, surely?'

'Yeah, right,' Molly grumbles, 'and anyway, where's Kate? Why isn't she here to cheer up this merry gathering? Has she had a better offer, or what?'

'She doesn't seem to be answering her phones,' says Jill, worriedly. 'I left her lots of messages though, I bet she'll be along later, perhaps she's having another of those important staff training meetings.'

'I sent her three messages too, she must be really busy if she hasn't checked her phones,' Poppy agrees. 'She normally has both her mobiles welded to her hip.'

'Hmm, doesn't Steve know where she is?'

'Molly, Steve never knows where Kate is – that's the way she likes it, you know that.' Jill sniffs. She always says she's very fond of Kate, but Molly's not entirely sure that's the case. Poppy refills glasses – although Jill hastily puts a hand over the top of hers –

and they grin at each other. Molly sneaks a look out of the window at Jake's usual parking spot, with a sinking feeling in the pit of her stomach. It's time to send the kids to bed and to try to get some sleep herself. Somehow, she thinks that sleep will be a long time coming tonight.

17

It's Saturday morning, the second day of Peggy's and Jake's mysterious disappearance, and Daisy is in her lovely warm kitchen making an early cup of tea and some buttered toast for her very good friend, the headmaster. She's humming along to one of her favourite hymns on that nice choral CD that Molly bought, but she's beginning to feel a bit jaded, to be perfectly honest. She's seventy-five, when all's said and done, and these young ones are wearing her out with all their stress and anxiety.

The post's late too – it's always the same on Saturdays – and the phone hasn't stopped ringing. The entire population of Mayfield seems to want to know if Daisy has heard from either of the wanderers. She supposes she's grateful they're bothered but is getting heartily sick of saying the same thing over and over again. Rob hasn't said much so far, but he did give her a nice smile, a kiss on the cheek and a bunch of freesias – her favourites.

Rob and Daisy first met two Christmases ago, when the schoolchildren began to use the chapel to rehearse their Nativity play. Daisy was in charge of opening up that day, as usual (funny how nobody else is ever available when you need them) and stayed to make sure the unpredictable heating had come on properly and that the children were not going to run riot amongst the pews that she'd spent most of her adult life polishing.

Daisy was quite impressed with Rob's way of showing he was in charge without shouting or being bossy – as a child, she had hated her own headmaster for his nasty sarcastic comments and the beatings he dished out without much cause. Daisy noticed that Rob seemed to really listen to them, and he could make them laugh, too. Mind you, the first time anyone was tempted to step out of line it was obvious that he was in complete control, oh yes, indeed.

Probably no one but barmy little Kyle Springer would have tried to have a drink out of the font, and she reckoned that no other child from that school would ever dream of it again. Rob's hiss brought every one of them to attention, and that lecture about respect for God's house would have shamed the most hardened criminal.

Daisy tried not to titter, but he heard her snorting into her hankie, and those wicked brown eyes of his met hers over the heads of the kiddies. Since that day they've been firm friends, and she had kind of expected he'd turn up this morning. Bad news travels fast in a village the size of Mayfield.

Looking at Rob as he crunches his second bit of toast spread thickly with butter and homemade marmalade, she wonders what he's really come for. He gives a huge contented sigh as he finishes the last crumbs, takes a big swig from his mug, wipes his mouth on the back of his hand and squares his shoulders inside his battered old leather jacket.

'Any news of your Jake?' he asks bluntly.

The post lands with a heavy thump on the mat. Diving to

pick it up, Daisy flicks through special offer catalogues for thermal vests, a chance to win a holiday in Ibiza, two credit card offers and a pension scheme, homing in on an envelope with a handwritten address. It's Jake's writing. He's always been keen on letter-writing, especially because he knows Daisy doesn't do email. The odd times Jake's been away for any reason, he's sent postcards to his mum or even a couple of pages of scrawl with mad little stick-man illustrations.

'I think this is it, love,' she says slowly. 'Would you mind if I read it on my own?'

Seeing that she's near to tears, he jumps up from his chair.

'Oh no – of course not. I'll just, erm...'

He looks disappointed to be ejected, but Daisy's got other things to think about now. Giving her another huge hug, he makes his way to the back door, shouting over his shoulder that he'll be outside if he's needed. She only half hears this as she sinks into her own chair, because the letter from Jake needs all her attention.

Sorry for all the worry I must have caused you, Mum. I did something stupid and I had to get away. Then I remembered I still had the spare caravan keys in the car from last holidays and I just drove here. Hope that's okay? Oh, and I think I've lost my phone, must have dropped it somewhere. I'll write again when I've sorted myself out a bit. Would you mind ringing Molly? It'll be better coming from you.

Love,

Jake x

So he's in Norfolk, at their old caravan. She might have guessed that he'd hide there. It's always been one of his favourite places. Daisy's eyes blur with angry tears. So Jake's, in the place where, actually, she would really like to be herself. He's put them through all this worry, and for what? 'Something stupid?' I'll give him something stupid, she thinks. What in heaven's name does he mean by that? And now he's probably sitting on the beach, feeling sorry for himself and soaking up the sun. Tell Molly? Yes, she bets it would be easier if she did that – for Jake. The injustice of it all takes her breath away, but Jake always managed to wriggle out of awkward situations even as a boy.

Suddenly Daisy is desperate to see the sea for herself. Leicestershire folk often seem to holiday in Norfolk – it's their nearest coast and if it's good enough for the dear late Queen, then it's good enough for anyone.

Daisy loves the North Norfolk coast with a passion. The pace of life's so much slower in a Norfolk village – there's still time to chat in the butcher's shop about what should go into proper sausages. In her mind's eye she sees the cliff path tumbling down to that vast expanse of firm golden sand. There were always shells and fossils to collect – the boys spent hours combing the cliff bottom for fossils, while Daisy and Reginald splashed in the shallows, hand in hand. Fish and chips at lunchtime, hot and greasy, and a crab to dress for tea. Daisy can almost taste the vinegar and the nutty brown bread; feel the sharp edge of a bit of overlooked shell in her mouth.

Pulling herself together, she re-reads the letter; she doesn't feel so confused now, and she can see that there are an awful lot of references to himself in it.

'Selfish young bugger!' Daisy yells furiously to the empty kitchen. 'What about Molly? The kids? Me?'

Angry tears finally flood down her cheeks as she screws the letter into a tight ball. Has she helped to make him this self-centred? Did she spoil him?

The door swings open and in comes Sam, closely followed by Poppy and Rob. They look at Daisy in floods of tears, and then at the crumpled letter.

'Is it Dad?' Sam blurts out. 'Is he coming home?'

His voice wobbles as he tries to snatch the letter out of his grandma's hands, but she holds on to it tightly. Poppy raises her eyebrows towards Daisy who nods wearily. The kitchen is very quiet. Finally, Daisy breaks the silence.

'Well, at least we know he's safe, I suppose. I'd better ring our Molly – she'll be wanting to go and find him, no doubt, although I'd like to get hold of him first and put him over my knee for panicking us all like this,' she says, heavily.

'Why are you so mad with him? What's Dad done? He might have just felt like a break.' Sam's eyes have never left the crumpled letter.

'It never ceases to amaze me how even grown-up kids can make you feel so responsible for them,' says Daisy. 'Never mind what your dad's done, we need to get him back here where he belongs. Molly will know what to do. Leave this to me.'

Poppy gives Daisy a thumbs-up and a hug. 'Right, well, maybe Rob can pop in and see Geoff on his way back to school – Molly's dad needs to know what's going on too.'

'Of course I'll go and see Geoff; I'll ring you later, Daisy, and see if I can do anything else. Do you want me to go with you to tell Molly, or anything?'

'No, love, that's a job for me, I think – I'll just ring her now, thanks.'

Rob smiles rather sadly, and shepherds everyone out of the kitchen. Daisy is so tired she hardly knows what to do with herself. Too exhausted even to make a cuppa, she heads for the phone, bolstering herself up with the promise of bed and a nice afternoon nap. She deserves it.

18

Nick stands outside Molly's door, annoyingly damp under the armpits. It's bad news to sweat when he's nervous, because it might put her off. Women like men to smell nice, at least that's what Kris reckons. To be fair, Nick's never found getting women a problem. Keeping them, now that's another matter. They bore him silly after a while and he seems to piss them off quite easily too.

He takes a few deep breaths. Okay, got to calm down now because he knows this is one of his better plans. Theo obviously fancies him, and the grandad is putty in his hands, in fact he's offered Nick a room for a few nights while he sorts himself out. Sam's suspicious, but he's been so busy worrying about his missing family that he hasn't really thought about what Nick's doing here, or wondered why he just happened to be in the right place at the right time with the shop job.

No, the problem is going to be Molly. For this plan to work, she has got to love him. Not be sympathetic or grateful if he helps her out, although that'll do for a bit, but she has to take him in and really, really love him. She has to be Nick's mum. So, to screw Theo at this point might be a bad idea – mums tend to be a bit funny about things like that. Now, if he married Theo, that would probably be different, because Molly would realise he needs looking after, and she'd have to take care of him properly. One or two more kids wouldn't be noticed in that house, even big ones.

Nick's already feeling much better just through being near Molly – his arms are starting to heal, he's eating pretty well, even had a bath yesterday, although he thinks his clothes might still be fairly high. Maybe Geoff'll let him use his washing machine tomorrow though. What next, then? Plan B?

Answering the door, Molly looks shattered. She must be relieved to know her bloke's safe and sound but that doesn't explain why he's still not been in touch with her himself. And still no word from Molly's mum. What a family – they're no better than Nick's when you scratch the surface, letting each other down and all that. After Nick and Kris were left to fend for themselves, they didn't bother about the other two much, *she* was the one that kept them together. Nick hates her. He would like to kill her for what she did to them, if she wasn't dead already, the bitch.

He tries to smile as Molly looks him up and down.

'Yes?' she says, frowning. 'Can I help you? Hang on, it's you – it's Nick, isn't it? Well, of course it is, nobody else has got hair like... I mean...'

Nick nods. Well, it's not really his name but he's got no desire to be known by the other one, the one *she* chose for him. 'Nick' is short, sharp and cool. You don't mess with someone called Nick.

'Yes, I work for your dad now, but I've come to see if you need a babysitter, and also, I think I know where your mum has got to,' Nick says, edging forward.

Molly opens the door, eyes wide, and he slides in.

In the kitchen with a mug of strong, sweet tea in his hand, Nick tells Molly about the phone call he intercepted earlier at the shop. Geoff had been outside in the garden having a little nap (Molly snorts at this) and so, after Nick shouted him and got no answer, he decided to answer the call himself in case it was urgent. Molly looks at him doubtfully at this point – perhaps he's going to have his work cut out here. He bets that bloody interfering Sam's been stirring it.

He carries on telling his story, hoping she'll lose that wired-up look soon – it's making him sweat again. There had been no one on the other end of the line, but then Nick had heard a muttered, 'Holy Mother of God, the bastard can't even be arsed to answer his own phone, so he can't.' He'd put the receiver down and rung 1471. Molly is clearly impressed at this quick thinking.

'Good thinking – so what was the number, Nick? Was it local?' she asks anxiously. She knows her mother wouldn't have the technical knowledge to block her number; by the sound of her, she's probably only just got the hang of putting your money in the slot at the right moment. In fact, how did she ever manage the whole call-box thing? You have to use a card, and where are you supposed to get one of those when you need to make an urgent phone call? Nick's been caught out by that one himself when he's had no credit on his phone. He bets no one in Molly's family has ever been so broke that they run out of credit though. Fancy leaving your mobile at home – and the bloke's lost his. What a load of morons!

'No, it was a Norfolk number – I went through the dialling codes in the phone book. I didn't know anybody still had those. Your dad's got a whole heap of them.' He's quite proud of finding that out. The whole phone call thing has really been a stroke of luck; Nick is sure the plan is meant to work this time. Molly is eating out of his hand now.

'Norfolk? Why would Mum be there? This is bizarre. They can't be together, can they; Mum and Jake?'

'Sounds like they might be – why is that so weird?'

'Well, Mum hasn't been to Norfolk for years, not since they came on holiday to the caravan with us and Hattie was teething. God, that was a terrible week. Sam fell halfway down the cliff and Theo got mumps and threw up in Dad's hat. Then we had a huge argument because I wanted to send the older kids to the Scripture Union Beach Mission, and Mum said it was nothing but Protestant brainwashing and we'd all go to hell.' She falls silent, remembering.

'Yes, well, she must be there now, it's got to have been your mum. I didn't know about your man being there though. I just heard he'd let his mum know he was safe. Anyway, shall I tell Geoff, or will you?'

Molly looks at him suspiciously – whoops, too familiar. Careful, careful, could lose everything now... Nick passes a hand across his eyes as if he's feeling emotional about it all, letting his sleeve fall back to reveal some of the network of scars and scabs that criss-cross his forearm. A horrified expression takes over.

'Christ, Nick, what have you done to yourself? Have you been in an accident?'

There is a silence, and he suddenly finds he can't meet her eyes. She's so bloody nice, this one. He sees realisation dawn as Molly struggles to think of something to say.

'Nick, how old are you?' she blurts out suddenly.

'Erm... nineteen last month, why?'

'Well, I just wondered – do you normally live on your own? Where's your family from? Doesn't your mum worry about you when you're away?'

There is a long silence, and he holds his throat as tight as he can but then he has to go and let out a sort of gulping sob. God, how embarrassing. He didn't mean to do that but it turns out to be the right thing to do – it works brilliantly.

'Oh, Nick, I'm so sorry – you don't have to tell me anything, of course you don't. Look, I've got to ring my dad. I need to tell him about the phone call, and then I think I'll probably have to go to Norfolk.'

Nick shivers. This is going almost too well. He's nearly in here. Careful, careful now. This is one hell of a dangerous game. One wrong move and she'll get all suspicious again. He can already tell that inviting a near-stranger into her house isn't something that Molly would normally do. He keeps his arms firmly by his side as Molly pours him a second mug of tea from her huge earthenware teapot. He doesn't want to do anything to put her off now he's come so far. The sweat is a dead giveaway. She mustn't guess how scared he is.

Molly goes into the hallway and Nick hears the rise and fall of her voice as she tells her dad the news. The words aren't clear but the agitation comes across, even through the wall.

'Mum,' Theo yells from the back garden, 'Max is all muddy! I told him not to...' She bursts into the kitchen and stops dead when she sees Nick lounging with his elbows on the table, about to dunk a chocolate digestive in his tea.

'Wh... what are you doing here?' Her face is redder than the newly dyed streak in her fringe and she takes a step back, lurching into a pile of plates and cups balanced on the draining board. They teeter and she reaches out a hand to steady them, but it's too late. They crash to the floor, shattering in a burst of sharp-edged pieces on the unforgiving quarry tiles and two terrified kittens make a dash for the safe space under the table.

'Oh, bugger.' They both look at the wreckage and Theo

continues, 'That's Sam's fault, that is. It was his turn to unload the dishwasher and he didn't, so I had to wash up in the sink because there's no way I'm doing his job for him, the lazy slob.'

Molly is back now, and when she sees the remains of her best breakfast pots, her eyes fill with tears.

'Bloody hell, I can't even turn my back for a minute round here, can I? I was going to say I'm off to Norfolk to talk to your dad, Theo, but how can I leave you all if you can't even stop yourself breaking the place up?'

'That's so unfair! It was Sam's fault, he should've... Hang on, what did you say about Dad?'

'Apparently, he's written to your gran.'

'Has he? Why not us?'

'I don't know why the hell he contacted her and not us, but that's the way it is. And now Nick here has found out that Nana Peggy's in Norfolk too. I feel as if I've fallen into some bizarre parallel universe where everyone acts totally out of character and does just what they like.'

Theo looks at Nick properly for the first time and he's stunned by the beauty of her huge green eyes. 'What? Has everybody gone crazy or something? Why would she go there? Why would Dad? What's going on?'

'I wish I knew, love.' Molly sighs and rubs her face, streaking her mascara and blinking sadly as she bends to pick up the pieces of pottery.

Nick and Theo help her, wordlessly, and between them the job's soon done. It breaks the ice somehow, and Nick suddenly feels very much at home.

'What are you going to do about all your kids if you go off to Norfolk?' he asks Molly.

'Kids? I hope you're not meaning me when you say that?' Theo's face flames again.

'Nah, but you've got to admit there's a houseful here. If you need a hand, I can help.'

'And what exactly do you know about childminding?'

'Theo, don't be so rude. Nick's only trying to help, and I can't leave you and Sam to cope with the other two on your own. But she's got a point. We don't know you really, do we, Nick? I've never left them for more than an evening.'

Nick's shoulders slump. So nearly there and he's blown it. Should've been more careful – there's no way Molly was going to trust him with her kids this soon, is there? But she's still talking.

'Look, Nick, I know you mean well with your offer and it's really kind, but if I go to Norfolk I'm going to be at least a couple of days. I've got no idea where Mum is, even if Jake will be easy to find at the van. Max and Hattie can be a bit wild at times and they haven't even met you.'

'And Sam wouldn't like it. I can tell you that for nothing,' Theo blurts out, pulling her fringe further over her face and folding her arms across her chest. She looks as if Nick's the last person she'd want to help with the kids but Nick isn't quite fooled. He's caught the furtive glances from under her eyelashes. Theo's not as anti-Nick as she'd like him to think. What is she, fifteen? A four-year gap's a lot at that age – he must seem like a proper grown-up to Theo. But she definitely fancies him, he's sure of it.

'Your brother will deal with it if I get Nick to help us all out, but even so...'

Molly's voice tails off and she chews her thumbnail, frowning at the floor. Nick feels a warm glow as he watches her. This is how a proper mum should be, not dashing off without a thought for her family, but thinking it through, wondering if she can trust a stranger. What can he do to convince her?

'Look, your dad's going to be around, isn't he? I'm staying there for a few days anyway, so we could come round here together some of the time – then you get two for the price of one.'

Molly's frown begins to disappear as the idea takes shape. Nick can see how torn she is. He smiles reassuringly at Theo and waits patiently. After a moment or two, Molly gives herself a little shake and squares her shoulders, as if she's preparing for a battle.

'Okay, well, it's incredibly kind of you, Nick, and with Dad around too, I'm sure everything will be fine. He'll probably say he wants to come with me to look for Mum but if I tell him he's needed here for the kids and the pets and the shop, I can get going almost straight away.'

Theo takes this information in, not completely happy with it all but on her way to seeing it's the only way to get the family back together. Nick can see she's not used to all this upheaval. He could tell her a thing or two about dealing with the crap life throws at you, but he won't. Not just yet anyway.

19

As she speeds past the Happy Eater on the Norfolk road, Molly can't help remembering the time, some years ago, when Jake finally gave in to Theo and Sam's pleading for burgers and chips and agreed to stop for a brief snack. He normally believed in sandwiches on the move, with only a toilet stop to break the journey, and only then if you really had to go. But this time, having just had news of a pay rise, and with redundancy unheard of, he cracked.

They sat round a very small table, baby Max howling on Molly's knee and Hattie grubbing happily under the table for cold chips, and already she knew this had been a very bad idea. When the food finally arrived, tepid and hard around the edges, Jake refused to make a fuss or send it back, but ate his meal in stony silence, glaring at each child until they did the same. Even Max, snuffling under Molly's shirt for nourishment, to the amazement of the middle-aged gentlemen on her left ('Bloody disgusting; you'd think they'd do that in private – no shame, some folks'), fell silent. Afterwards they'd filed out to the car, a family in disgrace.

Why, Molly thought with sudden sour bitterness, hadn't she shouted at him for punishing them all like that, just because she wanted a change of routine and a hot dinner? What right did he have to be so smug and self-righteous? Molly resorted to the packed lunch routine without comment on the next holiday, and the subject was never mentioned again.

In defiance, she pulls in to the next roadside café, freshens up in the cloakroom then orders an all-day breakfast, putting extra sugar in her coffee even though she hardly ever takes sugar and really can't stand fried bread. Feeling better, if slightly sick, she carries on with the journey, turning the radio up to full blast and opening her window wide (Jake hates draughts). Delighted, she recognises an old The Who track and starts to sing along to '5.15', belting out lyrics about girls of fifteen being sexually knowing.

Hang on a minute, when did those words change from an exciting idea to a frightening one? Could Theo be 'sexually knowing' yet? And what about boys of sixteen, for that matter? However is Molly going to deal with these sorts of thoughts without Jake to talk to? Although she probably couldn't mention Theo's possible sexuality to him without bringing on a panic attack anyway. She sniffs, supposing he'd think it was okay if Sam was sowing a few wild oats.

Molly drives on, past wide, flat expanses of cornfields, military rows of poplars and farms planted in the middle of nowhere. Occasionally, there are stern farmhouses, lonely galleons in the middle of windswept ploughed seas. What must it be like to live so far from your neighbours? No one to watch you, she thinks wryly, but then realises that a parked car outside an isolated cottage would be just as obvious as a headteacher's Volvo in a pub car park.

How *do* people have affairs? It must be unbelievably tricky.

You could never relax, surely? There would always be the chance that some well-meaning person would chirp up, 'Oh, I saw you the other day, Mr Jennings, popping into the Square and Spanner for a quick pint. Or your car was there, anyway – I didn't actually see *you*.' Very dodgy. She drags her mind back to her mission. How is she going to start when it comes to saving her marriage? And more to the point, does she even want to save it any more?

Does Jake want to drag them back from the brink or is he tired of it all? And do people really visit seedy hotels or Travelodges and sign in under 'Mr and Mrs Smith'? Oh God, Molly can't concentrate. She fixes her eyes on the ribbon of road disappearing over the wide blue horizon. Soon she'll come over the hill into Cromer where the children always yell, 'I saw the sea, I saw the sea, I saw it first, I saw the sea!' And that means that if Jake's where she thinks he is, and not out somewhere enjoying himself, it'll soon be showdown time.

Molly reaches into the glovebox for a humbug and decides to try to sort out her feelings about Jake, their marriage and their life once and for all, before she reaches the point where she needs to confront him in the flesh. Okay – what does she like most about being married to Jake? After a few moments, she shelves that question and begins work on the other side first, as she can't actually think of any positives today.

No, she mustn't give in so quickly. Surely there should be more on the good side? After all these years of marriage? And four children? And shared in-laws? She sighs hopelessly. Well, at least she still likes his knack for mending things, like the hoover, or a wobbly defective kite, but... surely there should be more? What about his sneaky way of making her laugh at all the wrong moments? They've got so many shared memories, funny things that nobody else could ever know.

Maybe having all the kids has pulled them apart? It's hard looking after everyone's feelings, his get missed out a bit, she supposes. But so do Molly's. There are all sorts of things she'd like to do, but there's never time.

Molly really wants to take up her music again – maybe even to play with a top-notch orchestra. To sing. Even karaoke's better than nothing. As a teenager she'd won competitions; felt talented and admired.

She'd like to sail a nippy little boat on the Solent. She's never tried it, but she'd really like to have a go before she gets too old. And she wants to go to Italy and China, and New York and Sydney. She'd quite like to jump off a cliff into the sea. She wants to have wild sex with that guy who played Poldark. She wants to eat only sushi and drink only champagne for a week. She yearns to dance on the beach in the moonlight with Rob Jennings, wearing nothing but a smile. Now where did that last thought come from?

Molly wonders if Rob's been in touch. She can't wait to check her emails but the part of Norfolk where she's heading is a black hole where communication's concerned. Is he somewhere thinking about her right now? Is she starring in his fantasies?

Half an hour later, driving down the rutty lane to the caravan site and trying hard to look inconspicuous, Molly's spirits are at an all-time low. The car stalls as she reaches her usual parking spot in the shade of a mighty oak. Abandoning it in disgust with a furtive kick, she thinks about everyone at home, with a lurch of her stomach. What sort of mother would abandon her children at the drop of a hat? Reaching for her mobile, suddenly desperate for reassurance, she rings Daisy, but the phone rings on and on. Maybe it's nap time for her mother-in-law? Or maybe there's a function on at the chapel?

Molly has kept Daisy up to date with her travel plans and knows she'll do her best to keep an eye on things, but it's not so easy now Daisy's moved to Hopton. When she was at the end of the lane, life was much simpler. She scrolls down and finds her dad's number, but there's no answer there either. At the third try, Nick answers Molly's call to the landline in her own house, with a terse, 'Yup?'

'Nick, I thought everyone had been beamed up by aliens. Are they all okay?'

He laughs, and now she can hear happy squeals in the background. 'Your dad's here – he shut the shop early and came round with me to check on everyone. We're ordering pizzas in for tea – they're all in the garden building a den right now. Their other granny's here too.'

'Great.' Molly clutches her mobile tightly as waves of relief battle with a ridiculous feeling of resentment that her family aren't even missing her a bit, or worrying about their missing dad and gran. 'Do you think Max and Hattie will be all right sleeping at the shop with Dad? Max isn't good at sleepovers as a rule.'

'Erm... well...'

'What's the matter? Is Max okay, Nick?'

'He's fine, only we're having such a great time here that we thought we'd all sleep at yours tonight. That is, except for Sam. He's staying over at the shop in case your mum rings again. I thought it'd be cool if Geoff and me both looked after the others?'

'I guess so, if the kids are happy with that?'

Wild screams echo down the phone as Max and Hattie get closer. Molly can hear them giggling as some sort of wild beast – hopefully her dad doing his Aslan impersonation – chases them through the hallway. She closes her eyes and imagines their flushed, laughing faces. If she can't get their dad back for them, how long will this crazy interlude last before reality hits home and they realise they're stuck in a one-parent family with a mum who has totally screwed up?

'Nick, this is really good of you,' Molly says, swallowing the lump in her throat that's threatening to choke her. 'I'm at the caravan now and I'm going in to see Jake. His car's here and the van windows are open, so I'm assuming he's here and not fishing or something.'

'It's fine, I'm having a great time. Your kids are wicked, Molly. Hope it goes how you want it to go, yeah? Bye now.'

Molly slips her phone into her pocket and takes a deep breath. It's time to face the music. But don't mess with me, Jake, or you might well be sorry, she thinks.

As she walks away from her car, a small gang of children burst out of a thicket screeching like banshees and running at full speed towards her. She closes her eyes and waits for the collision, but they manage to stop just short, whooping like maniacs. The wildest one dances in a circle round her legs.

'Hiya, Molly? Bet you don't remember me? It's Zac, Hattie's friend?'

His voice rises annoyingly in a question at the end of each sentence, and she remembers just how much that irritated her the last time the family was down here.

'Zac! Nice to see you – how's your mum?'

'Oh, you know, still nagging? Think she misses you, though? Like, she likes a good natter an' all that? Where's Hattie'n'-Max'n'the others?'

Molly hasn't been down to the caravan site since the May holiday, when things had seemed fine with Jake, and all the children had a great time, spending days on the beach, swimming, digging in the sand and generally behaving like a family should.

She stretches her shoulders and massages the base of her spine, wondering what to do next. The gang of children move away, bored now they can see that she's alone. Zac raises a hand in farewell, looking puzzled.

Molly gazes at the view of grassy clifftop and blue, blue sea. The sky here always seems so vast, and there are a few lazy clouds drifting around. It's a perfect September afternoon moving into an even better evening; warm, slightly hazy, and smelling faintly of wood smoke and leaf mould and all the classic things that usually make her nostalgic for Norfolk when she's trudging around Leicester or in the village, longing for the scent of the sea.

Suddenly, she remembers Jake's pleas, only last week, for Molly to think about his ideas for the future. She wishes she could just bite the bullet and go along with Jake's dream of living here permanently. She does so love the sea, and the beach, and the cliff paths, and the Broads, and the winding little streets of Norwich with their black-and-white timbered buildings, and... all of it, really. But is that enough? It's one thing liking somewhere for holidays, but dragging everyone down here, away from all their friends, grandparents, schools and so on is a different matter.

So, what now? Molly's anger's still there somewhere, but lethargy is slowly taking over – she needs a cup of tea and some good, squidgy cake before facing this crisis. A sudden longing to be with Rob washes over her. Guilt, anger and self-pity fight with each other and she began to cry quietly. She's completely knackered. The landscape swims into a gentle wash of green and blue. After a few minutes, she wipes her eyes. This is getting her nowhere fast.

In her pocket, Molly's phone vibrates, breaking the mood. She jumps guiltily then realises it doesn't matter who's texting, she's alone here, in more ways than one. She unlocks the keypad.

> Thinking of you, dreaming of you, dazzled and amazed by you x

Probably not the kids trying to find out where she is, then! Has anyone ever been dazzled by Molly before, she wonders? Or dreamed of her? Jake only seems to think of her when he wonders what he's getting for his dinner or if Molly's paid the gas bill. It's very seductive, all this 'thinking of you' stuff. She feels all bubbly and irresponsible, even though she's tired out with the crying and raging she's done.

Standing in the middle of the field, surrounded by caravans and discarded bikes, tricycles and other holiday amusements, Molly thinks maybe she should just go for it – have a torrid affair, throw caution to the winds, forget about a strange person seeing her stretch marks and marvelling at the size of her naked bottom? Actually, she reckons she deserves it. But, awful thought, what if Rob's just playing some weird game with her?

He could be one of those blokes who's into the thrill of the chase, and all that. If she goes back home, moisturises like crazy and then rushes to meet him with her best knickers on under a slip of a silky frock, he might just laugh nervously and pretend she's got the wrong end of the stick. And she can't help coming back to the practicalities – where would they meet? Molly's phone buzzes again and she's looking at the new message before she's had time to think.

> Come home, let me appreciate your finer talents! xx

Maybe he's heard about her meringues? She can't resist it – she has to answer.

> Oh, I so wish you were here.

The answer arrives promptly.

> Me too, my mind is so full of you I can't think of anything else, my sweetheart.

Now she's really torn; she's never been called 'my sweetheart' before. Is it lovely and tender, or is it naff? She can't decide, but the whole thing has taken the edge off the pain of having to deal with Jake. Molly doesn't reply this time.

An enormous gull swoops down and seems to be about to peck her, squawking ferociously. Molly automatically checks round for her children. Hattie in particular is scared of the gulls. She used to bury her face in Jake's neck when they came too close. Molly flaps her hands at it, just as her phone buzzes again.

> When will you be back? I need to see you very much, and soon xx

Just a minute, the last thing Molly needs at the moment is someone to check up on her. She stares at the words. She doesn't want to have to report her timetable to Rob as well as everyone else in her life, does she? And she hasn't decided if she will see him or not yet, anyway. Shivering, Molly takes a last look at the view of rows of caravans and trees that are all that's between her and the sea. She wishes she could have a walk along the sand before she tackles her husband, but all this shilly-shallying is ridiculous. It's time to sort herself out. As she puts her phone away, she plunges her hands into her pockets and feels for her lucky shell left over from the last holiday, a bit battered but still in one piece. She thinks she might need it today.

20

In his mum's elderly green caravan, three rows back from the beach, Jake has had a brilliant day of fresh air and exercise. Although he can't see the sea from his little garden because of all the vans, the smell of the salty tang of seaweed was all around as he mowed the tiny grass border around the veranda. He's going brown already, his shirt's been off since mid-morning and he thinks he's in pretty good shape, considering. If only Kate could see him now. He'd logged on to Instagram and seen that mistletoe, and it had been like a shot in the arm. Nothing has been the same since.

When his family used to come here years ago, Jake hated these gardening jobs and fought bitter battles with his brother Matt for the chance to go to the beach instead; he'd say he'd already cleaned the bathroom, done the shopping – anything to escape mowing and suchlike on holiday. Now, he's getting a weird sort of pleasure at the sight of this neat little lawn, and has really enjoyed pulling out the weeds and tidying around the steps to make it perfect; how pathetic is that, he asks himself? A patch of mint is straggling around the back door, past its best but still smelling great, and a few other herbs are still trying to grow, reminding him of Daisy's attempts at country living.

His dad called them weeds, but Daisy used to throw them into their dinner with wild abandon, sniffing the steam with a big daft smile on her face, and moaning at them all for being ignorant Midlanders with no soul. It was her one go at adventurous cooking, this patch of dreams. Never mind that the food tasted strange – Mum was convinced that this was cooking the French way. Why a Leicestershire woman, who loved bangers and mash, should suddenly feel the need to cook like a French peasant in deepest Norfolk was a mystery to Jake and Matt.

'Well, at least she draws the line at bloody garlic – be grateful for small mercies,' their dad would mutter, as he shovelled in a huge forkful of well-doctored beef stew, dunking wobbly slices of Mother's Pride.

Jake flops into a deckchair as tears prick his eyes. Where have all the years gone? How could he have got it all so wrong just lately? Mind you, that night (well, couple of hours) with Kate was fantastic. God, what a woman! She got him out of his clothes before he'd even had time to be embarrassed. Jake was shaking like a boy on his first date. And then... wow! He'd forgotten just how much laughing you can do, how much talking and teasing in between the steamy bits.

She seemed proud of her body too, not forever worrying about her thighs, like Molly. She wrapped her arms around him, cuddling him as if she never wanted to stop. Jake still can't believe it happened – he thought Kate hated him like poison. Afterwards, she cried a bit, and said that she and Steve never went to bed at the same time any more, and that he preferred his old motorbike to her.

He suddenly thinks of Molly and gets a lurch of guilt. She doesn't care about him the way she used to though, he knows she doesn't. He seems to annoy her all the time these days, can't do anything right somehow. Jake bets Molly wouldn't even care if she knew about Kate. Or would she? Of course she bloody would.

He hadn't planned it. He'd been passing the end of Kate's posh road on his way home from work, and yeah, she'd been on his mind after that Facebook status and the text she'd sent to make sure he'd seen it. But he would have gone straight home if he'd not checked into his X account in the canteen and seen the rumour that the brewery was closing down and they'd soon all be out of work.

And then Jake had just suddenly decided to call on Kate and get his guitar back. She'd borrowed it last year for one of her daughters to learn on, but Jake thought it probably hadn't been out of the case for months. It had just been a short-lived fad. He wanted it back to play himself anyway – it wasn't that he wanted to see Kate. Okay, he'd known Steve was on nights but still...

Lately, the restless feeling inside had made Jake want to write a song or two, just like he'd always used to do with his best friend Shaun. He misses Shaun. Maybe he'll go there next. Brighton will be quiet at this time of year. Then reality kicks in, and Jake remembers work and Molly and the kids and all his other responsibilities.

He closes his eyes and imagines Kate is here with him, walking on the beach, or finding one of those little beach huts... and maybe spending the evening eating mussels and fresh crab and crusty bread and then staying the whole night. Then he tries to substitute Molly for Kate in the dream, but she keeps telling him not to get sand in her knickers and says she never eats shellfish. It's just not working.

Jake's not sure how he feels about anything any more. Molly's bound to find out what he's done soon, and then there'll be a showdown. Jake hates scenes. All that shouting, and then having to talk about your feelings and all that boring crap. God, it's so embarrassing. And what about the kids? They're always around so there's no chance to really sort things out at home.

If only they lived here, by the sea, Jake is sure that life would be so much simpler and more relaxing too. He could get a job on a farm, or a market garden. He could learn to cook properly and do something with his flair for food. Molly could maybe work at the village school. He remembers a recent conversation with Molly about the very same thing, when he'd done his damnedest to persuade her to sell up and move to the Norfolk coast.

'But why not, Moll? Think how the kids would love it. They could play on the beach after school every day. It'd be safer for us to get about on bikes too; you'd like that, wouldn't you?'

'Don't talk to me like I'm a child – you can't bribe me to do something I don't want to do.'

'What's the problem though? I can't see any disadvantages at all.' Jake is beginning to get angry now. She must be able to see how much better their life would be if they just took that step.

'Well, that's just the thing, Jake. You never can see my point of view unless I spell it out. What about my mum and dad? And your mum, all on her own now? And our friends? And the kids' friends? It's not just about the place – it's the people as much as anything for me.'

'But they'd come and see us.'

She snorts at this.

'What? Why are you making that stupid noise, Molly?'

'Because you hate visitors, and that's when they only drop in for a short while. How are you going to feel when they descend on us for a week or a fortnight?'

'I like it when Shaun visits, and Matt. Anyway, they wouldn't...'

'Course they would. People who move to the seaside, or anywhere with holiday potential, find they're suddenly very popular. You remember reading *A Year in Provence*?'

'I guess so.'

'And have you forgotten Matt's horror stories about when he first moved to the coast? There were people who he never spoke to from one year to the next who suddenly couldn't wait to come and stay for a fortnight.'

Jake yawns. He supposes she was right, but he hates arguments; emotional stuff wears him out. Maybe he'll just have a bit of a nap, it's so warm here in the sunshine. And it must be about time for a nice cold beer...

The sound of the car stalling breaks into his doze. Who's that? He hopes it's not the people from the next-door van. If he remembers rightly, they were the noisy ones – parties every night, sausages and burgers being incinerated, fried onions with everything, inviting half the site round for drinks. And their dogs were a nightmare. Huge great Alsatians, slobbery and loud. Jake hates dogs. It's so peaceful here without neighbours of any sort.

Jake can't see the car from where he is, half lying in the deckchair, but he waits, holding his breath, for the onslaught. Nothing happens until the gang of children from up the other end of the site start charging around. Must be coming to meet one of their visitors. Phew. But then he hears the sound he's been dreading. Footsteps are coming towards the van. They stop. Are they next door? Horrified, he registers that the rapping on the door is much closer to home. Who can it be? Perhaps they'll go away. Then, even worse, the footsteps start to come round the side of the van, and a familiar voice shouts, 'Jake? Where the hell are you?'

Jake lurches to his feet, almost ending up on the floor as he wrestles his way out of the deckchair. Molly is standing in front of him, eyes blazing and cheeks pink with fury. Oh, God.

'Molly. I... um... wasn't expecting you here.'

'No, I don't suppose you were. But after everything you've done, where did you expect me to be?'

'Everything I've done?' Jake feels the shaking beginning in his hands. How has she found out so quickly? Surely Kate hasn't blabbed? In the letter he only said he'd done something stupid and he's pretty sure his mum wouldn't have shared that part with Molly, even if she'd somehow managed to guess what happened. Which she couldn't have, could she? He'd meant his mum to think he'd got into bad debt, or managed to lose his job, or similar.

'Yes. Did you think you could get away with this? Do you even care how I feel? How we all feel?'

She must know. But how? Jake tries to think quickly but his brain seems to be made of soup.

'Well? What have you got to say for yourself?'

'But it was only the once. I didn't mean to do it; it just happened. Kate was in her dressing gown. She was crying. I wanted my guitar. I only... then she... it's never happened before...'

As Jake stumbles on, he registers Molly's silence, and meeting her eyes at last, sees the total amazement there and grinds to a halt.

'Only once? With Kate? Are you saying what I think you're saying, Jake? Because if you are... if you're telling me you've got something going on with one of my best friends, I'll... I'll...'

Molly's voice has risen to a shout now, and Jake imagines

everyone on the site turning their heads as they get their barbe-
cues out and open a beer, listening to his and Molly's marriage
cracking open; a rotten egg spilling its disgusting contents all
over them.

'Come inside, Molly, we need to talk,' he pleads, gesturing
towards the rest of the site.

'Talk? *Talk*?' she repeats, but she seems to sense what he's
really saying and, glancing around, follows him up the steps and
into the van, where they face each other across the tiny lounge
area, like boxers entering the ring.

'You didn't actually know about Kate, did you?' Jake asks.
'I've been even more stupid than I thought.'

Molly shakes her head, eyes still wide with shock.

'You were just talking about me walking out and leaving you
all without saying where I was going, weren't you?'

She nods, speechless for the moment.

'But honestly, Moll, it was a mistake – a one-off. I just called
for my guitar, like I said. Kate was upset. I've never seen her cry.
I was trying to comfort her.'

'Ha! So, she made you do it, did she? She threw herself at
you and you couldn't help yourself, was that it? Poor little Jakey,
it must be so hard being you, soooo helpless and irresistible!'

Jake has the grace to blush. 'I never said she made me do it,
you're trying to put words in my mouth – she just made me feel
wanted, that's all.'

'And I don't make you feel wanted, I suppose?' Molly begins
to pace round the caravan, but soon runs out of space and has to
resort to furiously crashing pots around in the tiny sink and
wiping worktops. She knows Jake hates it when she does that,
after he's already made everything clean.

'Leave the dishes, I never asked you to wash up!'

'That's not all you never asked me to do, is it? What else did

Kate do for you that I don't? I bet she knows a few tricks, the slut!'

'Don't, Molly – she's your friend...'

'Friend? You have got to be kidding! That's not what friends usually do for each other – like, "Hey, Molly, you must be busy just now, let me shag your husband for you; it's no trouble, honest!" – was that how it went?'

Jake shrugs moodily. He doesn't like it when Molly uses words like 'shag' and he's always been really bad at arguments – he much prefers long stony silences and loud door slamming to discussing his feelings. Molly's always trying to get things out into the open but Jake thinks things like uncomfortable feelings are better kept in the dark. He has this vague idea that they'll sort themselves out eventually if they're left alone long enough, and what's the point in repeatedly digging things up? A person can't relax with all that *Oprah*-type soul searching going on around them.

'So, where did it happen then?' Molly spits the words out, still standing with her hands in the sink. Jake blinks and rubs his neck.

'Jake! What are you thinking about?' This is his least favourite question, only slightly ahead of 'Shall we talk about it?' Molly finally cracks, and pulling her wet, soapy hands out of the washing-up bowl, grabs him by the shoulders, shaking him until he has to push her away.

She reels backwards as if he's pushed her much harder and he reaches out to steady her, but Molly smacks his hand away, beginning to cry.

'You're thinking about her, aren't you? Well, answer me! Why is she better than me? What has she got that I haven't?'

Afterwards, Jake realises pretty soon that this was where he went even more badly wrong, but she asked, didn't she? He tells

Molly that he knew that all that sizzling-hot sex and stuff was a really bad idea, but, oh, it was such fun with Kate! She had made him feel... not just young again exactly, but somehow she had reinvented him as a brilliant lover and actually, quite an interesting bloke too.

Speechless, Molly doesn't react, except to sink down onto one of the sofas. Jake sits opposite her, thinking that at least they're talking about it, and that's what she always wants to do with problems. He leans forward with his elbows on his knees, still naked to the waist, hearing his voice going on and on about Kate – how he talked to her for what seemed like ages as they lay on her living-room floor on big heaps of squashy cushions, and they had laughed like teenagers, and...

'No! *No more!*'

'But you asked me...'

'You didn't have to tell me though, did you, you stupid sod? You don't even begin to understand women. Well, she can have you if it's all so wonderful. You can just clear off.' Then she seems to remember that that's exactly what he has done.

Leaping to her feet, Molly heads for the door, grabbing her bag and keys as she leaves the caravan. Jake calls her name, but doesn't go after her until it's almost too late and she's back in her car revving the engine like crazy. He doesn't honestly think she meant to run over his toe.

21

Sunday dawns with the smell of bonfires in the air. Daisy is in the chapel at quarter past ten, glad to get out of the mist. She settles into her usual pew, halfway down on the left, next to the aisle. The mingled scent of lilies and dust is everywhere, in fact there's a bit too much dust for her liking. And why lilies?

She thinks carefully about whose turn it is to do the flowers; it must be that Mrs Crabbit from the posh houses on the estate – she's a right old show-off. Who needs expensive shop-bought flowers when the gardens are full of beautiful things at this time of year? Berries and fuchsias and all sorts. It's sheer indulgence to buy lilies.

Come to think of it, the whole place could do with smartening up a bit, not only the dusting and polishing side. Just putting a flower arrangement on the table next to the cross isn't going to impress Daisy. The cleaning rota needs reorganising and it's time the committee bought some new cushions. These wooden pews are very hard on the bottom. Daisy sighs. It's the same everywhere these days. She noticed that the kneelers in Molly's Catholic place were getting very worn too when she went to that 'Churches Together' shindig – the younger generation don't think you need to kneel to pray, but Daisy can't help feeling that God is more likely to be listening if you're uncomfortable.

She glances around at the others; the Sunday School children are in their usual, fidgeting row at the front of the church, watched over by Sarah Slater. Daisy spots Hattie's new pink sparkly jacket and Max's hand-knitted sweater with its Wallace and Gromit design. She can't see the trickiest bit from this angle, but remembers the long hours spent on that particular labour of love. Jake laughed, and demanded one too and like a fool she started it straight away. It's nearly finished too. He doesn't deserve it now – Daisy is so angry with him that she could scream right out loud, even here in the quiet of the chapel, and her heart feels bruised. In fact, it's worse than building up to a dose of the flu; she's all chilly and clammy, and her fingers are tingling. Maybe it's the worry.

And talking of scaring them all, where's Peggy today, apart from somewhere in deepest, darkest Norfolk? Wherever she's hiding, she's giving her family grief. She was always a wild one, thinks Daisy, stubborn and wilful. Bloody Catholics – they think they can get away with anything, and then just go to confession. There's still been no word, other than that phone call, and she's got serious doubts about the wisdom of believing that young strip of a lad, Nick – who is he, anyway?

Geoff's half-crazy with worry – he wanted to go with Molly when she'd set off to search for the wanderer, but Molly had other ideas, and said that it was best that she went alone. Geoff argued that she might need someone to look after her, and if Peggy was somewhere there, he ought to be involved too. Peg's woken him up, and no mistake, Daisy can't help admiring her really. If it wasn't for this business with Jake, she'd probably be much less critical of a woman who showed her lazy husband what for.

Molly was adamant though. That Nick's wormed his way in and he's helping Geoff to keep an eye on Molly's brood. Daisy can see her daughter-in-law's point. They've got an address for Jake, but Peggy could be anywhere. Molly says she doesn't need looking after, thank you very much, and her marital problems are a private matter. Good for you, Moll, Daisy tells her silently.

Mellow music begins to play and Daisy cranes her neck to see into the organ recess – it must be Clive on the keyboard this morning. If it was Maud playing, Daisy wouldn't feel this relaxed. Sarah Slater reckons that Maud plays between the notes. Daisy sits up straighter as she notices Jill and her family slip in quietly. Those kids haven't been here for a month or two, she thinks, with a sniff. Then Daisy's mouth drops open before she can stop it, as she see that the smart woman behind Jill is Kate, clicking down the aisle with sideways glances at the occupants of each row. They nod to each other as Kate slides into a seat well away from Daisy, bowing her head as if she knows the drill.

'Now what's that all about?' Daisy wonders, as Rob squeezes past her to his usual seat on her left. Kate never goes to any sort of church, as far as she knows.

Well, the Good Lord's going to have his work cut out this morning listening to this lot, Daisy thinks with amusement, as Clive begins to play the introduction to her favourite hymn, 'What a Friend We Have in Jesus'. The congregation stand up in ragged lines and Daisy's eyes blur as she opens the hymn book and reads the lines:

> Are we weak and heavy laden,
> Cumbered with a load of care?

Precious Saviour, still our refuge –
Take it to the Lord in prayer!

As the congregation belts out the familiar words and tune –
no one sings like a Methodist – Daisy's voice, usually a sound
alto, begins to wobble and she needs to blink several times
before she can swallow the lump in her throat.

Outside the chapel, the wispy mist has lifted at last and the
September sunshine is warming the grass around the grave-
stones. Daisy greets old friends, and fields a few pointed questions about the disappearance of her son. The minister is new to
the circuit and doesn't know the families very well yet. He holds
both of Daisy's hands in a moist grip, and looks her straight in
the eye, asking if there is any way *at all* in which he can help.

Short of sending him off to Norfolk to give Molly moral
support, she doubts this, and by the look of him, the chances of
this gentleman giving up on his Sunday lunch are slimmer than
his waistline.

Looking around, Daisy sees that Kate has vanished, but that
Jill is hovering, waiting for Reverend Lightfoot to release her. He
finally lets Daisy go, with one last squeeze, and immediately Jill
homes in. Daisy edges backwards but Jill is too quick for her.

'Daisy, you poor love. How are you coping with everything?'

'Oh, coasting along, you know, ducky. At least I've had a
letter from Jake now – did our Molly tell you she was going to
find him?' *Poor love indeed!*

'Yes, and I offered to go with her, of course. I really felt that
she shouldn't be alone on that sort of drive. I've been praying for
her all morning, and I'm sure the Lord will give her the strength
to carry this through. If it's His will that Jake is to come home,
He will provide the means to work things out together.'

Daisy has always had a sneaking feeling that it's rather

unfair to pray for a person when they don't know about it. They could find themselves doing something that they hadn't meant to do. She doesn't really think Jake would appreciate holy intervention either – his commitment to God consists of attending the Nativity to see if Hattie has got the Virgin Mary's role yet, and a token attendance at weddings and funerals when he can't get out of it.

'Oh, well, I'm sure that's very good of you, dear,' she says doubtfully, 'but I think our Moll will be all right on her own.'

Jill nods earnestly. 'But surely, we all need to give our troubles to Jesus and He will show us His way, if we only open our hearts and minds to Him.'

Daisy begins to wonder if Jill has been 'got at' by that lot at the Anglican church in Hopton. This is a very strange way for a Methodist to talk, and Daisy doesn't go along with it at all. Smiling in what she hopes is a brave but discouraging manner, Daisy hastily takes her leave of Jill, who smiles, hugs her, and wishes her 'God's Peace'.

It's to be hoped that all this hugging and sharing the peace lark doesn't catch on in Mayfield, Daisy thinks, as she hurries round to Sarah's house for lunch. The problem with nits is bad enough without any of that nonsense.

As she gets near to Sarah's house, she rummages in her bag for the key. Sarah will still be sorting out the stragglers at Sunday School and Daisy has promised to put the veggies on. It was kind of Sarah to offer to cook for Geoff and the grandchildren too, so it'll be a family occasion, but very different to their usual get-togethers.

The rich smell of roast beef meets Daisy as she opens the door into Sarah's immaculate hallway. In the kitchen, she gets the spare apron on and begins to collect her weapons – six shining stainless steel saucepans, a huge carton of salt (Daisy and Sarah agree wholeheartedly that today's youngsters are far too worried about silly things like being lactose-free and low-carb) a long, dangerous-looking vegetable knife, and the bowl of Yorkshire pudding mixture made earlier by Sarah.

She heats up a roasting tin for the potatoes – Sarah has very sensibly par-boiled them earlier – shakes some salt and semolina over them and makes sure they're well coated to make them nice and crispy. She thinks she remembers getting the potato tip from that woman on the TV, the one who has some right tarty clothes but quite good ideas. Always licking her fingers though; can't be hygienic, surely? When the potatoes are safely cooking, she puts the radio on and gets to work in earnest. Soon the pans are full of an assortment of runner beans, chunks of carrot, parsnips, potatoes, leeks and mushy peas. Daisy adds plenty of salt, the kitchen fills with steam, and soon the puddings are sizzling and puffing up in their tins in the oven.

She gets out a cheery yellow cloth and lays the table in the dining room, and back in the kitchen, peers through the oven door anxiously – the puddings are rising, in answer to her own, more mundane prayers.

* * *

The family lunch party goes well, despite the absence of two of its key players. It's strange and quite horrible being here without Molly and Jake. Molly had the grace to phone Daisy saying she'd felt a bit dizzy on the way home and didn't feel safe to drive any further. She'd pulled into a little B&B just outside Cromer and luckily they'd got a room, so she'd decided to stay and have a good sleep, as Nick, Geoff and Sam seemed to have the younger ones in hand. It had been ages since she'd had a chance to catch up with the books on her Kindle, she'd said, and she was going to have a huge, bubbly bath and come home later on tomorrow when she's had a bit of a scout around Peggy's old haunts.

Daisy had tried to find out more about Molly's trip, such as if she'd seen Jake, and if so, why she'd left him so fast. All Molly would say was that Jake was staying in the van for a day or two to think things over, and that she'd realised looking for Peggy would be worse than the needle in a haystack problem so she'd rather do it after a good night's rest.

Even though Daisy's missing the other two, she's pleased to see everyone enjoying their Sunday lunch and she can see that Sarah is just as happy; there's something so satisfying about cooking a traditional dinner for the people you love. She and Sarah don't let themselves get lonely. It's perfectly acceptable to eat alone and Daisy knows for a fact Sarah makes a point of cooking delicious, healthy meals for herself, but in her heart of hearts, Daisy thinks this is better.

Sarah looks round the table and smiles when she notices that her guests are all using their napkins – she always likes to get the good linen out so that she can have the silver napkin rings on the table; they're all initialled, but their original owners are long gone. Sarah loves polishing them, and also the candlesticks, spoons, trays and tea set. When the teapot has just been polished it could easily grace Downton Abbey. Sarah's standards don't slip; that's how she keeps sane these days, she tells Daisy.

The spectacular joint of beef, gently pink in the middle, has complemented the high-rise Yorkshire puddings, golden potatoes and soft vegetables. Daisy and Sarah can't abide the modern trend for crunchy sprouts and rock-hard cabbage, and everyone seems to be absorbed in appreciating their cooking.

However, by the time Sarah brings in the steamed treacle sponge and custard, Daisy can sense restlessness in the air. As they eat, almost mechanically, the children murmur to each other under cover of the grown-ups' talk of gardening and the mild weather. Nick eats ravenously, and watches Theo under his eyelashes, occasionally making her blush with his cool stare. Hmm. Daisy wonders, not for the first time, where this strange boy came from and what is his game. There is something very disturbing about this Nick person.

He looks up suddenly and meets her gaze. What is it about him? Daisy looks straight back at him, and out of the corner of her eye can see Sarah's head turn too. What is it that's bothering them both about the boy? Daisy can't put her finger on why he's so unsettling.

Nick is the first to lower his eyes; such unusual eyes too, being one green and one blue, and Daisy remembers she had a kitten with eyes like that once – it was almost feral. This boy has the same air of inscrutability, somehow. He even holds himself like a cat; proud and wary.

Everyone has nearly finished when Sam finally flings down his spoon in desperation. He turns to Sarah, almost knocking over his water glass in his fervour.

'Mrs Slater, it's only half past two – if you borrowed that old school minibus, we could all go to the caravan and see Dad. I don't reckon Mum's in the right mood to make him come home and if she's gone and made him angry, he'll never come back!'

At this, Hattie and Max begin to cry, and Theo adds pitifully, 'Please, Mrs Slater? Mr Jennings won't mind; he said any time you wanted the bus, you only had to say.'

'Yes, but he meant for Sunday School outings, not joyriding,' Sarah protests half-heartedly. 'I can't just take the bus to the seaside for the day – it's not right.'

She looks around the table; so many pleading eyes, all asking for the same thing. She sighs.

* * *

An hour and a half later, as they drive through the light traffic around Peterborough, Daisy is sure they must all have taken leave of their senses. What on earth has she let herself in for? Jake will probably be furious to find his entire family hot on the heels of his wife, and she knows her tetchy firstborn, his disapproval will be blatantly obvious. But then, she reflects, she really doesn't know Jake, because she never would have expected him to do anything like this. She especially wouldn't have expected to hear about him leaving Kate's house after midnight on the evening of his disappearance. Sarah spotted him as she returned from the late-night meeting of the French film society in Hopton. Daisy wishes she hadn't told her in some ways, but she knows if Sarah had kept something like that quiet and she'd found out later, she'd never have forgiven her.

Daisy looks over at Sarah with deep affection as her old friend weaves the minibus confidently through the Sunday-afternoon drivers. It's not been an easy life for Sarah since her marriage ended, and Daisy knows it was a very messy break-up involving another woman, but she hasn't said a word against Jake, bless her.

When Sarah's life with Ken Slater was over, she told Daisy she'd promised herself she would never, ever, judge or try to understand other people's relationships. Not one of Sarah's friends ever really understood her own problems, not even Daisy, who knows her so well. So Sarah doesn't want to know what Jake was playing at, she doesn't want to know Kate's part in it, she doesn't feel the need to find out what Molly thinks – she tells Daisy she just wants this good, solid family to stay that way.

She has even prayed for them, even though she thinks Jake wouldn't thank her for it. Families should stay together; she

knows that to her cost, although that doesn't really apply to
Sarah and Ken – they never constituted a proper family in
Sarah's eyes.

It's many years since Ken left Sarah. Daisy can't even
remember exactly what he looked like, only that he was very
good-looking, in a Stewart Granger kind of way, with a taste for
dapper sports jackets and a clean, pressed handkerchief in his
top pocket. He was only medium height, but his silver sideburns
and upright carriage ensured that he looked like a gentleman.
It's a shame that appearances can be deceptive. He was the best
headmaster the school had ever had; if he'd stayed, he could
have been a real force to be reckoned with.

Sadly, Ken Slater was an inspirational teacher but a lousy
husband. When he went away, Sarah has told Daisy that she
was too innocent to realise why – it wasn't until much later that
she found out about the girl. But what really broke her heart
was hearing about his children.

Sarah would have dearly loved some children of her own in
those days, but she's fine now; she's got school, her niche at the
chapel and her friends. She would never depend on a man for
her happiness nowadays, there's no future in it. She won't pry,
won't give advice – she'll just be here as a taxi service and pick
up the pieces when it's over. It's what she does best, after all.
Daisy is grateful from the bottom of her heart for this. Without
Sarah, today would have been an endless worry. Now, it's almost
an adventure.

22

Poppy stands in the middle of the room with her hands on her generous hips.

'So where *has* Molly gone?' she asks Jill and Kate. 'You're not telling me she's really shot off to Norfolk to look for Jake? I wouldn't have bothered – let the silly sod stew in his own juice, clearing off like that for no reason!'

Kate has already polished off most of an excellent bottle of burgundy and several bowls of olives, crackers and pretzels. They are surrounded by the remains of plates of sliced ripe tomatoes with fresh basil and chives, dripping with walnut oil, and avocado, lightly tossed in lemon juice. A deep dish of home-made mushroom pate sits next to a basket of roughly cut ciabatta, and the cheese board is heaped with stilton, delicate goats' cheese, fragrant Sage Derby and a perfectly runny brie.

Poppy's kitchen is always so welcoming, full of homely touches like strings of garlic, shiny copper pans and the smell of wonderful things cooking. It's nothing like Kate's – all chrome and clinical whiteness, or Jill's stripped pine and chintz haven. Kate sighs. She's been waiting for the hidden agenda. It's so relaxing here that she couldn't resist Poppy's invitation, but of course there's a hidden agenda. She looks up at her friend warily, as Poppy gets to the point.

'Any ideas? Jill? Kate? Where and why do you think she's gone, and what happened to make her change from the sensible Molly we know and love to someone who'd leave her kids and not even pack a proper overnight bag, or so Sam tells me?'

'I see what you mean about Jake having no reason,' says Jill. 'He's never been one for snap decisions, as far as I can tell, has he?'

'Perhaps he did have a reason,' Kate answers slowly. 'Perhaps he was ashamed.'

'What's Jake got to be ashamed of? He's never done a bad thing since he got caught scrumping my dad's apples,' says Jill. 'He's a really, really nice man, and Molly's lucky to have him.'

Poppy looks at Kate sharply. 'What are you getting at, ducky? Something we should know?' She refills Kate's glass and it's promptly emptied.

'Only that he slept with me on the night he left – we didn't do a lot of sleeping actually.' Kate tries to keep the smile off her face, but it breaks out – she looks as if she's been dying to tell someone.

Jill stands transfixed at the sink where she has gone to fill a glass with water – she says drinking at lunchtime always makes her head woozy.

'But Kate – you've committed... adultery!' she falters. 'And Molly's supposed to be your friend!'

'Oh, don't be so sanctimonious, Jill. He was desperate, he was unhappy, and if you must know, I've always wanted to see what he was like in bed.' Kate drains her glass again, and reaches for the bottle, only to find it empty.

Automatically, Poppy goes to the cupboard for a less expensive replacement, uncorks it, and refills the glass. 'But you've always said he was a bit of a prat. I thought you couldn't stand him,' she says faintly. After a brief pause, she adds, 'So, was he any good?'

Tension released, Poppy and Kate begin to rock with slightly hysterical laughter.

'Stop it! Shut up, you pair of trollops!' screams Jill.

The word 'trollops' only sets them off again, holding their sides in agony, as Jill grabs each of them by a shoulder and shakes them.

'You've got to find Molly and say sorry – she'll forgive you if you tell her straight away!'

'Hang on a minute,' gulps a sobered Poppy. 'I don't want forgiving, thank you very much. It's Kate who's confessing, not me!'

Stung by this betrayal, Kate forgets her recent promise to keep a secret and flings back, 'Oh, come on now, Miss Perfect. You might as well get a quick prayer for forgiveness in while we're at it – I only screwed a proper grown-up. You seduced that innocent young bloke from the corner shop, and don't you forget it!'

'You did what? Mr and Mrs Mitchell's son, William? I can't believe it. You didn't, did you, Poppy? He can't even be twenty years old yet.'

There's a silence as Kate and Poppy try to avoid looking at each other.

Jill's white, open-mouthed face confronts them briefly before she flies from the kitchen with a sob, yelling, 'That poor man needs me now more than ever – I must go to Norfolk!' The remaining two are left staring speechlessly at each other.

'Did you really go to bed with Jake?' asks Poppy finally.

'Well, no – we did it on the living-room floor,' Kate replies with a giggle. 'What about you – surely you can't really have meant to lure young Will into your lair?'

'It was kind of an accident, to be honest. I didn't mean to do more than give him a hug when he was upset because his dog had been run over. But I told you that in strictest confidence. You weren't supposed to tell a soul – why did you have to blab to Jill, of all people?'

'Sorry. It just came out. I guess sex was on my mind, but for goodness' sake, Poppy, if you shagged everyone who cried, your life would take on a whole new focus.'

'And why not? I'm a free agent.'

Kate laughs enviously. She's always suspected that Poppy has a weakness for youngish men, but has never been able to get her to admit it. Poppy keeps her own counsel – she won't tell anyone her age and she never talks about her past. Her friends think she must be hovering around her mid-thirties but it's hard to tell, because her skin's so smooth and unlined – she tells them it's because she never diets and doesn't have to deal with tantrums of any kind, from any adult, teenager or child.

Poppy considers herself to be completely self-sufficient, but Kate doesn't believe her. Kate thinks that the sickening thing is that Poppy will sail through all this stuff with Sam, and at the end of it all no one will be hurt. Sam will always remember her affectionately and she'll have had a bloody good time. But as for Kate; she's tried to explain to Poppy that this was more than a bit of fun, and that she can't forget Jake's face when he left. She can't resist talking about it either.

How was it possible to have gone through all these years of knowing a man, been godmother to his children, teased him relentlessly, made him so cross, and then ended up all warm with him on the rug in the candlelight? She certainly hadn't planned to try and take him away from Molly, but now it's happened, she can't find it in her heart to regret it. Kate helps herself to more wine. She's had way too much but it's the only way to numb the longing for Jake that's kept her awake for the last two nights.

'Jake seemed a bit on the desperate side to me. Do you reckon Molly keeps him short?'

'Kate – they've got a houseful of children. When do you think they get a chance to roll around in front of the fire? There would be kids stepping over them saying, "Mum, what's for tea? And what are you doing to Dad?" Look, there's no time to worry about that now – we'd better hurry up and get after Jill before she completely wrecks the marriage for them. I've only had one glass of wine with my dinner and loads of water – ring your gang and tell them you're off. We're going to the seaside.'

23

The kindly sun shines down on Peggy as she sits on the caravan steps shelling broad beans and drinking strong black coffee. She can just see the sea through the gap in the fence, and the sound of the gulls is raucous. The last few days have been a bit of an eye-opener, to be sure; her hair is hanging down her back as if she was a teenager again, all grey curls and mess, and she's totally relaxed for the first time in years.

Peggy would never have described herself as a stressed-out sort of person, being fairly mellow on the whole, but she can feel the tension just trickling away the longer she is near to the sea and the cliffs. She can even think about Maria without wanting to cry.

There's a place near the lighthouse where people have planted trees for their loved ones who've died. Peggy thinks that she would have liked that for her baby. Maria didn't live more than a minute, if that, but if there had been somewhere to go to really be with her, Peggy might not have felt so bitter about letting her go. They wouldn't let them bury Maria – in those days a premature baby was just taken away if it was very early –

but maybe the pain wouldn't have been quite so bad if they could have had a funeral.

Peggy reckons that folks would think she was barmy if they knew how often Maria is on her mind. It was thirty years ago, but it's still like yesterday. They all said it wasn't anyone's fault, but Peggy's not so sure. She was so busy with the others. Rushing about, never sitting down to put her feet up. Resting was for those with nothing better to do, she'd always said. Ah, Maria, God love you.

She wriggles to adjust her cushion – the steps are wrought iron, and very hard on the bum, especially if you haven't the padding there. In the tall grass at her feet lies a long, thin lizard of a boy. He whimpers in his sleep, and she brushes a dusty twist of hair away from his open mouth. He wakes with a yelp as the hair catches his newly pierced lip, whirling to his feet and on the defensive before he remembers where he is. They smile at each other, a private, lazy grin of shared happiness.

'Are you hungry, my pet? How do broad beans and bacon grab you?'

Kris sinks to the floor, with a sigh of deep contentment. His eyes – one blue and one green – grow moist, and he rubs a grimy hand under his nose.

'Where do you reckon the dead go, Peg? I reckon my gran's still around somehow – she liked it better here than anywhere else, and she spent most of her life saving up to get this caravan, so why would she move on just because she's dead, eh?'

'You've got a point, love. Course, I was brought up to believe in heaven but don't get me started on limbo. Never could get me head around that one.'

Kris frowns. 'Don't know about limbo, but them couple of holidays she treated us to here were the best ever. Gran reckoned sitting on the sand with her back against a breakwater was her idea of heaven on earth.'

'Can't fault her for that. Mine too, come to think of it.'

'Yeah, but Mum never settled here, she liked towns best. She wasn't keen on Gran – said she was always trying to come between her and her kids. But Gran just loved us, that was all. Mum was a bitch. I bet Gran haunted her.'

Peggy shuffles uncomfortably; this is strong stuff and she's quite attached to him now – she can't let him burn in hell. Crossing herself furtively she says a silent prayer to Our Lady – Mary was a mother, she should understand. She must have had a lot of bother with our Lord when he was growing up, a right wilful little monkey by all accounts. What about all that carry-on with the priests in the Temple? She must have been frantic when he just disappeared without a word. And then he wasn't even sorry – kids! And this one isn't much more than a lad either. She'll have to try and educate him a bit, if she can.

'Don't know about that, love, and I know some folks say once you're dead, that's it, but us Catholics, we believe we'll be saved to go to a better place if we live right, not that it's easy, mind you.'

They sit in silence, both trying to make sense of their thoughts. After a while, Peggy carries on. It isn't easy but she wants to make him relax again, like he was when he was sleeping.

'It's like this, Kris. My Reginald always used to say that there's something good for everybody – some folks get theirs when they're here, some have to wait for the next place. He reckoned those that get all of theirs now miss out later.'

Kris looks up at Peggy trustingly and her heart twists, taking her breath away for a second or two. He's so bloody helpless, she wishes he'd talk about exactly what's gone on in his life to make her want to protect him like this – she thought she'd used up all her maternal instincts on her own brood and Moll's.

'Mmmm. I'm going to have mine now then Peg. D'you fancy goin' down the pier? We'll have dinner first though,' he adds hastily.

Peggy rises to her feet in one movement, feeling fit and stronger than she's felt for years. She's still tanned from last summer and from these precious days basking in the Norfolk sunshine. She gives a little wiggle – go Peg! She is still wearing the denim skirt she left home in, but has swapped the shop overall for a faded, red checked shirt that she found stashed away in the caravan wardrobe. It's a bit frayed at the neck but she's tied it at the waist and the whole look is quite snazzy with the flip flops left behind after the last holiday. Her sleeves are rolled up, workmanlike. Bending, she scoops up the colander, the bean pods and the empty mug all in one go.

As Peggy clatters around the small living area of the caravan, wrinkling her nose at the stink of cigarette smoke and damp carpets that no amount of fresh air and spray polish seems to shift, Kris gazes thoughtfully at the row of clean t-shirts steaming gently on the makeshift line.

'You making parsley sauce, Peg?' he yells, hopefully. 'Only, Gran used to say broad beans and bacon was naked without a bit of parsley sauce.'

'Yes, I'm making parsley sauce – it's instant though, there's no fresh round here – and yes, I do want to go to the pier, but you'll have to help with the washing up first. I've only just sorted this sink from when I got here. Honest to God, Kris – this place was a pigsty. They can't rent out a filthy dump like this, surely? It's a good job I'm not making proper sauce too – there's only this one beat-up old pan!'

Kris grins. Peggy knows he's got no intention of washing up.

He probably thinks the job's not worth doing until there are no pots left in the place. He sniffs the air hopefully.

'Nearly ready, Peg?' he calls, rolling to his feet and shaking grass from his torn old t-shirt and baggy jeans. 'I'm starving.'

'Get in here and give us a hand then, you lazy young dote... this sink needs clearing. And take those bloody great boots off in the caravan – I've just got this floor to look decent. Your gran would turn in her grave to see the state you live in.'

Reluctantly, Kris eases his feet from the battered, smelly old army boots. He flings back his hair, rolls his eyes and says he hopes that Peg's not going to be more trouble than she's worth because he can do without nagging women. Then he pads into the caravan, nudging her shoulder affectionately as he passes the greasy cooker, and she clips his ear for him.

How have they got so comfortable together, this skinny boy and the Irish granny? They are living in a run-down caravan with hardly any money to call their own. The key was under the mat, and Kris reckons it's not changed since his gran died. The site owner was meant to be taking it over but it looks as if the only people who've been on holiday here are a few mice, and no one's seen the bloke for the last few months – they say he had an argument with some visitors and had to disappear for a while.

The site's only a mile or two up the coast from the place where Daisy keeps her van, but Peggy thinks it's a world away from that manicured place with its clubhouse and swimming pool. This one's faded, seedy and stuck in the sixties. Secretly, Peggy loves it.

Anyway, the panic she felt as she drove away from her home and her man (and her fights with Molly, and, really, her whole life) has just melted away. Kris was standing by the side of the road not far from the turning for the quarry, with his shoulders slumped, looking sad, and very young. He glanced up hopelessly as the car passed; hardly even bothered to stick out a thumb. As Peggy reversed in a cloud of pebbles, he looked as if he couldn't believe his luck.

'Where to, love?' she asked, as kindly as she could, in the circumstances.

'Wherever you're going is good, 'specially if we can stop for some chips!'

'Bloody cheek – you want a lift *and* to get fed? How do I know you're not an axe murderer?'

'How d'you think I can afford a bleedin' axe?'

'Hmm, good point. Don't much care if you are, anyway. Tell you what – you can work for your tea; do you drive?'

'Course I do; no licence though.'

'Sod the licence – this is what you need to do...'

He caught on quickly, and they were soon on the train heading for the east coast, and freedom. She just can't figure out why he looks so familiar.

* * *

A couple of hours later, Kris and Peggy walk along the pier, eating hot doughnuts and making fun of the serious fishermen with their buckets of rancid crab pieces. The wooden slats of the pier structure are uneven, and glimpses of water can be seen through them. A small boy is sitting next to an older fisherman, posting small pieces of shell through the cracks and humming to himself. Kris is scornful.

'Where's the fun in that, Peg? They sit here all day stinking of fish, catch some tiddlers and a few crabs, then throw the whole lot back in and go home. Wankers. Pointless, or what?'

'Mmm, I can see the point if you eat what you catch, but this is just plain daft. Maybe they don't want to go home? Or maybe they haven't got homes to go to. And don't say that word; don't ask which word either, I wouldn't sully my lips with it, and you know it.'

That shuts him up, good and proper. He gets out his mobile and starts fiddling with it. He does that a lot. Peggy's already asked if there's somebody he wants to phone but he just shrugged and said he'd run out of credit. Now his shoulders are down and he looks so sad Peggy can hardly bear it.

'Okay, what's up, love? You've gone very quiet all of a sudden. I think it's about time you told me what's going on. Come on, let's sit in the sun on this bench, look at the sea, and talk about your worries. Then I'll tell you mine – that'll take your mind off your troubles, for sure!'

She gives the boy a swift hug, shoving him towards a nearby seat, empty of fishermen but still a bit fishy. Kris leans against her as they watch the tide coming in, the ripples of sunlight on the water and the salty tang in the air soothing some of the painful words as they boil out.

'Mum left us when we were quite little. She didn't like us much, or so our dad said. She was killed in a car crash not long afterwards. We had to go and live with anyone who'd have us, after *he'd* had enough, and then me and Nick managed to get fostered together.'

'Oh, pet – it sounds awful.'

'It wasn't so bad with the new people, but Nick's always been tricky. He was expelled from school after... well, there was a bit of trouble.'

'What happened?'

Kris's face is closed in now. He shrugs again.

'You might feel better if you let it out, you know. A trouble shared, and all that?'

'What about it?'

'You know the old saying – a trouble shared is a trouble halved?'

Kris laughs. To Peggy, the sound grates like nails on the blackboard when she was at primary school. There's precious little humour in it.

'Half of this trouble would be bad enough,' Kris says, shivering, but he carries on. 'Nick started hurting himself – razor blades, scissors, anything he could get hold of. After a bit it wasn't enough to hurt his own body. There was a girl...'

'What did he do, Kris?' Peggy's stomach is churning now, but she needs to know.

'No, I can't tell you, Peg.' Kris is weeping openly now and Peggy longs to hold him, but he flinches away when she tries. 'He promised it would be over. He's changed his name and everything. It's all behind us now. It never came to court.'

'What? What did your brother get himself into, for pity's sake?'

But Kris won't be drawn. It's getting cold now, and most people have gone home from the pier. Peggy is alarmed by the pinched, blue tinge of his face.

'Right, cup of strong, sweet tea and fish and chips for us before we do any more talking today. I'm hungry even if you're not – it seems ages since dinner; must be the sea air.'

Kris looks really ill, as if he's just getting over flu or something, thinks Peggy. They set off arm in arm, back down the pier, almost as if he's just learning to walk again. Peggy can tell how shaky he feels, and she matches her pace to Kris's. Inside, she's burning with anger and sympathy for those poor, motherless children. But what, in the name of all that's holy, has Kris's brother done?

'Maybe Nick will text me soon,' says Kris, 'he said it would be best if we separated to hunt on our own.'

'Hunt? What are you talking about now, pet? You didn't say anything about hunting.'

'Oh, erm... did I say hunt? I meant manage by ourselves.'

Peggy eyes him doubtfully. It's easy to see how close the twins must be. Kris has said several times that he wonders where his brother has got to. Even when Peggy and Kris were on the East Coast line after dumping the Rover, he'd muttered about not being able to shake off the feeling that he'd let Nick down; they have never ever been apart for this long before. Peggy has a feeling that Nick is still holding the reins, wherever he is now. It's not altogether a comfortable thought.

24

Molly sits behind the wheel of her car as she speeds back along the A47, radio on full blast and the window open to let in the warm breeze. It's been an eventful time in Norfolk but parts of it have been so peaceful that she feels guiltily refreshed by her break from the family. The previous evening had gone exactly to plan in the end. She'd dropped lucky with the B&B; it was right next to a village pub and they'd given her the only room left, a quiet one at the back of the cottage, right under the eaves, with a dreamy view of rolling fields and a distant forest.

Flopping down on the bed, Molly had propped herself up with pillows and done the necessary phoning to make sure everyone was safe and catered for. The team of Geoff, Sam and Nick seemed to be coping rather well, and after Molly had spoken to Daisy, her evening was her own.

But what should she do with it? The dizziness that she'd used as her excuse for staying over had been genuine, and now, in this beautiful place, she felt much better, and ready to do some serious thinking.

'Will you be wanting a meal tonight, love?' the helpful

owner of the house had asked. 'Only, the pub does a fantastic deal with us – the food's all home cooked and you get it half price if you're staying here. Want me to book you in?'

Molly's stomach had rumbled so alarmingly at this point that the woman had laughed out loud. 'I'll take that as a yes then?' she'd said, picking up the phone. 'Eight o'clock okay for you?'

So Molly had had a little while to tidy herself up as best she could with the random collection of things she'd thrown into her bag as she'd left home. She upended it on the bed and considered the heap of contents. Purse, spare knickers, notebook and pen, toothbrush and toothpaste, packet of crisps (?), lipstick, hairbrush and face wipes. Hmm. Good job the pub was a well-used walkers' place, according to her hostess. Molly would blend in nicely with the rumpled, windswept crowd.

It had been strange to be eating alone. Molly couldn't remember ever having gone into somewhere and ordered a meal for one. There was something luxurious about it, once she'd found a secluded table and tucked herself away out of sight of the gang of ramblers who'd piled in just as she was ordering steak and ale pie and hand-cut chips.

Molly took a swig of cider and shuffled her chair nearer to the blazing log fire. The evening was still warm but the flickering flames were comforting, and she felt her tense muscles begin to relax at last. When her pie arrived, with golden, crispy pastry and chips like mini paving slabs, she tucked in with gusto, and cleared the plate without once thinking about Jake or Peggy.

Back in her room, it wasn't so easy to distance herself from the events of the last few days. Her mind had whirled with snippets of conversation – Rob, Jake, Geoff, Nick... she ran an enormous bath and tipped in a whole bottle of complementary shower gel, and as the water swirled and foamed, she undressed without looking in the full-length mirror.

It was better under the water, with her bare limbs decently covered by the bubbles, but even as the warmth relaxed her again, Molly couldn't shake off an overwhelming feeling of failure. She'd flirted shamelessly with Rob without a thought for her husband, but in the meantime Jake had gone one better and actually leapt into bed with one of her closest friends. Now her marriage was in tatters, and whatever jaundiced view she'd had of it before, she'd never actually imagined life without Jake in it. And why did her mum have to pick this moment to have a belated midlife crisis?

Molly's relationship with Peggy had never been entirely straightforward but the love had always been there, hadn't it? Couldn't Peggy have told her if she needed to escape? Molly gave herself a shake as she dried herself on the enormous bath sheet and slipped naked between the sheets. This was no time for feeling sorry for herself. She sat up in bed and reached for her notebook, shivering at the unaccustomed feeling of smooth linen against bare flesh. Jake had often tried to persuade her come to bed without her pyjamas but she'd always made the excuse that when the kids shouted out in the night, she was the one who'd have to go and sort them out.

Now, she was beginning to see that, even through the blistering anger at his betrayal, there might have been room for improvement. She picked up her pen and began to get her tangled thoughts on paper. She'd never sleep without some sort of therapy, and this was the only one available. There wasn't much point in roaming around looking for Peggy – she could be anywhere in Norfolk, after all – and in her heart of hearts she was as sure as she could be that her feisty mother was just teaching her dad a lesson. She'd come home when she was good and ready. As for Jake, he could just stew for a while. Molly decided the best plan would be to have a lazy breakfast, just in case her mum did decide to make contact, and if not, to head home mid-afternoon and be back in time to get everyone sorted, ready for the next day's school run.

* * *

As she thunders back down the A47, Molly's unruly thoughts are still buzzing around her head like angry bees. She has already had three texts from Rob today, and she hasn't answered any of them, because she has suddenly become plagued with venomous feelings about scary Lydia Jennings.

Molly doesn't know Lydia well. She comes to school functions sometimes, and she's always got some incredibly rare ailment that means she has to sit down all the time and have cups of tea brought to her. She watches Rob constantly, and smiles graciously at everybody as if they should be feeling really honoured to have her with them. And she wears gathered flowery skirts and knitted short-sleeved jumpers in pastel colours. Molly doesn't get it – if it's cold enough for a jumper, surely you need sleeves? Has the invention of the T-shirt completely passed Lydia by?

Molly wonders why they don't have children? Perhaps it would have interfered with all that sitting down. Molly can't remember the last time she sat down and someone ran around with cups of tea for her. She usually ends up manning the cake stall at school functions or selling reams of raffle tickets.

Oh, this is so awful. Thinking about Lydia is only a distraction, Molly knows that really. She can't bear to think about Jake with Kate. She'd never imagined it would hurt so much, knowing your own husband has been with someone else, and done all that secret stuff that you only do together, but of course it does. It's hideous.

The phone on the seat next to Molly vibrates and she jumps so violently that she swerves into the middle of the road, causing a white van with three men in it to shout and gesticulate as they just avoid wiping her out. Sod the phone – if it's him again, she doesn't know what to say and if it's anyone else, she can't be bothered. She'll be home soon. They can wait for an hour or so. Molly has never, ever ignored her phone's demands before – mums don't as a rule.

It feels good.

She drives on, liberated in a small way, trying to face up to the fact that soon she's probably going to be liberated in lots of bigger ways too.

25

Molly doesn't even notice the school minibus as she dashes back towards King's Lynn. It's far too late to attract her attention by the time they realise who's just passed them, and Sarah's busy trying to avoid squashing all those hikers with their chill-proof anoraks and sturdy boots, so they don't even wave.

Theo tries Molly's mobile to tell her what they're doing. It rings for a bit and then it's turned off, so she leaves a garbled message. Privately, Daisy thinks that it's just as well the phone's gone to voicemail, as Molly hasn't quite got the hang of stopping to answer calls – her phone only buzzes, it never rings properly, and if she notices it, she just scrabbles in her bag, tipping out most of her things, causing chaos on the roads around her, and then shouting 'Hello?' into the wrong end of the phone.

Once, she rummaged so hard she flipped one of those tampon things into her dad's lap – he didn't know where to look. Daisy was surprised he knew what it was – she'd never have let her own husband see anything like that. She supposes that's what running a shop does for you. How must he feel if shame-less women come in and ask for... well... ladies' things? Daisy shudders and tries to bring her mind back to the subject in hand.

What a worry Molly is – much beloved, but no common sense a lot of the time. She usually makes herself available for her children every hour of the day and night in case they might want to get hold of her, so they never cease making all these demands on her time and energy. This is the only time Daisy can remember Molly being off their radar.

Daisy has tried to explain what it was like when her own kids were little. They didn't have a phone in the whole street, let alone one that they could cart around with them. Theo says she even takes her mobile in the bath with her. For goodness' sake – what's so urgent it can't wait a few minutes? Daisy remembers the time when a much smaller Jake fell out of a tree, the vicar's wife ran all the way from the other side of the village to summon help, and then Daisy ran all the way back with her to where he was lying, then the kind woman ran all the way home to the vicarage to phone an ambulance, and after that someone else ran to get Reginald... and Jake was fine in the end. It just goes to show.

The minibus carries the strange assortment of people onwards towards the sea; all either worried or grumpy, or both. They're still full of dinner – most of them would rather be sneaking a short nap, or a crafty smoke or watching a nice black-and-white Sunday-afternoon film; Daisy knows for a fact that nearly everyone on this bus would prefer to be somewhere else. None of them are sure what they should do when they get to Jake. Max spent the first part of the journey wondering if he was going to be sick (he was) and the sight of Molly flying back in the opposite direction has unsettled everybody.

'She's going home again already, and she was on her own. If

Mum can't sort things out with Dad, what chance have we got?' mutters Theo.

'Don't be so defeatist, she can't do it because she gets mad too fast – we'll be okay,' answers Sam, but perhaps he's not as sure as he makes out, because he won't meet Daisy's eye when she turns round to smile at him, and he keeps fidgeting in his seat, twisting and turning like he used to do at Sunday School.

'Hey, Sam, do you want a wee?' asks Max. He's perked up no end since he's been sick. Sarah's not so chuffed – he managed to hit the back of her neck.

'Course I don't, we're nearly there anyway,' Sam snaps.

'I've seen the sea already,' Hattie brags.

'You can't have – we never see it till we get to Cromer. You're such a liar, Hat!' Theo's getting edgy too.

'No, I am not a liar, I did see...'

'Quiet, all of you!' The bellow from Geoff startles them all. The kids are dumbfounded – he never shouts. Fat tears begin to trickle down Max's cheeks, and he chews on his nails. Theo looks thunderous. There's going to be trouble from that young lady before too long, thinks Daisy.

A gloomy silence falls as the bus reaches the outskirts of Cromer, and Sarah makes everyone wind their windows down, 'to appreciate the scent of the sea.' More likely to get rid of the smell of sick, Daisy thinks.

She would quite like to stop for a bit, really. She loves Cromer pier, and she's in no hurry to get to Jake now Molly's not there to worry about, but the others seem to want to press on. Gazing out of the window, looking enviously at the Sunday-afternoon visitors who are wandering around the town, Daisy notices that some of the shops are open – that would have never happened in her day; if they hadn't got it, they managed without.

The church is just as impressive as ever; strong and formidable with the solid tower giving it even more weight. No storms from the sea will ever touch it. Daisy suddenly wants to be inside the church, safe and cared for, singing 'Will Your Anchor Hold in the Storms of Life?' or 'For Those in Peril on the Sea', or any of those good old tunes. Still, the Good Lord hasn't let her down yet. She murmurs a silent prayer, a line from another of her favourite hymns – '...strength for today, and bright hope for tomorrow' – that's what they all need.

Driving through the lanes, everyone's spirits lift – the sea on the left is as blue as speedwells, or forget-me-nots, or Daisy's eyes, according to Reginald. The tiny flint-covered cottages huddle together against the breezes – it was Reginald's dream to buy one of those for his retirement so he and Daisy could keep their old bones supple by walking along the beach. It's bleak here in winter, but today is all puffy clouds, sunshine and big, blue sky.

The minibus eventually pulls up at the caravan site and everyone tumbles out in the car park by the entrance, relieved to be here at last. Mind you, once they've stretched themselves, they stand around looking at each other, like a right crowd of wallies. There is a brand-new clubhouse here, and Daisy can't help standing on tiptoe to try to see the soft furnishings. It's like a little Swiss chalet with bright red geraniums in window boxes and a sign advertising 'Fondue Nite' on Saturdays. Fondue? That's cheese spread, with a bit of garlic and brandy in it, Daisy reckons. Only £15.99 a head and a free pint of lager. She can feel Reginald turning in his urn again. She squares her shoulders and marches off down the path between the willow bushes, being careful to avoid the dog mess – they don't know about pooper scoopers in this neck of the woods. Nothing much else has changed, but the van looks very tidy. The grass has been cut, and someone's even cleared the herb bed – Daisy can smell the mint and thyme from here.

'Right, who's going in first, then?' barks Geoff.

'There's no need to take that tone, Gramps,' says Hattie. 'We could all be grumpy if we wanted to, but we're trying to be brave, aren't we?' She looks round, smugly.

'Oh, shut up, smartarse.' Theo's clearly still cross about who saw the sea first.

As Hattie builds up for a really good tantrum, her grandmother steps in – someone's got to take charge here.

'I'm going in first because I'm his mother,' Daisy says firmly. 'You lot can stay out here for a minute or two.'

They look a bit mutinous but Daisy thinks they're all quite glad they haven't got to face Jake just yet. She takes a deep breath and knocks – hang on, it's her own caravan, she doesn't need to ask permission to come in! The door opens straight into the lounge, and Daisy goes in, hoping she looks braver than she feels.

Her heart seems to stop for a second – Jake's lying flat on his back on the floor. Then she notices he's got a bag of frozen peas on his foot, and realises that not many people collapse after putting vegetables on their extremities. He opens his eyes and rolls them in her direction, then sits up, shouting out in pain and grabbing his toes.

'Mum! What the hell are you doing here? Oh, bugger, it hurts!'

Daisy bends down creakily to look at the damage, trying not to laugh.

'What have you done to yourself, son? Stubbed your toes again? You're always...'

'Stubbed my toe? Stubbed my bloody toe? No, I have not

stubbed my toe, Mum. I haven't done anything to myself – that silly woman ran over me!'

'Ran over you? Who ran over you?'

'Who do you think? Bloody Molly, that's who! Came flying down here, I thought she'd come to sort things out, but, oh no – she just has a go at me, shouting and stuff, then she runs over my toe.'

'That doesn't sound like our Molly, she's not normally violent. Still, you did make her mad taking off like that without a word. And what with her mum and everything...'

'Her mum? It's nothing to do with Peggy, this is between me and Molly. She needn't bother trying to interfere this time.'

Daisy is surprised to hear this – Jake never told her that Peggy had interfered before. Still, no time to bother about that now – save it for later.

'No, not interfering – *she's* disappeared too. Molly's been frantic with both of you going off like that.'

He has the grace to look a bit shamefaced.

'Oh, right – so, where's Peggy then?'

'Jake, are you not listening to me at all? I just told you, she's missing. Like you were, but more so.'

'But Peggy wouldn't just go off, would she? She never does stuff like that, she's always there. What about Geoff, what does he say?'

Bang on cue, the door opens, and in troop the rest of the party – Geoff first, looking sheepish, then the kids, with Sarah bringing up the rear.

'So, here you are – you've led us a merry dance, lad. Er... can I use your toilet, please?'

'Hang on, Gramps, I asked first,' whines Max, who is then knocked out of the way by Hattie. She slams the narrow door behind her and the rest of the group listen to Hattie doing what comes naturally – no privacy in a caravan. Max begins to giggle and everyone begins to talk loudly to cover up the splashing noises. Max's voice is by far the loudest.

'Hi, Dad. Where did you go? You were supposed to be helping me with my project on frogs for school this weekend. It's got to be in soon.'

'And you said you'd give me a lift to Maisie's sleepover tonight. Where've you been, Dad?' Theo pushes her way to the front of the huddle as Hattie emerges and Sarah moves quickly into the tiny bathroom, locking the door on their howls of anguish.

'Well, hard luck, everyone,' she says clearly, through the bathroom door. 'I smell of sick, I need a wash.'

Jake looks bemused, as well he might.

'But... but... what are you all doing here?' he stutters. 'I came here to be on my own and to think, not to host a holiday weekend. I need a break. Go home, all of you. Leave me alone.' And to everyone's dismay, he begins to cry – great heaving sobs that shake his skinny body. Daisy instinctively moves to comfort him, but Geoff steps in front of her.

'No, he's right, we shouldn't have come. But now I am here, if you'll have me, Jake, I reckon I'll stop a bit.'

'What, stop here? With me?' Jake looks dumbfounded.

'If that's okay? Only, Peg's down here somewhere, and I hate it at home without her. I left Nick in charge of the shop; he can shut it up for now. I can't be bothered with worrying about the business when all this is going on. Theo and Sam will help Nick out with everything, won't you, kids?' Sam looks dubious and Theo blushes.

'Sure, Gramps, but what about Dad – aren't you coming home? Ever?' she says. Her voice shakes, and Jake comes over to give her a hug, but she shrugs him off. Good for you, Daisy tells her, silently.

'And who's Nick, anyway?' Jake blusters, trying not to let on how upset he is at Theo's rebuff. He reaches out to ruffle Hattie's hair, but she somehow manages to be just out of reach.

'Ah now – who's Nick? Good question, lad. I've been wondering that myself, but the thing is, he's been an extra pair of hands when we most need it. He's really handy around the place, and Theo will keep an eye on him, won't you, pet?' She grins, suddenly more cheerful, and goes to put the kettle on – thank heavens for that, Daisy's parched.

The family range themselves around on the faded bench seats, just like they have so many times before, but never all together, and never quite like this. There's that faint, reassuring smell of damp and air freshener which always makes Daisy think of holidays, and Jake has obviously been hoovering because the seventies shag pile is in neat rows, like a well-cut tennis court. Daisy's old familiar nick-nacks are still on the high shelves – the crinoline lady, the blue and gold vases, the souvenir plates from the Broads and Yarmouth, and the photos of the grandchildren. Outside the windows, Daisy can see a group of children playing on the swings, and can hear the shrieks. She sees that Hattie and Max have noticed too, and are edging closer to the door, hopefully.

'Come on, kids, let's go and burn off some blubber,' says Sam, and the younger four take no persuading – they head for the park, whooping with excess energy.

Eventually, after a quick mug of tea and a team talk, Daisy accepts that Geoff really wants to stay with Jake. She supposes it might be the best thing for both of them if this Nick person really can be trusted. Who is he, anyhow? Nobody seems sure, but they all seem quite taken with him. Geoff says even Sam is getting over his wariness now.

After a lot of yelling, the children are rounded up and most of the party decide to carry on down the coast, to see where the cliffs are tumbling into the sea. That distracts Max enough to get him out of the caravan and away from his dad without more than a sniff or two – someone's garage went over the cliff last month and he wants to see if their car was still in it. But Geoff's adamant that he's not budging, and Jake doesn't say no. As the bus leaves, Daisy thinks that this is turning out to be the strangest Sunday she has had for ages... but it's quite fun now that the arguments have stopped.

26

Poppy's driving is speedy and skilful. It's too fast for comfort usually, but today Kate doesn't care, and in no time at all they are flying down the King's Lynn bypass in total silence. It begins to give Kate the creeps after a while. She switches the radio on – she has never known the two of them to stop talking for this long – they've always had something to say to each other, even if it's trivial stuff. Jill is somewhere ahead. She doesn't usually top fifty miles an hour even on a motorway, but she's so furious with Poppy and Kate that she's taken off like a bat out of hell, or an avenging angel on a heavenly mission.

Watching the traffic stream in the opposite direction, away from the coast and homewards ready for the new week, Kate thinks about the friendship between the women. She guesses that Jill disapproves of all of them in different ways, especially Jake, for some reason. Maybe she fancies him herself? She seems to feel personally insulted by their 'lack of respect for marriage vows' and 'selfish, thoughtless behaviour'. Her own marriage is so solid and caring, after all.

She probably just can't imagine ever wanting anyone else to

see her wobbly bits or to find out that she has the embarrassing problem of breaking wind during sex, Kate thinks bitterly, betting Jill wishes she hadn't told her friends about that one now. Well, she may have a point – it might be amusing in certain circumstances, with the right person, but Kate can't help thinking it could be a bit off-putting with a stranger. And anyway, Jill's always going on about marriage being sacred, isn't she? Come to think of it, Kate used to think that, too.

Kate's aware that Poppy's dying to ask more about what happened with Jake, but she probably daren't now, after being so grumpy, so Kate drifts off again into a glorious technicolour daydream – she can't stop thinking about Jake and she's not really trying to.

Jake has always been able to make her laugh – really laugh out loud, about silly things that other people would never understand. He seemed to understand her completely, and that was seductive too. The memory of the way his stubble felt on her face is still making Kate tingle all over – she keeps catching her breath unexpectedly when she remembers the sensation and her stomach has that elevator-going-down-suddenly feeling. She falls deeper into a daze, half-listening to the gentle music on the car radio. It reminds her of Jake, every song seems to be about them.

Why on earth hadn't the two of them got together before... years before, when Kate was young and not so cynical? They could have had a bunch of kids, a big house with a paddock and some horses, or even a swimming pool, and Jake could have had his own market garden and grown as many leeks as he liked. Okay, the actual sex itself hadn't been that great, but these things take time, don't they?

But it's too late now anyway, Molly got in first, as usual. Kate never dared to tell anyone how much she fancied him when they were all at school, it was easier to take the piss when Molly and Jake started getting all mushy.

All these years Kate's assumed Jake didn't much like her. He's always seemed to despise Kate's flash job and the power dressing. It wasn't until he got the social media bug that they started talking properly, and then it was mostly exchanging barbed, witty comments.

Kate can't wait to see him again, but is secretly unsure what he'll do when she and Poppy turn up out of the blue. Will he be pleased? What if he's had second thoughts and Kate was just a quick fumble on the carpet for him?

'Snap out of it, Kate, we're nearly there. Hadn't you better put your lippy on or something?' Poppy sounds peevish, perhaps she's jealous too. Kate would rather have the man than the boy any day, that thing with Sam definitely seems a bit gross.

'Thanks. I will, now you mention it, sweetie,' she says with a Cheshire cat smile, and gets out her instant repair kit. A squirt of 'Poison', and lick of gloss, a dab of powder on her shiny nose, and her short hair just needs tousling a bit more. There, ready for action.

'I was joking, actually. You're unreal, do you know that? He's just left his wife and driven to the edge of the earth, he's not going to be noticing your bloody lip gloss, is he?' Yes, definitely peevish.

'Look, Poppy, you might possibly know what makes young blokes tick, but leave the grown-ups to me. He'll notice all right. He's probably been trying to ring me anyway, but my battery's dead,' Kate says, with more bravado than she feels.

'Yeah, right. Well, I'm glad you're so confident because we'll be there in ten minutes.'

Trying to calm the fluttering in her stomach, Kate turns the radio up louder. He will be pleased to see her. He *will*.

27

Poppy crunches another mint imperial and snorts to herself at Kate's misty smile. The girl's got it bad; she's been gazing out of the window for the last fifty miles, mouthing words to the cheesiest of the songs on the radio and sighing every five minutes. She's heading for a fall. She thinks she's got it all in control – just a fling. Hah! There will be tears before bedtime, undoubtedly.

Messing with anyone else's marriage is always bad news. At least Poppy's not doing anyone any harm these days, and anyway, she reckons she's probably done young William Mitchell a huge favour. It's kind of a service to the community, really. Maybe it could be written into the job description for older female friends of a family, known to all as *Aunty*... or... hey... even godmothers. Poppy's never been chosen for that role but surely every boy should have a generous godmother – silver spoons when you're christened and fat wads of cash on your birthday are all very well, but Poppy's kind of present would be much more useful. She wonders if she should write to the *Guardian* about it – it could start a whole new trend in the choosing of the godparents before a christening. Their age and temperament would have to be much more carefully considered. It could definitely catch on.

Swerving casually into the one-way system in Cromer, Poppy winks at an angry man who is trying to get into the same lane. He stares in surprise and then winks back, to the disgust of his wife. See, there she goes again, spreading joy and happiness – they should give her some sort of medal; one more in her list of services to the community. She could become a national institution. They might erect a statue or build a posthumous fountain for her. No, not a fountain, that's a bit old hat, maybe a chain of spectacular food halls all over the country.

She drives on, lost in wonder at this splendid idea, trying to decide whether 'Poppy's Pleasures' or 'Poppy's Palate' would be best to commemorate her bountiful nature. She can see the sea through the gaps in the hedges now, speedwell blue. The fields are edged here and there with splashes of scarlet; her namesake flower lines the cornfields with bright patches.

With a start, Poppy is aware of flashing lights in the rear-view mirror, and a wailing siren. Bugger, she doesn't need a fine, that'll be the end of her licence after dodging all those stupid cameras and then the time when they got her – the speed awareness course was mind-blowingly dull.

But the blue lights aren't for Poppy this time, and she pulls over just in time to let a speeding ambulance overtake before a bad bend slows them both down. She sees his red taillights as he screeches to a halt and her stomach flips. She hates accidents. Well, obviously nobody likes accidents, but Poppy really hates them.

She has good reason for this fear. Her mum and dad were so badly mangled that the police had to use their dental records to identify them, so she never looks when she goes past an accident on the motorway – honestly, some people are so ghoulish, you can see them slowing right down and craning their stupid necks and saying to each other, 'See, I told you he'd end up in a ditch driving like that on wet roads.'

Poppy looks round anxiously, wondering if there's a turn-off that she can take so she doesn't have to drive by whatever's happening round the corner, but she can't see one, so she sets off again, ready to avert her eyes if it's nasty. Kate's just realised something's going on – at least that's wiped the soppy smile off her face.

They crawl towards the bend, joining the line of cars waiting. Oh my God. Poppy can see the back end of a yellow VW beetle sticking up out of the ditch at a sickening angle, and just make out the little fish sticker in the back window. How many times have they told Jill that it's tempting fate to drive around advertising the fact that you're a Christian – almost as if you expect to get preferential treatment in the safety stakes. Tears begin to pour down Poppy's face, and her hands are shaking so much that she can't turn off the ignition, but Kate's already out of the car and racing towards the accident, pushing a little group of onlookers out of the way in her hurry.

'Jill! Oh no, Jill! Let me through, you silly buggers, this is one of my best friends, and it's all my fault,' she cries out, standing on tiptoe to see.

A kindly looking paramedic moves her to one side as the tiny broken body is lifted from the car, oh so gently, and placed on a body board. Kate, shaking all over now, climbs into the ambulance with Jill, and Poppy desperately tries to pull herself together to go after them as, after what seems like an age, they race towards the hospital. She can't do it. Everything was manageable until the accident, she could cope when Mum and Dad were alive.

Being an only child, and an orphan to boot, is no joke. Who cares about Poppy now? Who would she ring to tell them she is parked in a ditch, crying and shaking, and can't control herself enough to follow her friends? Pathetic, that's what her life is.

After what seems like ages, but can't be long because she can still hear the siren, Poppy rubs her eyes and starts the engine. Jill and Kate need her even if no one else does.

28

It's weird without them; Nick had got kind of used to having them around. They're none of them so bad really and Geoff and Nick are getting on really well already. Nick reckons Molly's dad needs him just now, what with his missus doing a runner and all the fuss with this Jake bloke. He's not at all sure he likes the sound of Jake.

Nick was too busy watching Molly to pay much attention to Jake last week, and then all of a sudden he upped and went, without so much as a note. Rude, Nick calls it. What she needs is a man to pay her some proper attention. But she's not used to that, and in his experience, not many other women are either.

Anyway, Nick's done himself a big fry-up and got the shop issue sorted. He's made a really good notice for the door with a big bit of card and some of the felt-tips off the stationery shelf. Nick's good at art; not as good as Kris, his brother can draw anything, but at least Nick can knock up a decent poster. This one says:

*Due to family problems, this shop will be closed for the fore-
seeable future.*

There, who says he's thick? Didn't even need a dictionary for
'foreseeable'. And that means he can open and shut whenever
he likes, and even if that snotty old bat from the big house bangs
on the door, he can just shrug, and point to the notice. Brilliant.

There's even been time for a bit of a tidy up and reorganisa-
tion of some of the shelves. There's a bargain area now, with all
the things on it that are looking a bit seedy. Nick's thinking of
persuading Geoff to branch out into wholesale pet food next –
buy in bulk, and deliver to all the old dears who haven't got cars
or can't lift the heavy boxes. But maybe he'd better wait a little
while for that one.

He found Geoff's credit card while he was tidying around
earlier too. Now, that was silly, leaving his card around, wasn't it?
Good job Nick's got scruples, or he could have got the old bloke
into a right mess. As it is, he only uses it for one thing. A
hundred quid, that's all it costs, and he reckons it's going to be
money well spent.

29

Molly's really tired of driving now, and her back and neck are aching badly from being in the same position for so long. She's listened to all of her favourite Spotify playlists, especially the Al Green mix, and the words 'Here I am baby, come and take me' are going round and round in her head like a mantra.

Nearly home. She decides to stop for a quick cup of what passes for Costa at the next services, and she's just trying to drink it, wondering why it needs to be so scaldingly hot, when she notices her phone is flashing 'three new messages'.

The first one is from Theo's phone:

> Mum, why don't you answer your phone? We are visiting Dad, back later.

What? Theo in Norfolk? Who's 'we'?

The second text is easier to understand but even more disturbing:

> Molly, where are you? Please text me, my arms are aching and it's just for you. R x

Oh no, he's turning into Lionel Ritchie. Maybe he'll appear under her window with a full orchestra and serenade her. Still, there's been very little romance in Molly's life these last few years, and even though she feels all sweaty and travel-battered, she can't help feeling the tingle beginning again. Rob wants her. Does she want him? Next message.

> At hospital in Norwich, Jill had car smash, Kate
> with me. Ring now. Poppy

Molly's fingers are shaking as she scrolls through the numbers in her contact list, but after a few false starts (the Po Yung Chinese takeaway and Pop's Taxis) she manages to dial Poppy, who – thank God – answers on the second ring. Molly hears a muffled voice say sternly, 'But I'm afraid you are not allowed to use your mobile phone on the ward – I have mentioned this several times now.' There is the sound of swearing, quick footsteps and gasps, and finally Poppy wheezes, 'Molly... about time!'

'What the hell's going on? What's happened to Jill? Why are you in Norwich? What's Kate doing there?' Molly yells.

'Calm down and listen to me, Molly. Jill's been in a terrible car accident – I reckon she was driving too fast because she was so angry with me and Kate. She knows about Kate and Jake, and... and anyway, she was going to see him because she thought you shouldn't have to deal with it all on your own.'

'Knows about Kate and Jake? But I've only just... Oh no, I can't believe it! Well, yes, I can, I suppose; she's always trying to look after me. Is she okay? And why's she angry with you? I can see why she'd be mad at Jake, but...'

'Never mind that – no, she's definitely not okay. She... she...' There is the awful sound of Poppy's sobbing. Molly has never heard Poppy cry before, and she takes a deep breath, trying not to shout at her any more. Why can't she just spit it out quickly? Poppy gulps a few times but carries on more calmly.

'She's in a coma, she smashed her head really badly. They don't know... oh, Moll, they don't know if she'll ever wake up. I've had to ring Roger and tell him. It was awful. He's on his way here now, but their kids will need some looking after. I rang Rob Jennings' (even in the middle of all this awfulness, Molly's heart does an involuntary lurch when she hears Rob's name) 'and he's looking after the boys.'

'Right... well... let me think a minute. What can I do?' Molly carries on with the deep breaths, wishing she could wake up from this horrible dream. 'Look, Poppy, it's probably going to be best if I carry on home – I'll be there in about half an hour – and I'll go and see Rob and help out if he needs it. I don't think Lydia will be too happy with playing mum, they might put their sticky fingers on her cream sofa.'

'Cream sofa? How do you know what colour her sofa is?'

'Well, I don't, obviously, but she looks like the sort of woman who would have a cream sofa, that's all.'

'Hmmm... anyway, you get on home and do that, and I'll wait for Roger, then I'll join you if he can cope. I don't know what to do with Kate – she's in a right state.' Molly sniffs loudly, and Poppy gets the message.

'Ring you in a bit, Moll. Oh, and how did things go with Jake?'

Molly sighs. 'Tell you later. Give Jill my love. Tell her anyway, she might hear you...' Tears are trickling down her cheeks again, she's cried more this week than she has in the last ten years. 'Tell her I... oh, I don't know, just give her my love. And you can tell Kate from me that she's never to come near me again, and if she does...' Molly runs out of steam, and disconnects before she really loses the plot. Draining the now chilly coffee, she sets off again, with an even heavier heart.

Only twenty minutes later, Molly pulls up in Camberwick Close, behind Rob's shed-like Volvo. Well, no one can say she picked him for his sexy car, she thinks. Each house has a subtle antique-effect lantern by the door, and solar-powered lights up the pathways and all the windows have their curtains open. Dignified light spills out onto the paved courtyards between each house. It looks like a stage set.

They never draw the blinds round here – Molly found that out when she was collecting for charity last year – but they still don't answer their doors to cold callers. She got more cash going round the council estate, and *they* didn't set their dogs on her.

Molly automatically checks the mirror – dishevelled, sticky and crumpled; not a good look. She fishes for her hairbrush and lipstick just as the front door opens and Lydia peers out suspiciously so she abandons trying to look respectable and gets out of the car. Lydia comes out onto the porch, sheepskin mules finishing off a truly awful trouser and jumper combo.

'Who is it now? Oh, it's you, Molly.' She's remembered Molly's name. Why? It's enough to make the situation even edgier.

'Robin told me you were coming, your friend Posy telephoned us a few moments ago.'

'Hello, Lydia. It was Poppy who called, actually. It was nice of her to phone ahead though. I'm sorry, I'm a bit messy – been on the road for hours and what with all the upset of Jill's accident...' Molly tails off, trying to tidy her hair and brush fluff off her jeans.

Lydia's own hair is in a round blonde bob, stiff with hairspray. Her lipstick is peach, and her earrings are small pearls. She is wearing a short-sleeved crocheted jumper in a bilious shade of lemon and, as a concession to the late hour, large lounging trousers in beige. Her slippers match the jumper exactly. Molly wonders vaguely if she has a pair for every outfit?

'Yes... I can see that... never mind, you'd better come in, I suppose. Have you come for the children?' She frowns. 'Robin's given them some supper, they seem a little unsettled.'

Molly gapes at Lydia. Is she mad? Unsettled? How else would Jill's children be when their mum's just been involved in a serious road accident? 'No, I haven't come for them – I thought you two were looking after the children for Roger?'

There is a thunder of feet as Rob and the boys come down the stairs two at a time, landing in a heap at the bottom. Lydia shudders.

'Molly, you're back!' Rob beams. Molly smiles back weakly.

'Hi, Aunty Molly, have you been to see Mum?' Tim blinks at Molly through his thick glasses, and attempts a brave smile. 'Is she better now? Dad said he'd ring, but he hasn't yet...'

'Course he hasn't, stupid. He only went a little bit ago, he won't even be there yet, will he?' George, at seven, is the leader even though he's two years younger than Tim.

'No, pet, I haven't seen her yet but Poppy said she'd ring me as soon as she had some news for us. Are you sleeping here?' There is an uncomfortable silence, broken quickly by Rob.

'Yes, of course they are – the twin beds are made up ready, and I'm just off with the boys to fetch their 'jamas, Dad forgot them in the rush, didn't he, lads?'

George looks mutinous, and Lydia sighs heavily. Tim comes over and slips his hand into Molly's. He looks up piteously.

'Would Max like me to stop with him, d'you think, Aunty Molly? He said he wanted me to help him to pick privet for the stick insects.'

'That sounds like fun, Timmy,' Lydia jumps in.

'Tim, not Timmy. I'm not a baby. George is the baby.' Tim's bottom lip juts, and George glares at him.

'But Tim's staying here, aren't you? That's what we arranged with Dad. And we're happy to have you both, aren't we, dear?' Dear? Whoever calls their wife *Dear* these days? Even Geoff doesn't do it – he calls Peggy Gorgeous or Poppet. Molly looks at Lydia with loathing. She really is quite obnoxious; Molly's sure she's wearing one of those pull-you-in-body suits – she's got that constipated look that they give you after a few hours, and her chest is suspiciously pointy. Lydia moves her mouth into a more friendly shape.

'Well, of course we are, and I'm sure Mummy and Daddy will be home very soon.'

Rob looks doubtful, so Molly adds quickly, 'We'll see you tomorrow at school, and then if Mr and Mrs Jennings can spare you, we'd love to have you to stay with us whenever you can fit it in.' The boys look relieved, and make a move to go back upstairs. Lydia gazes meaningfully at their shoes.

'Oh, boys, I don't think you heard me earlier when I asked you to remove your shoes in the house. I know you'll under-stand; these carpets are rather special and some of my rugs are *Egyptian*, you know.' The boys look down in surprise and slip off their trainers, then glance at Molly. Suddenly, the tension of the last few days is too much, and an inexplicable giggle escapes her. The next moment, all three of them, Molly, Tim and George, are holding their sides and laughing like proverbial drains. Rob is startled, but is soon unable to stop himself join-ing in.

Lydia's eyes are like chips of ice. 'Yes, laugh, all of you – I suppose the idea of keeping up standards is funny to some people. I'm off to bed, my head is pounding after the day we've had. Robin, if you could bring my tablets up? Any time, darling, no rush. After all, you've got your visitors to entertain.'

She smiles sweetly, and sweeps past them up the staircase, putting a trembling hand to the small of her back as she climbs. Rob freezes, red in the face and obviously uncertain of how to deal with this situation.

'Erm, sorry, guys,' he mumbles, 'I forgot to remind you about the shoe thing. Well, Molly, how about a nice cup of tea? Glass of wine? You must be shattered, all that driving…' He seems to remember why she was doing 'all that driving' and becomes even redder, but he sends her a heart-rending look which pleads with her not to go. The boys fix her with their sad spaniel eyes too, but she's had enough of this evil house and its aristocratic carpets. Molly edges towards the door, giving the boys a hug on the way.

'No, I really need to get back, my lot will be home soon, I expect. I've got to see if there's any news of Mum and sort out the school stuff for tomorrow. I'll be in touch if Poppy rings, or perhaps she'll ring you herself? Right, see you all soon then.'

With difficulty, Molly hardens her heart and walks down the path, the sharp edging stones reminding her of Lydia's teeth. She sinks into the car, so weary she can hardly get the key in the ignition. One more lap, then home. But what will home be like with only one grown-up in it? Suddenly, unexpectedly, she wants Jake very badly.

As Molly pulls onto the drive, she notices two things – one, that the house is in darkness, and two, there is a large package of some sort lying on the steps. She staggers towards the door, stiff legged, and gasps at the sight of the most enormous bunch of flowers she's ever seen. There are lilies, gladioli, strange stiff curly bamboo things, fronds of giant fern – it's amazing! Is there a card with it? She fumbles around and finally finds a small white envelope. Inside the house (which, as expected, is chilly and unwelcoming) she switches on as many lights as possible and rips open the little packet. The tiny piece of cardboard is mostly covered with a print of some rather garish roses but the message is succinct:

Please be mine, Molly.

Molly gulps and sits down on the nearest available seat. She had pretty much convinced herself not to see him again but how can she resist flowers like these? She's never seen such a beautiful bouquet in her life. They must have cost a fortune. Not that the price makes a difference, of course it doesn't. It's the emotion behind the bouquet. They say it's the thought that counts, don't they? And the thought is the most dangerous thing ever, right now.

30

After a great deal of soul searching, Kris thinks that he probably needs a new mum like he needs a hole in the head. The last one did a great job of messing with his brain and it seems as if he's only just feeling okay about her. Well, not okay exactly, he still hates her for leaving them, dying and all that stuff, and mostly for what she's made Nick do, but he can think about her without crying now, and that's down to Peggy. Still, a deal's a deal, and the bet was that Kris could find them a proper mum before Nick could do it.

Kris would like to stay with Peggy by the sea forever if he could get his brother here too. The only problem is that the money has run out. They've got away with staying in his Gran's caravan; Kris supposes no one wants to rent it out these days, and this site's not one of those smart ones where they ask you to scrap your van if it's too old. If anything, it looks as if this is where caravans come to die – there's some right pigeon sheds here. Some of the people are a bit dodgy too – Kris managed to sell Nan's old radiogram yesterday to a bloke with only about three teeth. It's a collectors' item now, so they say. So that paid for dinner, because Peggy forgot her bank card in the rush to get away and now she's down to her last few quid.

Peggy says she's happier here than she's been for years, and that makes Kris feel good. He doesn't usually make people happy; he tends to bring them down if anything. So, back to the problem. How are they going to raise enough cash to exist? They don't need a lot – they won't be going out much in case someone's looking out for Peggy – for all they know, her photo could have been on the TV. Kris has sold the TV too but he only got a tenner for it.

He's planning to get into the habit of hanging round the local market at the end of the day to pick up cheap stuff to eat, and he thinks there may be the chance of earning a bit of cash helping to clear up at the end of market days – Kris has never had a job before, but then neither has Nick. If he did something like that he'd be able to support Peggy, she could cook the meals and fuss over him. Just like having a mum, but without any of the bad feelings. He wonders how his brother is. He misses Nick so much. His twin'll ring soon, he's bound to, isn't he?

31

The wanderers are back from Norfolk now, except for the man of the moment, obviously, and Geoff too. Molly can see why her dad wants to be on the spot if Peggy's there somewhere, but it's one less ally for her in this crazy time, and she needs all the support she can get at the moment.

Hattie and Max are in bed at last, and Nick is reading them a story. Molly's not quite sure how that happened. He just seemed to appear when the minibus arrived, and the next thing, he was cooking dinner. He'd brought pasta sauce from the shop, and frozen mince, and tagliatelle, and even some dried parmesan. Theo rummaged in the freezer for a couple of packets of garlic bread and organised the table – even paper napkins and candles. Nick is having a good effect on her; what a treasure he's turning out to be.

Molly still doesn't know where he came from though; Theo's got some story about a troubled childhood and a mother who died in a car crash, but that could be just Nick finding his way in. Theo's always been a sucker for a hard luck story. Molly's caught him looking at her a few times, and Theo's doing a lot of hair tossing and wiggling at the moment. Sam seems to have cut Nick some slack now, but he doesn't like him being around all the time. Probably just being a bit over-protective. Molly hopes her eldest son doesn't feel as if he's got to stand in for Jake and be the head of the house, and all that sort of thing.

There's a fire blazing in the living room so she takes her iPad and snuggles up in front of it on the saggy old sofa (no cream leather here), trying to relax. This room is Molly's place really. Oh, she knows they all use it, but when she and Jake were doing the house up, Molly said she'd got to have at least one calm place to unwind at the end of the day, even if the bathroom was a wreck and they were cooking on an old primus and a tatty barbecue.

There are loads of squashy cushions both on the sofa and the floor, and a big rust and green ethnic rug. It's definitely not Egyptian – Molly picked it up on Leicester market years ago and brought it back on the bus; not a popular move with the other passengers.

There are lots of deep rusty-orange-coloured shades on the lamps so the light is very gentle in Molly's room – the bookcase is groaning with all her favourite children's books and the fire bucket is made of battered old brass that gleams in the firelight, when she remembers to polish it. She wriggles deep into the sofa and tries a bit of meditation, but there's an annoying lump underneath her and she can't get comfortable. She rummages under the cushions and finds a screwed-up t-shirt.

Unfolding it, Molly's eyes prickle as she recognises one of Jake's favourite items of clothing – an ancient, faded Coldplay top. He likes to wear it with his battered denim jacket and his oldest Levis. She snuffles instinctively to see if any scent of husband remains but there's only the faintest whiff of deodorant.

'Mum, we're going out for a bit, do you mind?' Theo's voice brings Molly back to the dismal present. 'Nick wants to show me what he's been doing at the shop and check the burglar alarm; he's changed things round a bit.' Theo and Nick are standing in the doorway, looking shifty. He clears his throat.

'We won't be long, honest; I'll walk Theo back, we'll be home by ten.'

'Well, that's fine, but take your phone, Theo,' Molly says uneasily. She has a primal urge to wrap everyone up in cotton wool and keep them here, even Nick. Jill's accident has made Molly feel very vulnerable and she can't stop thinking about her friend, lying in a horrible metal bed, with wires and drips and things, just like on one of those horrible TV hospital soaps.

'My phone's flat, can I take yours, Mum?'

'Erm, mine's even worse than yours, I should think,' Molly stalls.

'No, it's not. I just heard it bleep – you've got a message. Somebody loves you!'

'Yes, ha ha, well, I'll look at it in a minute. But I'd better keep it here in case Poppy needs me.'

'Don't be silly, she can ring on the house phone, can't she?' Theo is impatient, but Nick seems to sense Molly's discomfort, and says, 'I've got mine here, no credit though, Mrs White. But I'll write the number down and you can ring if you want?'

'Thanks, Nick – tell you what, I'll treat you to some credit for cooking the dinner – take ten quid out of my purse and please try and call me Molly. You're making me feel like a teacher, it'll be "Miss" next!' He looks mortified.

'I don't want paying for cooking your dinner, Mrs Wh... I mean... Molly.'

'Shut up, Nick, and let's go before she changes her mind.' Theo helps herself to some money and drags him away. Immediately, Molly starts to feel uneasy. Theo's sparkling like the fairy on the Christmas tree. But her mind is soon on other matters, because as the two of them disappear into the distance, Molly hears a car approaching, and gravel sprays as Poppy makes her usual big entrance.

Opening the front door wide, Molly folds Poppy into her arms as she sobs and shakes. After a few minutes, she calms down enough to sit in front of the fire with some hot chocolate and a box of man-sized tissues. Molly wonders fleetingly why big tissues are called 'man-sized'? It's not often men have such a big cry as this. Women are generally the ones who use all the hankies.

'Thanks, Moll, I've been looking forward to that hug for the last four hours,' she says, still hiccupping gently and blowing her nose from time to time. She looks most unlike her usual glowing self – her eyes are bloodshot, her mad curls are drooping, and her clothes are in disarray. Even her face looks different, thinner and shadowed.

The firelight improves things a bit, and Molly watches the flames dancing and listens to the quiet crackle of the logs burning while Poppy takes great heaving breaths.

'You look awful, sweetie,' Molly tells her.

'Oh, cheers, love.' She grins at last – that's more like it.

'So, what's happening?' Molly asks, hardly daring to listen to the answer.

'Jill's stable, they say, but she looks bloody awful to me. She hasn't come round yet, and she's so little and pale, Moll... and Roger's just sitting there crying and holding her hand. He can't bear to leave her for a minute.'

'Now, that's the sort of man who'd be faithful no matter what.'

'Well, yes – but would you really want to be married to

Roger? Seriously, Moll? I'm sorry, but lovely as he is, the teeth would put me off.'

'Poppy, Jill loves him.'

'It does seem weird...'

Poppy's face looks older suddenly. 'It was seeing Jill being dragged out of the wreckage, it reminded me of Mum and Dad...' She breaks off, the tears threatening to start again. Molly reaches out for her friend's hand and holds it tightly.

'Poppy, try not to think about it, love. What will Roger do? Will they let him stay?'

'Yes, there's a flat you can use, apparently, so Roger's moving in there. I said I'd pack some clothes and stuff and take them back tomorrow, I'm due a few days off work. Do you think the boys will want to come with me to be near their mum and dad?'

Molly shivers, thinking about where the boys are. At least half of her wishes she was there with them. She's got no doubt the poor little souls wish they were safely here, away from Lydia's stringent regime.

'I don't know, they're very young to deal with intensive care, aren't they?'

'Yes, but, what if, you know... if she doesn't make it? They won't have seen her to say goodbye. And that feels bad. I can tell you that for nothing.'

Molly looks at her watch. It's nearly ten o'clock already.

'Tell you what, let's leave it till tomorrow to decide. We might have better news then. Do you want to sleep here? The spare bed's made up. I'm just going to look if Theo's anywhere about – she's off with Nick and I'm a bit edgy about it, somehow.'

'No thanks, I need my own bed tonight. Who is this Nick everyone's talking about anyway?'

'Good question. A very pretty, very mysterious stranger.

Sharp cheekbones, a bit aloof, looks like a throwback punk version of Legolas. Theo never got over the first time she saw Legolas in the film – you know, Poppy, in the *Lord of the Rings* series, you must have seen them by now? He didn't come over as that sexy in the books. Don't think J. R. R. Tolkien saw his elf as a sex god, somehow.'

'Lego Land? No, you've lost me there, if Hugh Grant's not in it, I'm not interested. See you tomorrow, honey. I'm dead on my feet... I mean... oh, you know what I mean!' They hug briefly and she's gone. As Molly peers into the gloom, she remembers that she'd had a text message ages ago. She must be preoccupied to forget that. She fetches her phone and gasps.

> Meet me down by the all-night garage on the
> main road, half 9, please! Just 5 mins?

Sod it! It's just ten o'clock now. Oh well, that saved a big decision. And here come Theo and Nick. Molly's filled with regret, longing and relief in equal measures. Should she text to apologise? No, best to let him think she was too high minded to meet him. Would she have gone? She really doesn't know.

Did he wait, and if so, for how long? Theo bounces in and gives her mum a radiant smile, waving Nick off casually. Ha, you don't fool me, Molly thinks cynically. She can see her daughter's eyes glittering. Is that a mark on her neck? Don't think I'm not watching you, young lady, Molly thinks, God, she sounds just like her own mother, which brings on another pang of anxiety.

The landline rings and Molly rushes to get it before it wakes the younger kids. It's Geoff, and Molly listens carefully to his update. She feels as if she's at last learning how to put her life into pigeonholes. There's one for her disastrous marriage, another for her possible extra-marital flirtation, and now here's her much-loved Pa opening another one.

Resolutely turning her thoughts away from young love, missing parents, middle-aged lust, faithless friends and straying husbands, Molly says a quick Hail Mary for Jill, and goes to bed. Her phone will be on all night in case of hospital news, but if Rob texts, she'll ignore him.

32

This is just heaven on earth. Jake feels as if he's lived here forever and it's only been a week. He and Geoff have settled down nicely together, considering Jake's just cheated on Geoff's daughter and Geoff's wife has deserted him; not a great combination of events, you'd think.

But in fact, if he wasn't so preoccupied with finding Peggy, Jake thinks Geoff would be as contented as his son-in-law. Jake knows neither of them should feel like this. By rights, Geoff should be distraught and Jake should be full of guilt and beating himself with a big stick, but Jake can't seem to help the sheer joy of being by the sea and living for the moment, and Geoff is the same.

The rest from being anxious all the time is great. Jake's worries about being made redundant have been going on for so long now, they're part of his life. Jake's been secretly wishing Molly would get a better-paid job to help out, and wondering what they would do if the kids all wanted to go to university. All his dreams have been about a new beginning by the sea, and now; here he is. This is the first time since Sam was born that Jake has just pleased himself.

After he rang work and said he was under stress and had gone on the sick, life became so much simpler – if he'd known cracking up was this easy, he'd have done it years ago. And it's not just a wind-up. He really does feel as if he was at the end of his rope. The thing with Kate was just the catalyst, he supposes. What a catalyst, though. It had been a very bad move to tangle with one of Molly's best friends. Bad, and stupid.

There were some of Jake's old trainers left in the van, and he and Geoff have been into Cromer and bought some basics; comfy, sloppy clothes to go down to the beach in. They climb down the cliff and walk along the firm sand near the water's edge at least once a day, and then they take off their shoes and socks and splash in the shallows, maybe pick up a few shells for the kids. After that, they sit on the rocks and just soak it all up – the wildness in the salty air, the ice cream caps on the waves, the people walking their dogs, throwing sticks into the water; just the sheer joy of it all. Jake has never been a poetic sort of bloke, but he can feel a song coming on – it's hovering at the edge of his mind, teasing him. He'll get it one of these days. He's playing the guitar a lot now, just strumming and picking out the odd tune.

When they're not on the beach, Geoff spends most of his time looking for Peggy, walking the streets, wandering up and down the pier, putting up notices on lamp posts, looking in the papers and talking to the locals. In fact, he's getting on so well with the landlord of the pub up the road that he's been asked to start a folk club to boost business in the winter season.

Jake had his guitar in the car when he arrived, and Geoff's borrowed another one from a bloke he met in the pub, but Jake never even knew his father-in-law could play. Jake is not preoccupied with Kate, but then he's not thinking about Molly either. The kids are on his mind though, he rings most days from the phone box on the site and they do talk to him a bit, but they're all angry, he knows that. Molly's told them Jake just needed a break from work because he's not felt too well, which was good of her, he supposes.

Geoff wants to stay a bit longer, until he finds Peggy. He never gives up; yesterday he thought he'd cracked it.

'I thought I saw her today, Jake, but when she turned round, the woman wasn't much more than a teenager. Shows how good Peg's looking for her age though, eh?' His smile was sad, but proud even so.

'Yes, she's a lovely-looking woman, just like her daughter,' he carried on, 'but you know that, don't you, lad? You shouldn't leave it too long to go back to our Molly, Jake, she might not be there forever.' Jake had looked up.

'What are you getting at, Geoff, has she said anything to you about us? About what's going to happen next?' Geoff looked back innocently.

'Course not, but she's not going to hang around on her own indefinitely, stands to reason. She needs a man.'

'Does she? She didn't really seem to need me.' Molly's such a strong woman, why would she need a man, now he's done his job and fathered her children? Jake suddenly feels close to despair. What about him? Doesn't he get to have a life of his own? He sighs. 'They can all do without me now, Geoff. She doesn't need me for anything.'

'Need you? She needs you all right, mate. You wait and see. I'm just worried in case someone else starts to appreciate her while you're waiting, that's all.'

'What are you talking about? Who's going to start appreciating Molly? What are you getting at?' Jake gibbered.

'Oh, no one in particular,' said Geoff, and he wandered off to talk to Bob at the pub about whether Simon and Garfunkel would go down better than The Everly Brothers. Or maybe a bit of Tom Paxton?

So, anyway, that was yesterday, and Jake is still not sure what Geoff was trying to do there. Scare him, maybe? Well, it isn't going to work, Molly can do what she likes. He's forfeited the right to mind now. And it's not strictly true that he doesn't think about Kate. At least he doesn't ring her though. Well, he hasn't yet, anyway.

33

Rob is pacing his plush, sterile living room, restless and miserable. The only living things in this house are Lydia's orchids. They're spreading like triffids. The kitchen windowsill used to be able to hold them all but now there are so many that they're everywhere. Rob dislikes orchids. There's something prissy about them, so stiff and perfect.

The day outside is glorious but September sunshine always makes him melancholy. He supposes it's the knowledge that another summer has gone by and he's still here with Lydia. He looks into the mirror over the pretend log fire and speaks firmly to his reflection.

'I hate my wife. There, I've said it. After ten years and four house moves, after five cruises and numerous mini-breaks, "whisking her away" for rest after rest (and what does she need a rest from, for God's sake?). After what seems like a lifetime of different migraine treatments and alternative therapists, I've finally found the guts to admit it. I hate her. I bloody hate her. I absolutely fucking detest her.'

The funny thing is, Rob thinks Lydia likes him better now

he's stopped being so relentlessly nice to her. He's always been patient with her illnesses and tried to understand her but this week he has finally realised just how selfish she can be and how they never really laugh together, or talk about anything other than... well... Lydia.

She seems to spend her entire time thinking of new ways for Rob to please her. He drives her around from one quack doctor to another and she never gets any better. Perhaps it would have been better if they'd had children but she always said she wasn't strong enough for pregnancy and childbirth.

Rob's glad they didn't really; what if there had been a child who turned out like Lydia? What if he couldn't love his own children because they were too much like their mother, how awful would that have been?

So, anyway, Rob has finally decided to leave her, whether Molly wants him or not. He waited at the garage for half an hour the other night, until he thought there was absolutely no chance of Molly coming to meet him. She must have been offended by the text. Maybe she just couldn't get away – he hopes that was it. Rob can't stand the thought of Molly just not wanting to see him.

Lydia is approaching the lounge now; she'll be wanting her dinner, although she's started a new diet this week, ready for their next holiday. They're meant to be cruising round the Greek islands at Easter – oh, joy! And there's Christmas to get through before that. Rob really has to leave, and soon. Maybe Lydia's sister will step in and save the day – Lorna can invite her for Christmas and then perhaps join her on the cruise. Hang on though; her sister doesn't like Lydia much either.

Rob quickly moves into the kitchen to rustle up some brown pasta with pine nuts – Lydia won't countenance meat at the moment and she is only allowing herself to eat wholewheat pasta. He can hear her calling him already and he's only been in here two minutes. He breaks a flower off one of the smaller orchids and stamps on it.

'Robin? *Robin!* Have you remembered not to put any olive oil in the pasta? I'm watching my weight.'

'Yes, no oil, Lydia. I didn't forget.'

Rob doesn't really think a spoonful of oil will make much difference to the size of her backside but he puts the oil back in the cupboard regretfully and looks out of the kitchen window to the immaculate garden; a tiny water feature surrounded by manicured lawn and decking, with colour-coordinated chairs and parasol that no one sits on because the sun brings on Lydia's headaches, and so does the cold, oh yes, and breezes, and wasp stings... Rob doesn't usually sit out there because he's usually just got comfortable with the paper when Lydia calls out again.

'Robin? Are you all right? What are you doing? You sound peculiar.'

Peculiar? That's a good one, his whole life's peculiar just now. He starts to rehearse what he'd like to say. 'Well, actually, darling, I've fallen in love with a wonderful, beautiful, caring, funny woman who could change my life – she's sort of married at the moment but not to worry because I'm leaving you anyway. I'm going to be a father to her children, maybe have another couple of babies if we feel like it, have shedloads of wild sex and never hear the word *migraine* again.'

'I'm fine, just busy in the kitchen, would you like a sherry?'

'Oh, no, Robin, of course I don't want a sherry – are you mad? You know I can't have alcohol, you of all people should remember that; it doesn't suit me.'

'Right. Fruit juice then?'

'Too acidic.'

'Cup of tea?'

'Robin, you know I can't take caffeine.'

'Decaffeinated coffee?' *Strychnine?*

'What are you having, darling?'

'A very large whisky.'

'Is that wise? You know how it keeps you awake.'

'I'll risk it.' It's not the whisky that keeps me awake, you silly old bat, it's wondering how best to smother you with your hypoallergenic pillow, he thinks bitterly.

Silence falls – she must be watching one of her *Inspector Morse* episodes. She says she finds Morse really attractive, but then he's dead. She used to find Rob quite attractive too, in the early days. He's a bit scruffy today, but his old blue shirt is soft and comforting and his cords have got just the right level of bald patches and baggy knees.

He wonders if Molly would like this look, she usually only sees him in the smart stuff. Rob wishes he could see her right now. He wants to wrap himself around her and smell that wonderful lemony scent, and slide his hands... Oh, God, this is torture. The radio plays Nina Simone. She's singing about being independently blue. Well, quite.

Rob dances funkily around the table, imagining Molly in his arms.

'Robin?' *Oh, for fuck's sake.*

'Yes, dear?'

'Can you come in and fiddle with the channels for me? I think it's Netflix I need but I can't get that nice gardening man. It's all fuzzy. Hurry up, dear, I'm missing it.'

'I'm busy getting your supper, Lydia, it'll have to wait. Have a go yourself, why don't you?'

'*I* can't do it. Bring my tablets when you come in, please.'

'Fetch them yourself, I told you I'm busy!' There is a short silence, and Rob can see her sitting with her feet up on the leather pouffe, bought to match the enormous corner sofa which could easily seat eight. He doesn't know why they bought that; she hates having friends round; they might mark the carpets.

Then he hears the sofa creak and the tell-tale noises of a substantial wife shuffling towards the kitchen. He gulps nervously. It's all very well being brave in here but he's not used to offending her face to face yet. He picks up the trampled flower and drops it into the bin.

The kitchen door bangs back and she glides stiffly across to the worktop where her drug collection lives, both medical and alternative, looking neither right nor left. She takes tiny steps like a geisha, but there the similarity ends. Rob smiles to himself but unfortunately, she notices.

'And what might that little smile have been for?' Her voice is like cyanide trickling over ice.

'Nothing, dear.' He goes for an innocent look, but it doesn't really come off.

'Robin, I honestly don't know what's got into you lately.'

There's a moving wobble in her voice now. Hardening his heart, Rob begins to wipe the already gleaming marble surfaces. This kitchen is so clean you could eat your dinner off the floor. He has a sudden vision of his newly brave self making Lydia do just that, as a punishment for all the years of misery, but then remembers that he didn't have to stay. He could have left years ago when the sex dried up and the affection went with it. He supposes he was too cowardly; afraid of what she'd do to him, and even, perhaps, to herself? Threats. The revenge of the cowardly.

'Robin, look at me. Have I done something to upset you, dear?'

Ha! How long have you got?

'Not really, nothing specific anyway. It's just that if I'm busy cooking for you...'

'Excuse me! For *us*, actually,' she interrupts, wiping her eyes with a trembling tissue. Rob's doing rather well, he'd normally have caved in long before this, and be soothing her with little pats, apologising for his short temper and promising to do better.

'Whatever.'

She huffs – she hates 'playground language'.

'Look, Robin, you've made me very sad tonight. I'm going back into the parlour now' – *It's a living room, you bloody snob* – 'and I hope you'll soon come to your senses. I shall expect an explanation for your boorish behaviour.' *Oh, right. The words 'pot' and 'kettle' spring to mind.* 'You really can't blame pressure of work this early in the new term, can you?'

She smiles bravely, a woman in difficult circumstances showing understanding and fortitude, and leaves the room. Rob turns off the cooker, grabs his old donkey jacket from the cloakroom, slips his wellies on and leaves by the back door, raising two fingers to the living-room door as he goes.

* * *

Up on the hill above the canal, the recent shower of rain has filled the air with the scent of leaves. The young trees are doing their best to grow in the poor soil. The ground is grey and full of lumps of clay and rock. This part of the village used to be slack heaps when the mine was open, and no amount of topsoil can make up for the rough stuff underneath. Still, they've done a great job with the landscaping. Rob didn't live here in the coal-mining days, but he's seen all the old photos, and this nature reserve has really changed the area for the better.

He climbs as high as he can, and perches on the stone wall surrounding the statue of the miner. The miner looks bowed with care, but for once Rob's not feeling that way, thanks to a huge burst of energy and excitement whizzing through his veins.

How long is it since he felt like this? The job gives him massive amounts of satisfaction, but this is different. He digs out his phone from the pocket of his old cords. It's never far away from him now. Clicking frantically, he writes:

> Am sitting on the top of the world, by the old miner. If you happen to be free, I'll be here for the next half hour. X

No pleading this time; must try to be less cringing. He's been forceful once tonight, he can do it again. Rob looks down at the winding trail of the canal, as a brightly coloured narrowboat makes its way towards the town lock. He can see an excited Jack Russell on its roof, barking at the trees and cows. A boater stands on the back wearing an old hat with a wide brim and a waxed jacket – he's puffing contentedly on his pipe, and it looks like he's got a pewter tankard in front of him.

What a life. Rob's so eaten up with envy that he can hardly breathe. Lydia was persuaded into a narrowboating holiday some years ago – she disliked the lack of space, the slowness (Rob can't think why, she never breaks into a sweat at home) and the way people insisted on looking into the boat when they stopped to lock. Rob loved every minute of it. They've never done it since, needless to say.

He glances at his watch. Fifteen minutes have gone by. So why is he still with Lydia after ten years of frustration? Because he's a pathetic, feeble-minded idiot? Because he's a soft touch? Or just because he needs someone to look after? That's what being a headteacher's all about really, being everyone's daddy. Well, the worm is turning. Fifteen minutes gone.

It's not far from here to where the path emerges from the bushes by the pub, and that's where Molly will probably come from... if she comes. Rob can see the chimneys of Molly's house from here; thin tendrils of smoke drift upwards, and he imagines her surrounded by her children, by the fireside playing Monopoly, roasting chestnuts, toasting crumpets, laughing, doing the things that families do in all the best stories.

But Molly's family has a gap in it now. Rob knows Jake hasn't come home yet because the White saga is the talk of the playground. He tries to picture himself in the middle of them all, filling the vacancy for a father figure, helping Max with his homework, ferrying the girls around and teasing them about their make-up and clothes, playing football with Sam. He knows he could do it.

The time has almost ticked away, and Rob's about to give up, when out of the bushes comes a brightly clad figure. He can't breathe for a moment. She's coming; all flushed and out of breath, her hair flying and a big smile on her face. She's wearing a huge sweater in shades of green and red and rust; she looks like an autumn leaf with those amazing hazel eyes.

'Rob! I only just found your text. I missed the last one – the garage one – so I just wanted to...' She runs out of puff. Rob can't stop smiling. He tries to take her hand but she pulls away.

'It's a bit close to home, be careful, Rob.'

'Sorry, it's just that I've waited so long to see you. I've got something for you. I've made you a CD.' She looks puzzled.

'*You* know, it's sort of a mixture of all my favourite songs, 'specially the ones that make me think of you.'

'Oh, wow! That's so sweet. No one's ever done that for me before. I think we've still got a CD player... somewhere...'

'Really? You don't mind? I thought you were going to say, "Oh God, another compilation CD – I'll put it with my others!"'

'No chance. Poppy once bought me one called something like *Now That's What I Call Music to Cut Your Throat To*, but that's the nearest I've ever got to a meaningful musical present. I can't believe you did that for me. It must have taken ages.'

Rob thinks of the snatched minutes spent downstairs after dark in front of the laptop, listening for Lydia's slippers on the stairs, thrilled to be making something for Molly. It did take ages but every bit of time was filled with excitement and hope. He grins.

'No, not really. I hope you like it.'

'Course I'll like it, but I'll have to go back now, I told the kids I'd only be ten minutes.' Rob's heart sinks but he carries on smiling down at her. The way to Molly's heart might be simply by means of giving her some space.

'Well, it was great to see you. Shall we walk back together or is it too dangerous?' She looks up sharply, but sees he's not being sarcastic.

'No, it's fine; we could have met by chance, couldn't we? So if we see anyone we'll just act all innocent.'

Rob likes this, it makes it seem as if they're in it together, some sort of brilliant conspiracy with the two of them on one side and the rest of the world on the other. They begin to walk slowly down the hill. Molly looks up at Rob and away again quickly, then stumbles over a brick end in the path. He catches her just in time, puts her back on her feet, and then very gently squeezes her shoulders before releasing her. It isn't easy to move away. Her shoulders feel blissfully warm through her jersey and it's very hard to let her go. It's all Rob can do to resist her. He clears his throat and tries for a bit of sensible conversation instead.

'Any news of your mum yet?'

'Ha! You might well ask. She phoned again while I was out yesterday but she was only on the line for two minutes, so Sam says, just long enough to say she was fine, and not to worry.'

'But you are worrying, of course. It's hard for you.'

'Yes.' Molly digs around with the toe of her boot in the earth and looks as if she's on the verge of tears, so Rob seizes on a new subject quickly.

'So, how are the boys? Poppy says they're going to stop with her for a bit.'

'Yes, Jill was conscious for a moment or two while Poppy was there, apparently, and made her promise to take care of them from now on, for some reason.'

Molly looks shifty, and Rob knows she must be aware by now of how much Jill dislikes Lydia, and that even when she's desperately sick she wouldn't allow Lydia to look after her sons for any longer than is absolutely necessary. He supposes Jill is bound to remember meeting Lydia briefly on that holiday years ago on the canals when she and Roger had been doing the same route in the opposite direction. It was when they'd all lived in Yorkshire, before Roger had come down to work in the brewery laboratory and Rob had got this job – his very first headship. Lydia hadn't come out of the encounter very well. Best not to think about that now.

Molly carries on hurriedly. 'Hmm, anyway, it was really good of you to step in – it's not easy looking after children when you haven't got any of your own. I mean...' She breaks off in confusion.

'No, it's okay, I know just what you mean. We're just not geared to it, somehow, even though I spend all day with children it didn't seem to work very well. Mind you, I'm not sure I can see Poppy being so great at family life either.'

Rob tries to give an amused grin but only manages to sound bitter. She pats his arm comfortingly and he covers her hand with his. They stand still for a moment, and he wants to hold her so badly that he aches.

They both glance around at the surrounding scrubland and grass – the trees aren't big enough to hide them yet. They would have to stand there for decades while a Sleeping Beauty-type forest grew up – then they could do whatever they liked. But for now, they carry on walking, lost in their separate thoughts.

Rob's wondering what he's going to say to Lydia and, after he's said it, when he can reasonably leave. He supposes the authorities will have to be told, and there'll be an extra governors' meeting, with much pontificating and self-righteousness. He doesn't know what Molly is thinking though. If he did, life would be so much easier.

34

The clock in the hall strikes three. Poppy turns over for what seems like the millionth time and swaps her pillow to the cool side, sticking one leg out of the quilt to let some air in. She is totally shattered but still can't sleep.

Over the years she has been working on a revolutionary new technique for getting rid of unwanted memories – this is how it goes. First, you take a few good deep breaths, nice and steady, and when you're calm, you look your bad memories in the face, without blinking or flinching, for five whole seconds. Then, you take another deep breath and push the worries and memories – with both arms – into a massive carved wooden wardrobe that just happens to have appeared in your bedroom (because the really bad memories only seem to pop up in the night).

Anyway, this wardrobe is a bit like the one that gets you into Narnia, and it takes up the whole of one wall, big enough for anyone's memories. Now, this is the tricky bit, you slam the wardrobe door, really loudly and turn the little gold key in the lock.

Then, you look at yourself in the mirror on the wardrobe

door, and say 'I am strong, I'm invincible. I am woman' (or bloke obviously, but perhaps men don't have the same sort of problem with foolish memories) and then you lie down, with a large brandy if necessary, or a cup of nasty herbal tea if you're on a health kick, and sleep will wash over you in large and luscious waves. Brilliant, eh? Only, tonight, it's not working for some reason.

Well, of course Poppy knows the reason really. It's all down to those boys asleep in the spare bedroom. It all started to go wrong when she took the clothes and things for Roger. She wanted to help and thought she would be safe, but the sight of him, his chubby chin and his grey ponytail and his tear-stained face – it just finished her off somehow. And then, just as Poppy was leaving, Jill opened her eyes. Well, all hell was let loose – it was the first time she'd woken up and there were tears and hugs and wall-to-wall emotion, and of course she wanted to know how the kids were straight away.

To cut a long story short, Jill threw the most amazing wobbly when she found out that Lydia was looking after her boys and the next moment, Jill was making Poppy promise to keep them safe and out of 'that odious woman's clutches'. Whatever can Lydia have done in the past to bring this on? It must have been pretty awful if she still remembers it when she's wired up to drips and monitors and heaven knows what else. This is some-thing that needs investigating. Poppy wonders who'd know? She decides to follow this up in the morning.

So, anyway, the boys are sleeping in Poppy's flat, and really they're no bother at all. They get their own cereal and toast in the morning and then they come to meet Poppy at work at the café for their tea after school. Rob takes their washing – she's not telling Jill that, but she bets Lydia doesn't dirty her hands with it anyway, he must do it himself. But Poppy can't sleep with them here, so she lies awake and thinks. That's a luxury she doesn't usually allow herself.

Poppy hates thinking. Sleeping children are innocent and beautiful. They always manage to look fragile, even solid little boys like these two, and they hurt her heart so badly that she can hardly bear it.

She starts to wonder again about Lydia and remembers that Jill once mentioned knowing Rob and his wife from years back. Ah – got it. They'd all met up on a narrowboating holiday, that was it! Poppy casts her mind back. She has, over the years, developed a very selective memory; she can ditch anything painful or unnecessary, and at the time she'd had no interest in Lydia or Rob. Poppy thinks hard but in the end decides that she probably never had all the facts; she seems to remember there was some sort of incident with Lydia and a lock-keeper but now she comes to consider it, Jill was very mysterious at the time. An argument and a tussle of some sort?

Well, if all goes well, she'll be able to ask Jill herself soon. Poppy knows for certain that Molly doesn't like Lydia; something to do with the way she treats Rob, which as far as Poppy is concerned is their own business. But of course, it's getting to be Molly's business. Poppy's not daft – she can see which way the wind's blowing. The last time someone looked at Poppy in the way that Rob looks at Molly, she married him. Whoops, scrub that last thought, pretend she didn't even think it. Poppy likes to leave her murky past to take care of itself.

She stretches in her comfortable bed, wriggles to settle into a better position, and feels the familiar little pain. Something else to deal with... if not tomorrow, then soon.

35

It's a snap decision for Daisy to head over to Molly's tonight. She almost can't find the energy, as exhausted as she is with all the worrying she's been doing. She's just sitting in her kitchen and wishing she could sort them all out, when a thought occurs, making her leap to her feet and shout, 'I can make it right if I put my mind to it! I just need to give 'em a good talking to, that's all, and I can't get at Jake down in Norfolk, so I'll start with Molly.'

Without further ado, she rings a taxi, which is something she never, ever does because she hates spending money on unnecessary things like that. Buses usually suit Daisy just fine, but there's no time to be lost tonight. She quickly changes out of her slippers into her smart lace-ups, buttons up her chapel coat and is there within half an hour, never even warning them she's on the way. She wants to surprise them.

It's Daisy that ends up being surprised though. Dear Lord, whoever would have thought it? Such wickedness happening, right here in Mayfield, and almost in the shadow of the chapel too.

There's no answer when she knocks on the door and then rings the bell at Molly and Jake's, and Sarah is out too, so Daisy looks for the key – yes, still in the same old place. Not very safe, must remember to tell Molly. Anyway, she goes in, and she can smell him straight away, that boy Nick.

She's never been sure about him – always thought he was up to no good. And it turns out... oh, heavens, she was right. She sees them, caught right there in the act. Loud music playing – no wonder they didn't hear the doorbell. It's the sort of music that Daisy hates – bump, bang, boom, and no proper words.

Daisy doesn't let on she is there to begin with, she's much too shocked. She stands just outside the door of the kitchen, peering into the brightly lit room, beginning to shake. Never in all her born days has she seen anything so disgusting. What in heaven's name are they doing?

Daisy can't hold back a gasp, and the boy suddenly looks straight at her, and opens his mouth to speak. She turns on her heel and gets out of there as quickly as possible, and is home again in next to no time, because a bus comes along just at the right minute, and that's the only good thing that's happened today.

She's back in her own kitchen now, and she feels dreadful; better to have some hot, sweet tea and a lie down and then she'll have to phone Molly and tell her. That boy mustn't have anything to do with any of them any more, especially Theo... he mustn't... he mustn't...

Okay, thinks Molly sadly, so now we've established that I'll jump if Rob texts me and I've got no willpower whatsoever. Right, what other degrading roads can I go down? Maybe I'll start hanging around outside school at odd times of the day, or driving past his house, although it must be quite tricky stalking someone who lives in a cul-de-sac.

She never realised how lonely her life would be without Jake in it. He doesn't say much as a rule and just lately he's been making her want to scream most of the time with his high-minded principles and his nagging about moving house, but it's miserable without him. She knows he doesn't seem to do much around the house, but nothing at all is getting done now he's gone. They all just wander about looking forlorn and sniping at each other.

Even the kids seem to be avoiding talking to her. Last night she'd left the younger ones with Nick and Theo. The two littlies were safely in bed and asleep, Sam was at a friend's and Molly just couldn't settle any longer. She had to get out. She'd only gone into Hopton to stock up at the supermarket but by the time she'd come back, all the lights were out and Theo's bedroom door was firmly shut.

Molly had knocked but Theo hadn't answered. Nick must have gone home early, which was annoying because she'd not have left Theo on her own with the others if she'd known he was going. Oh, well. Another half hour and she could be in bed herself. She'd unpacked the shopping and taken a mug of hot chocolate up but sleep had been a long time coming.

Theo had been a bit weird this morning, come to think of it. She'd made an excuse for Nick, saying he'd remembered he hadn't locked the shop till up properly and had to dash off, but her eyes looked heavy. Maybe they'd had an argument, but it seemed unlikely – they were as thick as thieves usually.

Molly sighs – something else to worry about. And it really isn't helping that her mum has chosen now to make some sort of feminist stand, or whatever it is she's up to in Norfolk. Molly's painfully aware that she irritates Peggy, and that her dad's laziness drives her mum mad, but surely they could have talked about it? Molly never seems to be able to get on her wavelength these days.

It wouldn't so bad if Molly and her mum had ever had long chats about meaningful stuff. It's all just trivia as a rule. They've never even talked about the saddest thing that ever happened to their family. Peggy seems to think Molly doesn't remember much about Maria, but she was nine when the baby died and she was so excited at the thought of a new sister.

Molly was sure it was going to be a girl; she was really fed up with the way Sandy and Paul were so close, being twins. She remembers thinking, 'This one's for me, my special sister.' They even let Molly choose her name (she was going through a pious phase at the time). After Maria was born and died, all in the space of a minute, no one told Molly for ages but she knew

something was up. She so wanted to help her mum and dad, but Peggy wouldn't even let Molly cuddle her, she got on with life as if nothing had happened, and Geoff just spent more time in the garden for a while.

So, on the whole, with all these thoughts floating round her head, Molly's feeling pretty unhappy. She knows Rob's unhappy too. Why not cheer each other up then? Jake obviously doesn't care what she does – he'd be here with her if he did, wouldn't he? And her mum would rather sort out her troubles away from her daughter. Molly's just waiting for Rob's next text and then she'll make a decision... probably.

As Molly drives to work on the first really nippy morning of the autumn, she feels her phone buzzing in her pocket, and her heart flips – this is it! Tonight will be the night. She's going to go for it. Rummaging around until she finds it, she pulls up in a gateway. Hang on, it must have been ringing, not a text coming through at all. The 'I missed call' message looks back at her – that's a new development, Rob's never rung her before. She checks the number but doesn't recognise it, so she takes a deep breath and rings it anyway. A crisp voice answers.

'Accident and Emergency, Sister speaking, can I help you?' and Molly almost drops the phone in horror.

'Who... erm... it's Molly White – you rang me...' she burbles.

'Oh yes, Mrs White, thank you for returning my call so promptly.' Molly can't speak. Sam? Theo? The school would surely ring if something is wrong with the other two?

'Mrs White? Are you still there?' Sister sounds anxious. Molly gulps.

'Yes, I'm here, tell me quickly, who's been hurt? Is it one of the children, or...?' Her voice doesn't sound right. It rasps a bit and gives up.

'No, not one of your children, and no one's been hurt exactly, but your mother-in-law, Mrs Daisy White, has been admitted this morning and we have tried both sons without any luck. You're our next port of call, Mrs White. We needed to notify someone as quickly as possible.'

'Daisy? What's happened to Daisy? Has she fallen or something? Is she ill?' Molly hears the unfamiliar croaky voice asking these idiotic questions, not giving the Sister a chance to reply. 'Because you won't get Jake – he's disappeared without his phone, and Matt's in Portugal for a little while, and the signal can be really bad, so...'

'Of course, Mrs White,' she manages to stop Molly's babbling at last, 'but Daisy didn't fall – a neighbour happened to see her lying in the open doorway and called an ambulance. She was admitted a short time ago and we're giving her some emergency treatment and finding out the cause of the collapse. Could you come to the hospital, do you think? We may need some consent forms signing.'

Sister pauses enquiringly, but Molly can't speak. A picture is now firmly in her mind; Daisy, all on her own, lying in the doorway, cold and frightened, maybe.

'Mrs White?'

'Oh, sorry, yes, of course I'll come – just give me ten minutes. Sister! Before you go – is she... is she conscious?'

'I'm afraid not, but we're working on her at the moment, Mrs White. She's having the best possible care. I'll see you shortly then?'

The drive to hospital is short but nightmarish – all the lights are on red and every route into town seems to be clogged with idiots crawling along, chatting and wasting time, probably listening to Radio 2 and laughing at the stupid jokes, just like Molly would be doing on a normal day. Eventually she reaches the car park and there are no spaces so she breaks a lifetime rule and parks in a disabled spot, leaving the car at a bizarre angle and sprinting for the lift.

Molly's mind is chanting, 'No, Daisy, don't die, don't go...' over and over as she runs along the echoing corridors and into the Emergency ward. Suddenly, she screeches to a halt as a stretcher is wheeled in front of her, carrying an elderly man obviously in pain, grey faced and thin, with a blood-soaked shirt and no teeth. She makes herself slow down as she approaches the nurses' station.

The receptionist sits behind a plastic grille. A bow holds her flowery shirt close to her neck, hiding the folds and wrinkles, and she bares slightly yellow teeth at Molly when she finally reaches the front of the queue.

'I'm Molly White – you rang me earlier. I came as quickly as I could...' The receptionist looks tired and not a little cross. Her phone is ringing incessantly and Molly can see someone being violently sick into a bucket out of the corner of her eye in the cubicle adjoining them.

'Ah, yes, Mrs White – you need the next ward. Mrs White senior is on the left down the corridor marked "Observation". I'm sorry to keep you waiting' (another flash of the yellow teeth) 'but we're very short-staffed today – the stomach bug, you know.' The sound effects from the cubicle bear this out, although a discreet curtain has now been drawn across the doorway.

'How...?'

'I'm sorry, I can't give you any more information here, just pop along to the desk in the next ward, thank you.' Her eyes are already on the couple behind Molly, who are clutching a wailing baby between them and getting impatient.

Molly sets off again at a brisk pace, only to find her way blocked by two paramedics pushing a trolley carrying another aged gentleman, this one shouting 'Gladys!' at the top of his reedy voice.

'It's all right, pet, Gladys is on her way, just relax and we'll get you a doctor to check you over,' says the first man.

The other paramedic looks surprised. 'Is Gladys coming then?'

'No, she died ten years ago,' his colleague whispers, 'but let's not get into that one just now.'

'Fair enough.'

They move on down the row of cubicles, and Molly follows them in a daze. Finally she sees an efficient-looking nurse behind a computer and heads for her like a shipwrecked sailor spotting a bit of floating wreckage.

'Excuse me?' Molly murmurs politely. There is no response. She coughs. The woman raises her eyes briefly and carries on tapping the keys.

'I've come to see Daisy White.'

'Is she in here then?'

'Well, so the Sister told me on the phone.' Molly begins to sweat. 'She seemed to think it was urgent. Can you find out for me, do you think?'

'Just a minute. Oh, that's the phone, I'd just better...'

'No!'

The woman jumps, and glances round nervously. An older nurse dressed in navy blue moves towards them enquiringly.

'Any problems, Sharon?'

'This lady seems a little bit upset.'

'Upset? Of course I'm upset! You ring me and tell me to get here urgently because my mother-in-law is unconscious, I get stuck behind every slow-moving vehicle in Leicestershire, I can't park, everyone's trying to stop me finding Daisy, and you wonder why...' Molly breaks off as the tears finally come, and

Sister ushers her into a small day room with a withering glance at the younger nurse.

There are six green upholstered chairs in there, and it is a most depressing green. Not the green of grass or the greeny-blue of the sea, or even a pale, delicate green. No, this is an acidic, bile-like colour and the chairs have interesting stains as if they have seen the harsher side of life for some time. A pile of dog-eared magazines is on a low table and Molly has the ridiculous but overwhelming urge to sit down and read her way through them – to find out all about the stories behind the lurid head-lines, to lose herself in candid snaps of celebrity cellulite and fashion gaffes.

'Mrs White – I'm sorry about all that, we spoke on the tele-phone. I'm Sister Marshall.' Her voice is still crisp and refined but the whole effect is less intimidating face to face.

'But what about Daisy, is she okay?' Molly manages to blurt out, trying to dry her eyes on her sleeve. 'Is she conscious yet?'

'Well, not yet, but we're giving her a good check over and the doctor will speak to you shortly.' She smiles kindly and passes Molly a handy box of tissues, but Molly's past pleasantries now.

'But... what's the problem? Is she going to be all right?'

'We're not sure what the problem is yet, Mrs White, but as soon as the doctor has finished...'

'Can I see her?'

Sister sighs, patiently. 'Just as soon as the doctor has completed his assessment, so the best thing will be if you could just come and sit down and have a nice cup of tea. We'll let you know as soon as we've some news.'

'But I want to see her *now*. There's only me here – the kids are at school, my mum's disappeared, my husband's run away to Norfolk, and my brother-in-law cleared off to Portugal when everyone kept saying he was gay. My dad's no use at the moment, he's too worried about my mum.' Molly runs out of steam and Sister gently moves her towards the least horrible chair.

'Are you sure there's no one we can ring to come and support you, Mrs White? I can tell this is a very stressful time for you, and it could be a while before we can fully assess your mother-in-law's condition.'

And suddenly Molly realises that, yes, there is someone she can ring. Someone who loves Daisy and seems to care about Molly too. She stands up abruptly and Sister takes a step back but when Molly explains what she's going to do, she motions her to the phone on the table.

'The signal in here is terrible; use this one,' she says, patting Molly's arm. Molly scrolls through the numbers on her mobile and begins to dial, her heart in her mouth.

Rob is in the playground when the phone call comes, but Ma Baker's frantic waving from the office window brings him inside at a gallop. At first, he thinks it must be the Ofsted announcement; they've been on tenterhooks all term and the visit has got to come soon, but Ma B soon puts him right.

'My heart was thumping, Mr Jennings, and no mistake – I felt like I was going to have one of my dizzy spells. I'm wondering if I should just pop home and have a lie down actually. You know how I get, and once I start, well...'

'But who was it? What's wrong? *Just tell me!*' he bellows, almost shaking the bloody woman.

'There's no call to take that tone, my lad – a bit of respect wouldn't go amiss.' She sniffs, and reaches for a tissue from the ruffled packet on her desk. Well, you could say desk, but it's actually an old table with a cloth over it in the corner by the window. She does like to see what's going on outside, even though she feels it's really not her business to interfere in playground crises.

Rob sighs and bites his lip – you can't get information out of the old battleaxe by shouting; she just weeps pathetically or has one of her turns.

'Sorry, Mrs B – I was just worried there was a phone call – you know I'm waiting and it could be any day because...'

'No, no, no! This is much more important than your silly inspectors!' In her haste to blurt out her news she forgets to be offended for a few moments and quickly fills him in on the call from the hospital. '...although I really don't know why Mrs White should ring *you*?' she says. 'There must be a family member more suitable to help out. After all, you're *supposed* to be teaching in five minutes.' Her voice is heavy with sarcasm – she's remembered she is cross with him and he will have to pay if their strange relationship is to resume its normal (frosty, but reasonably even) footing.

'Mrs White probably realised that you would be the one to answer the phone, Mrs B, and that you would have everything sorted out in no time. You know how I rely on your skills to organise us all, especially in a crisis, and I think this is definitely one of those.'

Rob's itching to be off, but he can't leave his school in the lurch, and Mrs B needs to be on his side for this to work. He holds his breath and tries not to beg. After a moment she bridles, but picks up the telephone, with a martyred sigh.

'Very well – how hard you do work me, that's for sure, Mr Jennings. I hope I can get through the day, my head is niggling and I'm starting to see colours, but I'll try to sort things out for you, seeing as it's an emergency *and Mrs White needs you so badly*.' She peers at Rob over her bifocals, and if it wasn't such an unlikely prospect, you might almost think she winks.

After a frantic few minutes rearranging the morning, there's a supply teacher on the way and the Year Six class split up in the meantime, to their delight. If they're lucky some of them will get to do 'choosing' later, which means water and sand, Lego and playdough. The parents might grumble, but Rob couldn't care less at this moment.

At long last he's in the car speeding towards town, heart banging. He's fighting wild elation and trying to feel more concerned about Daisy. Of course he's worried about her – she was so good to him when he was trying to settle in Mayfield and he and Lydia didn't know a soul – but it's hard to believe the fact that Molly rang *him* when she was desperate for help. Well, he guesses she really didn't have much choice in the matter as no one else is around, but even so...

The worst of the rush-hour traffic has gone now, so he reaches the hospital in no time. The slip road leading to the car park is lined with quite gracious-looking trees, trying to make visitors feel as if they've stumbled into a little bit of countryside, but most people are too anxious by this point to notice their surroundings.

On the one hand, Rob would have quite liked the journey to take longer while he decided how to handle the situation, but most of him is just frantic to get to Molly, scoop her up and love her better. She sounded frantic. Bloody Jake, clearing off and leaving all the dirty work to his wife. Rob's never met Matt, but he doesn't sound much better, rushing away to Brighton just because one or two people made comments about his sexuality. And now he's even further away for a while.

Who cares if Matt's gay, anyway? Well, his dad might have done by all accounts, but he'd have got over it. Rob bets Daisy wouldn't have minded so long as her boy was happy. He could probably have wrapped himself in PVC and been the only gay in the village for all his mum cared.

He remembers Daisy talking about Matt's tendency to dress up as a princess when he was in the reception class, or whatever it was called in those days – she asked Rob if that happened very often and if he thought it was in any way strange. Rob went for the soothing approach, because wearing a frock when you're a five-year-old boy can just be a sign of a sensual nature and a stylish, creative outlook. On the other hand... oh, well, Daisy has probably guessed about her son by now, and she's much too sensible to mind.

It's difficult to park; Rob seems to have arrived just at the time when there's often a fight for spaces as all the clinic appointments start at nine o'clock. As he nips into a space in front of a red-faced lady who waves her fist at him, he spots Molly's car dumped at a strange angle near the entrance, and gets inside the hospital as quickly as he can, passing the huddle of grey people in dressing gowns having a smoke outside the revolving doors, underneath the 'Thank You For Not Smoking' sign, coughing and spitting in unison like some sort of alternative choir.

There's only one woman with them. She's wrapped in something that may have once been fleecy and was possibly white in a previous life. She's having a great time, enjoying the banter and sucking in as much nicotine as she can before she gets rounded up, flicking her fag ends into the scrubby bushes and tossing her greasy hair.

Rob tries not to look disapproving. Mind you, a couple of them look as if their days are somewhat numbered, so he supposes they might as well enjoy their vices. If he was dying, he'd definitely want to have a go at all the vices he could handle. Excellent wine, a family-sized bucket of fries, smoked salmon, caviar and prawn canapés, and a very posh hotel room with Molly. A roaring fire for when they finally got out of bed, and a good long stretch of beach to walk along in between bouts of earth-shattering passion. Maybe some fine old brandy?

Rob drags his mind back to the present crisis and sees Molly huddled in a chair watching the door to the Emergency ward. She catches sight of him and leaps to her feet, almost knocking over a small child with its leg in plaster and mumbling apologies as she moves forward, arms open. Her face is grubby and tear-stained and her clothes look as if she's slept in them already.

And he's dreamed of this moment – not just daydreamed, really dreamed, night after night, but he usually wakes up before the most wonderful bit, where he buries his face in her soft, sweet-smelling hair and kisses her neck, and she wraps herself around him so tightly that you can't see the join.

Eventually they pull apart and Rob holds Molly by the shoulders as she tries to explain what's happened. Then he puts an arm around her as they head for the A&E doors. He can sort this out. He can get her some answers. He can ease the pain. And who knows what will happen next?

38

Well, Nick's really done it now. All that planning and scheming, and minding the shop, and cooking great dinners, and being nice to everybody – all wasted, just because Daisy had to turn up at the wrong moment.

It was Theo's fault; she's been following him around for days now. She thinks he hasn't noticed that she's always 'just passing' the shop when he comes out, or 'just popping in' to see if he needs any help. Anyway, he was coming round to see if Molly was home last night – he'd had a vague thought that he'd cook them all something stodgy, maybe a cheese and potato pie with a lovely crispy crust.

His mum used to do that, with beans. Nick's been thinking about her a lot this week, and it doesn't seem to hurt quite so badly at the moment. He wonders what she'd look like now, if she hadn't gone and died? Still skinny, and still dancing in the garden? He supposes after a certain age that might seem a bit sad.

Anyway, he 'just happened' to meet Theo on the way to her

house and when they got there, Molly was looking all wild-eyed and crazy.

'Nick, are you busy for a little while?' she'd said. Well, Nick wasn't, as it happened. They'd all had their tea early and the little kids were snoring already – they'd had some sort of fun day at school and they were wiped out, Theo said. That meant Nick's cooking plan was a non-starter but he was sure Theo would be able to find him a pizza or something in the freezer, so he'd nodded when Molly had asked him to hang around with Theo.

Theo's mum hadn't been out of the house for more than five minutes before Theo had made her move. Nick still can't believe what happened next. Suddenly, she'd ripped open her shirt (guess what, no bra), shouted, 'Look, Nick – this is, like, ridiculous, I want you, and I know you want me!' and fallen to her knees in front of him. Next thing Nick knew, Theo had his jeans unbuttoned and... well, you can probably picture the scene. Bloke looking like all his Christmases and birthdays have happened at once and woman on knees performing lewd sex act. And then she'd got her hair caught in Nick's zip.

It was at that point that he saw Daisy watching them. Nick could have died. She just shouted, 'Lord save us!' or some such rubbish, and she was off like a rocket, leaving them frozen to the spot. Poor Theo, Nick felt really sorry for her at that point. She probably doesn't go in for this sort of thing as a rule. Neither does Nick, as it happens, but he knows enough to tell Theo's no expert – she made his eyes water, to be honest.

Still, she cried for about an hour once Nick got her untangled, hysterical at one point, she was. He'd thought about slapping her like you're supposed to, but it'd be just his luck for her mum to come in just as he was knocking her for six.

Eventually she calmed down enough for Nick to go back to

the shop, and he'd had to dip into Geoff's best malt whisky to calm his shattered nerves. His arms are bleeding again; he's not sure how that happened though. He thinks maybe he'll lie low for a day or two until things calm down. Then he'll see if he can salvage the plan.

Back at the shop and desperate for something to take his mind off this mess, Nick spies a pile of old photo albums in the bookshelves. He usually hates that sort of thing – smug little groups of people, grinning at the camera and congratulating themselves on playing happy families. But tonight, he's curious. This lot are so weird – maybe their old photos will help him to understand what makes them all tick.

The first one he takes down is really old, and he hardly knows anyone in it; Peggy and Geoff look all scrubbed and innocent, but the others are strangers. He picks another, a newer-looking burgundy plastic one this time. Ah – Molly. She was a very cute teenager, and he can see where Theo gets her sex appeal from... no, don't go there.

He turns the pages quickly until one picture makes him stop suddenly and look much more carefully. He reaches for his wallet – bugger! Must have left it at Molly's house. Nick looks at the old photographs for a long time, but he doesn't come to any conclusion because what he's thinking is too ridiculous to even contemplate.

39

Oh. My. God. This has got to be the worst day of Theo's life. Worse than Dad going, worse than the guinea pig getting caught in the waste disposal unit last year, even worse than the time she got lost in Debenhams and then accidentally wrapped herself round the wrong daddy's legs and bit him for losing her.

How is she ever going to face Nick again? Let alone Gran, who thinks swearing's rude, so you can guess what she must think of oral sex. And Nick... oh God, oh God, oh God... she is so red in the face that she might just explode. That'd solve all the problems in one go. Just a huge splat on the kitchen floor and that would be the end of the embarrassment once and for all.

Theo puts the kettle on for yet another cup of tea, and rinses her best Shrek mug, but then she remembers that Daisy bought it last Christmas and goes all hot again and puts it away, dragging out an old Bovril one instead. She wishes she was twelve again, or ten, or five, or... anything but fifteen, really. Anything but stuck in this horrible moment with no chance of ever feeling better and no one to talk to and the beginnings of a really huge spot on her chin.

Why did she ever try to get off with him anyway? She should have known that someone like Nick was way out of her league – he must have had loads of girlfriends that know all about rude stuff, not like Theo, who gets all flushed and ends up getting her fringe caught, and a pubic hair between her front teeth. How uncool is that?

She wishes she'd never met him now, with his bloody sharp cheekbones and his ridiculous hair. Oh God. And why did she say such a stupid thing about wanting him, like they were in some cheesy soap? And then Gran coming in too, as if things couldn't get any worse. She must think Theo is such a tart. They probably hadn't even invented oral sex in her day.

Theo wishes she'd never heard of it either – she thought Nick would think she was so experienced and liberated if she made the first move, because, let's face it, he was never going to start anything. Not with a dumpy, ignorant idiot like Theo. And now she's found his wallet under the chair and doesn't know what to do with it – if she takes it round, Nick will think she hid it on purpose as an excuse to see him again. Maybe she should just have a little look in it while it's here though. There could be clues about him. There might be something that explains why he's like he is...

She opens the wallet carefully – it's quite old and cracked. There's no money (not that she thought there would be) or cards, only a phone top-up one, but there's some really tatty bits of paper in the back. They're photos, mostly of kids. There's quite a new-looking one of Nick but with dreads in – hang on, here's one with Nick and his Mohican and the dreadlock boy is on it too.

Two of him? And some little kids. And a really creased one of a thin blonde woman in an Indian-type dress, with wild hair and bare feet. She's got a really nice smile, with her hands up covering her mouth like she's been laughing for ages and just tried to calm down for the photo. The woman reminds Theo a bit of somebody but she can't think who.

Anyway, back to today's problems. She'd better get to school, and then call in with the wallet later when she's brave again, if that ever happens. The embarrassment keeps coming in big waves, and now the message light's on the answering machine. Maybe it's him. Yeah, right. Oh, sod it – Theo's not going to school. She's never bunked off before, but now seems to be a really good time to start. This is all Dad's fault, going away and stirring everyone up, so he can help her to sort it out. That's where she's going – Norfolk. She can leave the wallet here and hitch, and if she gets murdered on the way, who's going to care anyway?

40

So here's Molly, with the man she wants to be with more than any other man in the world right now, but in totally the wrong place for the things she has in mind to happen.

She's had to leave him outside the ward, because apparently they have some sort of bug going on here and Molly has had to rub her hands with gel that smells of gin. It takes her right back to the Covid days, and the risk of infection seems rife again, even if in a different way. Molly has to put on a plastic apron before she can even get into the place. They've been here for three hours already and Sister only just let Molly in to see Daisy.

Molly's full of disgusting coffee-machine drinks, jittery with caffeine and still no nearer to contacting Jake or Matt. She's also very tired of being civil to rude receptionists who sit behind signs warning people that they will not tolerate any acts of aggression on the part of patients or their visitors.

Molly and Rob have slipped into the waiting routine to such an extent that when they finally come to escort Molly to Daisy, she's almost forgotten to be worried. However, the panic returns with a lurch as they approach the final bottle of gin gel on the wall near the nurses' station. She slaps some more on for good measure and tries her hardest to look brave.

Daisy is in a four-bedded ward with curtains round her which are failing miserably to cut out the sound of her neighbours who seem to be singing, vomiting and calling 'Nurse' and 'Toilet' alternately. The nurse with Molly, a small, pale girl in purple, smiles at the singer and tweaks the curtain round the hurler so there are no disturbing gaps.

'Now, Barbara,' she says brightly, 'you know we've just taken you to the bathroom, you don't need to go again yet, I'm sure!' and bustles Molly into the next enclosed space without further ado.

And then the world stops turning for a minute. Daisy lies flat on her back, not just pale but much worse – as grey as dirty washing-up water. In fact, there are no words to describe how dreadful she looks, and no way of expressing how Molly's heart twists at the sight of her much-loved face, immobile on the pillow, sunken cheeked. Her mouth is slightly open and she is snoring gently.

'Visitor for you, Daisy!' trills the nurse.

'But... can she hear you?' Molly asks, beginning to shake with the effort of not losing the plot.

'Of course she can. She's just resting at the moment, aren't you, sweetheart?' answers the nurse, adjusting Daisy's pillows with a deft flick of the wrist, and adding a note to the official-looking clipboard at the foot of the bed. The machine by the bed begins to wheeze alarmingly and Molly jumps up, looking at the nurse for reassurance.

'Don't worry, Mrs White – we're just monitoring Daisy's blood pressure for the time being, while we wait for the doctor to come round.'

'But surely, she must have seen a doctor by now? We've been here for hours.' The nurse looks wary. Has Molly overstepped the mark? Is she going to be classed as violent and disruptive and be ejected from the ward?

'Of course Daisy has seen a doctor in A&E, but the doctor will be coming to see her in here shortly, and then he'll explain everything to her sons personally. I appreciate that you must be concerned. Have you had any luck in contacting her family yet?'

'I *am* her family!' Molly says, keeping her temper in check with a mammoth effort. '*I'll* see the doctor, there's no one but me here anyway!'

Molly hears what she hopes is the doctor's step in the corridor.

Relief floods the nurse's face. 'Here he is,' she says, opening the curtain to welcome him.

Molly can tell that the doctor has become embroiled in a discussion with Vomiting Lady on the way who is enjoying describing some details that Molly would rather not be party to, especially given the amount of hospital coffee sloshing around in her poor tummy. Singing Lady is in full flow – it sounds like 'Distant Drums' – Molly isn't much of a Jim Reeves expert, but the bedside table seems to be coming in handy for the percussion. Shouting Lady has either gone to sleep or slipped into a coma; peeping round the curtain it's impossible to tell the difference.

At last Dr Khan is in Daisy's cubicle, shaking Molly's hand and bowing with tired politeness. He is immaculate – small and dapper with thick black glasses and a tiny moustache, which he strokes lovingly as he speaks. The nurse almost genuflects, she's so excited. He's obviously a force to be reckoned with, and her cheeks are rosy pink. She gazes admiringly at him and explains kindly that Mrs White junior has been rather agitated and wishes the doctor to update her, in lieu of immediate family. At this, she shoots her a nervous glance but Molly lets it pass.

The doctor attends to business first, checking the paperwork, listening to Daisy's heartbeat briefly, and lifting one of her eyelids, revealing a bloodshot nightmare. Molly shudders, and he gestures for her to follow him away from the bed, down the long, tiled corridor, past little huddles of visitors making determined small-talk, and behind the nurses' desks into a tiny office.

They sit knee to knee as he explains, as best he can, that Daisy may or may not wake up today, and that she seems to have suffered a slight stroke and probably a mild heart attack, both of which have rendered her deeply unconscious.

'But surely, if it was only a slight stroke and a mild heart attack, she should be awake by now, Doctor? She seems so very far away...' Molly mumbles, beginning to cry. He pats her on the arm and passes the handy box of tissues; there must be one around every corner in this sad place. Molly wonders how many people have sat here and been glad of them.

It really is a very depressing office, looking out onto a scruffy, flag-stoned patio with a rather tired shrub or two in pots. If she wasn't miserable when she came in, Molly decides she definitely would be when she left. She pulls herself together to try to take in his words.

The doctor seems to be saying that Daisy is basically strong and healthy, she seems to be in some sort of shock, possibly following an incident, or exertion of some sort, and does Molly know of anything that could have caused such an outcome over the past few hours? It must have happened fairly recently, whatever it was, he muses, continuing to pat her arm absent-mindedly. Arm patting is really quite soothing; she's getting to like it.

Molly tells him that Daisy has had a difficult time lately; there have been various family problems to contend with, and so on, but he clearly feels that something more serious and sudden has triggered this attack. Molly is mystified. What can Daisy have been up to?

'So what might happen next? Is there any treatment that Daisy can have to bring her out of this deep sleep?' she asks hopefully.

'I'm afraid not, Mrs White. We must just watch and wait. We'll set up a saline drip so that Daisy doesn't become dehydrated, but further than that we cannot go at this stage.'

'A drip? That sounds serious?'

'Just routine, I assure you. I recommend that her family visit and talk to her peacefully, perhaps play some music. Nature has a way of righting the balance,' he advises gently, and walks back with Molly to Daisy's bedside, smiling and waving at a number of eager nurses, patients and visitors en route.

Molly feels a bit like a member of a royal entourage; perhaps the lady that carries the floral tributes, or the one in charge of the royal wallet? As they approach Daisy's room, she notices that 'Distant Drums' has been replaced by 'Roll Me Over in the Clover' – obviously a lady with an interesting past. Vomiting Lady has, mercifully, nodded off, and Shouting Lady seems to be watching one of the soaps, with the volume turned up to stun.

Looking down at Daisy's apparently sleeping face, Molly takes her hand as gently as possible so as not to disturb, before she realises that she doesn't actually want Daisy to stay asleep. She squeezes the motionless hand but Daisy shows no sign of feeling anything.

Oh, Daisy, my lovely mother-in-law and friend, how would I ever manage without you, thinks Molly, fragments of memories of their shared past spinning in her mind like kaleidoscope pieces. Tears trickle down Molly's face as the song changes to

'Delilah' – Singing Lady belts out the lyrics about the cheating woman and what becomes of her, as she holds onto Daisy's hand and wonders if she'll ever escape from this sad, mad world.

The nurse swishes the curtains around them again and Molly hears quick, rubber-soled footsteps. After a while curiosity gets the better of her and she peeps through a gap in the curtains but there's nothing to see. All the other beds are screened off too but a very old lady with a zimmer is tottering towards Daisy's cubicle.

As she sees Molly, she lets out a small, excited squeak and, balancing with one hand on the frame, reaches into her dressing-gown pocket.

'Is it teatime?' she asks hopefully.

'Erm... not yet.' Molly glances at her watch. 'It's only just past lunchtime. Why? Are you hungry?'

The lady sways alarmingly as she rummages again in her pocket.

'No, dear, I don't get very hungry in here, but I saw you come in and I wondered if you'd like a tomato?' Molly's not sure if she's misheard, but the lady holds out a small container. 'Go on, dear, have one. They're home grown.'

Molly smiles nervously and takes the container – it contains a set of false teeth, smiling up at her.

'Go on, don't be shy, dear,' the old lady says cheerily.

'Oh, well, perhaps later,' Molly says, and her new friend shrugs, unconcerned, as she begins the long totter back to her own territory.

A nurse pops out of the cubicle where Vomiting Lady lives, and says, 'Lily, off back to bed now, my love – come on, chop, chop!'

Molly looks at the nurse with barely disguised irritation.

Surely there's no need to be so brusque? The nurse catches Molly's meaning and whispers, 'We need her out of the way because we've got to remove Barbara, and the others get upset if they see us wheeling them out.'

'Why, is Barbara going to another ward?' Molly asks.

'She's gone.' The nurse looks at Molly and widens her eyes, gesturing with her head towards Barbara's bed.

'Gone? But you said you were taking her... oh!' Light dawns, Shouting Lady will cry 'Toilet' no more. Molly feels an intense wave of sadness for Barbara, and for the world that Daisy now inhabits, where tomatoes can easily be mixed up with teeth, and people 'go' and don't come back. Suddenly, she needs Jake... or Rob... but who can make it better? Can either of them help?

But whichever man Molly herself needs, of course Jake should be here, and so should Matt. Somehow, she's got to let them know about their mum, and fast. If Barbara can slip away so easily... but Molly daren't even finish the thought.

Molly goes back to Daisy's side and gives her a kiss, murmurs how much she loves her and says a prayer to the God who she has recently been doubting. It never hurts to hedge your bets, as Geoff likes to say. She hurries from the ward, tearing off the horrible plastic apron as she leaves. Someone will have to go to Jake and give him the message. It can't be Molly; she needs to stay here. Who can she send?

41

Poppy is just not cut out for this motherhood lark. Even Tim knows it, with his undeniably quirky needs that she isn't meeting in any way, shape or form. She's not so bad at the practical bit; feeding them, getting them up for school and all that. It's the listening, and entertaining, and... just loving them, she supposes. Poppy's crap at all that, always has been, maybe always will be, although she'd like to think it's possible to learn if the chance was there.

As it is, they muddle through with a little help from their friends. Molly does the mothering, Rob does the laundry and discipline, and Lydia does bugger all, as usual. That woman is the nearest thing to a complete cow that Poppy has ever met, and she's met a few. Lydia is just pure selfishness – Poppy can't imagine why anyone would stay with her. She moans constantly, she wears clothes that even Daisy wouldn't be seen dead in (whoops, unfortunate turn of phrase in the circumstances). And, what's more, she is *so boring*.

Poppy was unlucky enough to have to chat to her yesterday and now she knows all about Lydia's migraines, her dietary

requirements, her unfortunate digestive issues and her delicate
emotions. It was tedious in the extreme. If Rob had smothered
his wife a few years ago, he'd be out by now. Even Jill clearly
detests Lydia, and she never says anything bad about anybody.

Jill is getting a little bit stronger every day, or so the nurses
on the phone report, and Poppy really wants to believe them.
Roger's still there, and Poppy will take the boys to see her at the
weekend.

Poppy has started to take stock of her own life too, starting
with Sam. Now, that's got to stop. She must stop acting like a
one-woman sex therapy unit. She's such a sucker for a sad face,
a 'my wife doesn't like sex' line, or the boyish innocence-need-
ing-experience scenario. But all that must change. It's time for
Poppy. Or whatever her name is. Or was.

Talking of sex therapy, something pretty explosive is about
to happen around Molly and Rob, if Poppy is not much
mistaken. It's as if there's an electric current sparking between
them every time they're in the same room. Jake wants to get
himself back here pronto if he knows what's good for him,
although Poppy reckons Kate would have other ideas if she got
the opportunity.

It's all going to be happening this weekend. Kate must
already be on her way to see Jake to tell him about Daisy – she's
not the ideal choice to break the news but even Molly can see
that someone's got to do it.

Molly's kids are going to be at the hospital – they hope that if
they stay with Daisy round the clock talking and singing and
playing her favourite tapes that she might wake up, and Rob has
put his foot down and said Molly needs a break from all this
visiting. Max, Sam and Harriet are getting a lift in with Rob then
Sam is taking the younger ones home on the bus later. Molly
said that this Nick person might help too. Poppy still hasn't met

Nick – he seems to have burrowed right into the heart of the family though.

She can't help feeling suspicious. Who is he anyway, and where did he appear from? Perhaps she'll pop round casually and just see if the kids are okay later in the evening. Molly has always collected waifs and strays. It annoys Poppy when people seem to batten on her friend's good nature, but Molly likes to be needed. Come to think of it, this must be the first time ever that Jake hasn't needed his wife for one reason or another.

Poppy suddenly realises that all this business with her children being organised and out of the way will leave Molly and Rob pretty much to their own devices, because the lovely Lydia is going on an alternative therapy break in Cleethorpes. She's going to be colonically irrigated, analysed, and every other purging or in-depth questioning you can think of. Whoopee! Maybe they'll find a nice kind woman hiding inside the outer layer of unpleasantness. Or maybe not.

And as for Poppy – well, she's got some detective work of her own to do, which has already been left for far too long. It's time to face up to a few things. She's not been feeling so great just lately, and all the tests so far have come back with inconclusive results. But it's not difficult to know that there's something wrong, so after the next doctors' appointment later today, Poppy is going to bite the bullet and do what she should have done years ago. She's going to find her husband.

42

If it wasn't for the gnawing worry about Peg, Geoff would be thoroughly enjoying this time with Jake. Everywhere he goes, he looks for his wife, and every crowded street has a Peggy in it. He has lost count of the times when he's run after a woman in the street thinking it's definitely her. He's even got as far as grabbing a couple of them and spinning them round – how he's got away without being arrested is a mystery.

Anyway, they're carrying on as near to normal as possible, Geoff and Jake, even though this is all so weird and they are not at all sure how to behave. Jake has cheated on Molly, and his father-in-law could cheerfully kill him for that. But if there's one thing Geoff is learning, it's the old chestnut that there are two sides to every story. He doesn't know their story at all – the two men don't talk about it, it's too tricky to be impartial. And Geoff doesn't even know the other side to his own story either, Peg's side, so there's no point in trying to sort it out.

Maybe if they were a pair of women, they'd talk about nothing else but the mess they're in. As it is, Jake and Geoff get on with this new, temporary life and hope for the best. Geoff wants Peggy back, as soon as possible; in the meantime, they've got their first gig tonight! Two acoustic guitars and two not-so-bad voices. Okay, it's only a pub folk group but so what? They're going to be good. Geoff has thought long and hard about their playlist and he thinks that the admittedly small audience will go for it:

'Mrs Robinson': Simon and Garfunkel (to wake them up and set the tone)

'The Last Thing on My Mind': Tom Paxton (from Geoff to Peggy)

'Catch the Wind': Donovan (Jake wants this one – he won't say why, but Geoff guesses it's something to do with Kate)

'Blowin' in the Wind': Dylan (to get them singing)

'Walk Out in the Rain': Clapton (just because Geoff loves it)

'Moonshadow': Cat Stevens (again, no reason, it's just a happy one)

'My Sweet Lord': George Harrison (another one for Jake)

After that, they could maybe see if there are any requests. And if the audience hates them, they'll get steaming drunk and just carry on the singing back at the van with any of the punters who want to come back there. Geoff is really enjoying the caravan thing – it's so nice not to have loads of jobs to do... or not do.

The two men take turns keeping it clean and it's honestly no bother. Geoff can go outside for a smoke and sit in the sunshine whenever he wants to, can be quiet when he likes and talk when he feels like it. Jake is very moody though, and he spends a lot of time mooching around on the beach. Geoff goes with him when he can, but he's got to make finding Peggy his top priority – he can't think about the future until he finds her.

On the funny side, the pub landlord, Martin, rang Geoff (at least *he* brought his mobile with him even if Jake forgot, although he keeps forgetting to charge it, so it's stone dead now). Martin said that the local TV station had asked if they could come over and film the folk night! Fame at last... So, tonight's the night. The nerves are kicking in now, but Geoff reckons it's going to be great.

The bar staff all know them now – it's like being part of a big new family in the pub, especially with Suchada. She's from Thailand originally, and she says her name means 'beautiful'. She's certainly that, in Geoff's opinion. Not in the first flush of youth, but with a sort of dignity and calm that he finds very relaxing. And the others are much younger, but they treat him like an extra uncle. Geoff's loving his new life.

43

Kate is on her way out of Leicester, following the teatime traffic. She's trying to avoid all the roadkill and is just about to start bypassing all the pretty little villages when who should she spy but Theo, standing in a lay-by and holding up a big cardboard sign saying *Cromer* in large red letters.

Kate only notices Theo because she's wearing that hideous lime-green leather coat that she bought from the Age Concern shop; surely no one else would wear anything so disgusting? Pulling in and winding the window down, Kate is glad to see that Theo takes a step back and looks wary. Good, at least some of her mother's warnings have sunk in. She stoops to see into the car, still keeping her distance, but when she recognises Kate, she takes another couple of steps back and nearly falls into the hedge bottom.

Kate jumps out and shouts, 'Theo, what on earth do you think you're doing hitching? And where are you going anyway?' although as soon as she utters the words, she realises where Theo must be heading and suddenly can't seem to stop herself blushing.

'Where do you think I'm going? I got a lift with a lorry driver the first bit but he was a bit weird so I told him I lived on a farm near here. Anyway, I've got every right to go to see my dad – it's me who should be asking you that question, don't you think?' She spits the words out and starts to walk away, but Kate catches up with her.

'What do you mean, love? I'm off to see Jake to tell him about Daisy, we can't get in touch with him any other way because Geoff's phone doesn't seem to be working now, or maybe they've got no signal in the van, and of course, your other granny, Peggy I mean, isn't here…'

Kate is rambling on trying to cover up for the red face when she notices Theo is now staring at her in terror rather than disgust.

'W… what about my gran? W… what's happened now?' She must be in a state, Kate hasn't heard her stutter for years. Theo grabs Kate by the shoulders and shakes her frantically.

'Tell me! What's happened to Granny D?'

'Theo, stop panicking and let me speak. She's had a bit of… well… a funny turn and she's in hospital – I can't believe you weren't told, where were you?'

'I… I… had to leave in a hurry… b… because…' She's making a huge effort not to stammer and she finally gives up the struggle and starts to cry, big gulping sobs that shake her from head to foot. Kate puts out her arms for a hug but Theo resists stiffly.

Finally, Kate manages to nudge her towards the car, gets the door open and eases her into the passenger seat. Theo is still howling and shivering alarmingly. Bloody hell. Kate is stuck in a lay-by with a hormonal teenager who obviously knows about her dad and Kate, and now is in hysterics about her gran being at death's door, and… oh good, it's starting to rain.

Kate sighs, and reaches into the glovebox for her emergency cigarettes and lighter – it's going to be a long day.

44

Of all the people who might have picked her up, why, oh why did it have to be Kate? They're nearly at the turn-off for Thursford now, and at the sight of the familiar signpost, Theo's mind wanders to the simpler days on holiday, when going to see the fairground organs and have a go on the old-fashioned merry-go-round was a really big deal. Granny D and Grandad Reginald loved it there.

They said it took them right back, and they would sit and wait for ages to hear the mighty Wurlitzer. Dad said it reminded him of Monty Python, something about a naked man in a bow tie, but only Mum ever laughed at that. Must be one of those in-jokes that married people have. Don't suppose they'll have those now, thanks to *her*! Theo looks sideways – she knows what Kate's after; she's going down there to the caravan to try and get her claws into Dad.

Theo saw him going in there, to *her* house, on the night he disappeared, but she didn't tell a soul. She knew she should have said something when everyone was so worried about him but she couldn't grass him up, somehow. Theo heard the guitar too, that night. Dad never plays at home.

Sometimes Theo goes out late, by herself, for a little while – they all think they know everything that goes on in that house; hah! She can get out of her bedroom window and onto the potting-shed roof dead easy, then it's just a bit of a jump, minding the compost heap, and out of the back gate into the little lane. It's a bit spooky and she's not sure about how safe it is on the roof but who cares? A person needs their freedom. Theo doesn't see why they have to know what she's doing every minute of the day.

Sam gets out that way too. He's rigged up a stack of crates so they can climb back in afterwards and sometimes they even go prowling at the same time, but Theo hasn't told Sam about Dad and *her*. She hasn't told anyone what she saw that night; she's been trying to decide what to do about it. When she came face to face with her dad at the caravan, she was too embarrassed to let on that she knew about his cheating. And even if she could have got him on her own, she wouldn't have known where to start.

To begin with, Theo had just been furious with her dad, and especially with the evil woman sitting next to her in the driving seat, but as time goes on, she wonders if her mum might be partly to blame too. All those sneaky text messages, and extra make-up. Something very strange is going on, and Theo has definitely meant to get to the bottom of it, but everything else is getting in the way right now.

By the time they get to the turn-off for the caravan, it's getting dark. Theo is glad to see that The Other Woman, as Theo thinks of Kate, is getting edgy. She's already smoked half a packet of fags (bet Mum and her mates don't know about *that* little habit; they don't approve) and she's started on her nails now. Or extensions. Hope one of them comes off and chokes her. Theo won't give her the kiss of life, the sneaky cow.

They get out of the car under the big oak tree and look at each other. It's still raining. Even in the shelter of the tree, water drips down their necks. Theo starts to shiver again.

'Well, are you going to speak to me, or not?' Kate says, trying to look cool. Theo ignores her.

'Theo, I don't know what I'm supposed to have done to offend you' (Theo snorts) 'but we don't want to upset your dad any more than we're going to anyway, if you see what I mean. He's going to be frantic about Daisy and if he thinks you've got a problem with me, it's going to be even worse.'

Theo glances round, playing for time, and suddenly realises that there are no lights on in the caravan. Several of the others round about have got their curtains drawn against the gloom and the rain, and she can hear the sound of gentle folk music from the next-door van, but theirs is in pitch darkness. Her heart drops even further, if that's possible.

They walk across the grass quickly; both under-dressed for the weather. Theo doesn't do running and she imagines Kate can't even run if she wants to. She's wearing very tight jeans, high boots with spiky heels and a soft black jumper with lots of cleavage showing. Theo thinks Kate might as well have a flashing sign above her head saying 'available'. Her heels sink into the soft soil and her stupid hair is getting plastered to her head. Good.

Theo tries the door – locked. She lets out a loud wail, without meaning to, and in the next-door caravan, a door bangs open and someone shouts 'What the...?' The man peering out at them is unfamiliar. He's naked but for a bath towel and his chest hair is gross – silvery grey, loads of it – and he's got one of those tans that have got to be out of a bottle, or sunbed at the very least.

'Are you looking for Jake or Geoff, ladies?' he asks, flicking back his curly grey hair.

'Well, either one of them would be good,' *she* says, in a sarcastic voice. Theo thinks Kate's rattled – she's come all this way and Theo bets she expected to have a fantastic, sloppy welcome and it would be all lovey-dovey – *yuk!*

'You won't find them here, babe, they'll be down the pub by now. You know, the Malt Shovel, just up the road? They've got a gig tonight.' He looks worried. 'Is something wrong? I can tell you how to get there if you like, or if you wait five minutes while I get me glad rags on, you can give me a lift down there. Going to be a good night, by all accounts.'

'Gig? We're not talking U2 here, you know! What gig? Have I wandered into some sort of weird parallel universe where everyone's a rock star?'

'There's no need to be like that. It's their first time. And I'm going down there to support the guys even if you're not.' He slams the door firmly in their faces, muttering something about stuck-up townies.

'Oh, well done!' Theo shouts, before she remembers she wasn't going to speak to Kate ever again. 'Now what's the plan?'

'Looks like we're going to hear some live music tonight, Theo. Back to the car, as quickly as you can. I've got to get inside somewhere warm and dry, and repair this bloody rain damage. Good job there's an old towel in the car, and I always carry a spare set of make-up.'

She seems to be thinking out loud, as if she's forgotten who she's talking to – like Theo cares whether she resembles a wet dog or not? The messier the better, as far as Theo's concerned.

But at least all this has taken her mind off Gran for a bit, and it seems as if she'll see Dad and Gramp soon.

There's a big lump in her throat again, and she kicks the car tyre as she gets in. She gets a glare for that one but they're soon off again, down the lane, out of the site, and racing over the potholes up the road to the next village. The lights of the pub look welcoming but suddenly Theo really wishes her mum was here.

45

It had seemed like such a good idea at the time. Small, local pub, friendly punters, music that everyone knows, lots of real ale and pork scratching. Well, guess what? Jake is scared and he wants to go home, right now. To be safe inside, with only his guitar and a beer for company. But it suddenly occurs to him – which home does he want?

If he had a choice, and he's frankly not sure if he's got that any more, where would he go? Would he choose his rambling family house, with Molly in the kitchen making soup, or fruit cake, or scones, or any of the five thousand things she does so well, radio playing soft rock, glass of wine at her elbow?

He can see it, smell it, hear it, feel it – a kitten on the worktop with butter on its nose, mewing for food, Molly swearing at it but with hands too pastry-sticky to give it a clip round the ear – the squeals of the kids in the garden, fighting and falling off the swing.

Or would he stay here in his new home – living the bachelor life with a man he is only just learning to appreciate; Geoff, with his amazing dry wit and endless repertoire of folk tunes?

Cramped living conditions, plenty of time to experiment with cooking unusual dishes away from critical eyes and with an appreciative person to test them out, clean socks and under-pants only every other day (turn 'em inside out – who's to know?).

Jake sees Geoff raise his pint and give him a huge wink. They both take a huge slug of beer, and Jake instantly feels better, and looks round properly for the first time at the cosy snug of the pub. The floor is made of the original flagstones, uneven and worn – it's comfortable, with wooden settles and very low beams, bunches of herbs hanging down and a row of pewter tankards hanging from the bar. Geoff's new buddy, Suchada, is polishing glasses and laughing at something one of the customers is saying, and Geoff is tuning up, looking cool and relaxed.

Jake often misses the fug of tobacco in pubs – the crowd of smokers are already clustering under the green umbrella outside but inside smells of pine disinfectant and toasted cheese baguettes. It's weird, it's as if Jake has gone back in time and can do whatever he likes. He can drink too much, eat cholesterol, sing too loudly, and roll back home at any time he likes. But tonight, he's still scared.

46

Blimey, Geoff can't believe how much fun this is. All these people and they're all going to be listening to his playlist soon. Geoff and Jake were only expecting a handful of old geezers to show up, but there are people of all ages here, and the babble of voices is getting louder by the minute.

The pub has the usual sharp scent of disinfectant and sweaty bodies – like Jake, Geoff has a brief pang of nostalgia for the days when smoke would have been the predominant smell, and he could puff away on his pipe and enjoy a pint at the same time. He doesn't enjoy huddling under an umbrella in the yard at all. He contemplates nipping outside now but it's nearly time for their first number.

Jake has been looking horrified and quite pale, but Geoff feels calm. He winks at his son-in-law and exchanges a thumbs-up sign with Suchada. She grins back and blows him a good luck kiss.

Geoff's been waiting for a night like this for years, and he's going to enjoy it. His old blue suit is even more baggy round the knees than it was when he got here but that goes with the image

– 'ageing folk hero' – and he's bought a nice black t-shirt in Cromer; his new/old trainers look good, just the right level of beaten up, so... Geoff is ready for 'em. Jake's in a checked shirt that's been washed so often it's faded to pale and soft; good job he was wearing it when he decided to come down here, that and his favourite jeans.

They've discovered the laundry room on the caravan site this week, luckily. Jake said he didn't even know there was one. There's an ancient spin dryer that dances all round the floor when you switch it on – amazing! And an antique iron and board, and a drying ground with proper wooden pegs. Geoff loves this place. If he could just... no, let's concentrate on the music tonight.

He strums a few gentle chords and slurps some of the excellent ale, and then he sees Martin waving to him from behind the beer taps – they're on. The TV cameras for the local station are set up and running – it's going out live, apparently. Jake looks as if he'd like to do a runner, but he drains his pint and follows Geoff into the other room, where the corner is set up ready for them. There's a bit of idle applause and they're away, straight into a really pacy version of 'Mrs Robinson' that gets the toes tapping from the start.

This is great, and the audience are loving it so far. But as they launch into the next number, Geoff hears Jake falter and looks up to see... bloody hell! Kate! And Theo with her? What's going on? Jake grins and goes straight into the intro for 'Catch the Wind', and the next thing, Kate's gone all misty-eyed and stupid and Theo's banged out towards the ladies' room, crying her eyes out. Now the lad's done it. He's really blown it this time.

47

So, just as Jake was really getting into his brand-new life, he's in the car with Kate, driving back to the old one. It's dark now, and the lights of the pub are far behind them. He never got to finish his very first gig but that's the last thing on his mind. His mum'll soon bounce back, won't she? He's always said that Daisy will outlive them all. It was hard to leave his temporary refuge but Jake's left Theo with Geoff, so he'll have to come back and sort things out with her – his eldest daughter is furious with everyone; Jake doesn't know which of them has annoyed Theo the most, or why. Hopefully Daisy will soon be back on her feet and Jake can come and make things right with his daughter and then carry on where he left off.

Kate's profile is confusing – she sometimes looks just as angry as Theo but Jake keeps seeing her looking at him sideways, and when he catches her eye, she blushes and goes all girly. She looks a bit of a mess – hair standing on end, damp clothes, but gorgeous all the same, and her jeans are so tight that there's no way she can be wearing any knickers. Like last time...

This is very difficult – worrying about his mum, lusting after Kate and dreading (but somehow looking forward to) seeing Molly. The radio's playing old songs, mainly Motown dance stuff, and to take his mind off all the stress, Jake starts toe-tapping to 'It Takes Two'.

Kate joins in on percussion, tapping the steering wheel in time, and before they know it, they're singing at the tops of their voices. As the song ends, she pulls off the road into a winding lane, and from there she coasts into a handy gateway under some trees, where she cuts the engine. And Jake finds out quite quickly that he was right about the knickers, or lack of them. But there's no time for this – his mum needs him. Pushing Kate away, with difficulty, he tells her to drive on.

48

Kris and Peggy have just settled in for the evening, slumped on the lumpy caravan sofa with mugs of tea and a plate of crab sandwiches each. Kris has picked up an old transistor radio at the charity shop and they're contentedly listening to a local station when Peggy lets out a loud scream, jumps up and almost scalds herself.

'Careful, Peg,' Kris shouts, reaching for a cloth to mop up the spilt tea – he's getting quite domesticated nowadays. 'What's up, for... goodness' sake?'

This time last week he wouldn't have used the word 'goodness' in that sentence, but Peg has very soon made him realise that swearing doesn't pay. She really hates it, especially the 'f' word, and he doesn't like upsetting her after she's looked after him so well, and listened to him moaning and whining at all hours of the day and night. Kris reckons, wherever Nick is, he can't be doing any better than this. But now, Peggy is on her feet, gibbering, red faced and almost in tears.

'Listen! I hear him... I'd know that voice anywhere. But... it can't be... yes, it is! What the feck...?'

He looks at her in amazement – this must be serious.

'Can't be what? What did you see? Come on, tell me!'

'Ssssh, listen, I tell you...'

Kris hears the announcer going on about the beautiful local area, the friendly people, the real ale, and suddenly realises that the place he's talking about must be right here.

'Well, that's nice, Peg, but there's no need to swear, surely? It's just live music from a—'

'Shut up! It's here! It's the pub up the road! And I heard Geoff, I know I did!' Peggy holds out a hand to stop Kris replying and they both hear the voiceover continuing his patter.

'Here we have a brand-new duo. It's Geoff and Jake, all the way from the Midlands, and they're going to take us back in time with some oldies but goldies.'

He starts to tell her not to be so daft, that it can't possibly be Peggy's husband and son-in-law on a mangy little regional Norfolk radio programme, but she shushes him again, and sure enough, he can hear the background noise of bar-room chatter and the strumming of guitars.

Peggy is listening open-mouthed as the interviewer sets the guys up with quite a nice little intro, all about how this little country pub, the Malt Shovel, is trying to get back to its roots by giving the punters what they want, real ale and proper home-cooked food, with old-style troubadours and minstrels in a traditional setting, log fires, spit and sawdust, blah blah blah...

'But what the...?'

'Shhh – I'm trying to find out what the stupid old dote's doing down here.'

The interviewer's well into his stride now, chatting to Geoff, who seems all sort of relaxed and confident, talking about his playlist for the evening and how hard it was to pick his favourites. And who's Tom Paxton anyway? Kris has heard of

Dylan, and Simon and whatsisname... but his mum was mainly into Bowie from the bits he can remember, and his dad only really liked classical stuff. He shrugs the painful thoughts away and listens again.

'Now, Geoff, just before we hear a bit more of your set for later tonight – can you tell us how come you two city boys have ended up playing here in this sleepy backwater; Leicester born and bred, weren't you?' Geoff nods, starting to look a bit shifty. 'So, anyway, what brings you to this neck of the woods?'

'Well, um...'

'Yes, you lazy old bugger, what made you get up off your arse and actually *go somewhere*?' Peg is on her feet again, yelling at the radio, bright red in the face.

'Peggy! No need for that language,' Kris says, only half joking. But she's only got ears for Geoff.

'Well, we've always loved our holidays down here,' (Peggy sniffs loudly) 'and we just thought... why not give a bit back to the area that's given us so much pleasure over the years?'

'Ye haven't told us what ye're doin' here in the first place, sure you haven't!' Peg is getting more and more Irish as her anger gets a grip of her properly. Kris wouldn't like to tangle with her in this mood... hang on, she's getting her jacket and shoes on and heading for the door.

'Where are you going? Wait for me,' he yells, setting off after her, grabbing his hoodie. 'Wait, I've got to lace my boots up.'

'I'm off down the road to that dive that's let these two cretins show themselves up for the eejits they are. Quick, I'll bring you with me if you hurry up.'

And she's off, with Kris limping after her, trying not to trip over his laces and pulling his jumper over his head as he stumbles out of the van. Hastily, he turns back to lock it – no point in taking risks with the few bits they've got, that's what Gran used to say anyway. God knows when they'll be back and what sort of state they'll be in – Kris is not looking forward to this gig, somehow.

It's only a short gallop down the lane to the Malt Shovel. In next to no time – much too soon for Kris's liking – they are at the pub. It looks a bit of a dive but it's nice in a way; sort of olde worlde with a red climbing plant thing round the door and up the walls, and some pots and baskets of flowers. There's a black-board propped up outside saying:

Tonite for one nite only – live folk music. You saw them here first; 'The Leicester Lads'

'Lads? I don't t'ink so!' sniffs Peg, kicking the door open and marching in. A gang of old guys move out of the way sharpish to let her through. Kris doesn't blame them.

'Right, where are the two great lumps of useless shite?'

The landlord looks worried but Peggy looks past him round the door frame.

'There he is, there's Geoff,' she says, through gritted teeth. Kris follows her gaze and sees a man with a guitar sitting in a corner strumming away happily to himself with a... well, just *the* most incredible girl curled up next to him on one of the big fat comfy chairs that are dotted about everywhere. She's right next to the fire and the flickering flames are making all her piercings catch the light and look like diamonds and she's got wild black hair with a purple and red streak. Peg launches herself towards her husband with an outraged howl.

'What in the name of God are you doin' here, ye auld goat?'

Geoff looks up in amazement, as does everyone else in the place.

'Peggy, love! How did *you* get here? Do you know how long...

I've been so worried...' He jumps to his feet and wraps her in a huge bear hug, lifting her off her feet – they're both laughing and crying at the same time, and even Kris feels a bit emotional. The girl is blinking back tears too, and Kris steps out from behind the door and smiles down at her in the firelight. The only person who doesn't seem to be entering into this love-fest is the older barmaid. She's all dark, flashing eyes and she's got her arms folded tightly across her generous cleavage.

'I reckon you and me are kind of in the way here, don't you?' Kris says to Theo. 'Do you fancy a walk down to the beach? There's one of those American clam-bake things goin' on tonight – I'll treat you to a bag of mussels?'

She looks at him as if he's dropped off another planet.

'But... but you're that "Nick with dreads" boy? How did you...'

Now this is strange – how does a girl like this, all these miles from Leicester, come to think he's Nick? And why has she gone so red? She's shaking too.

Kris holds out his hand and tries to sound soothing.

'Come on, girl. Maybe you and me can find something to talk about. And I'm Kris, not Nick.'

She gets up slowly and looks doubtfully at the outstretched hand.

'Mussels? Oh, go on then... Kris?' She takes his hand and they both give Peggy and Geoff a wave, but they're totally oblivious. Kris has got a feeling that Peggy won't miss him for quite a while. They head for the beach huts. Kris thinks he might be in love.

49

The long day at the hospital has taken its toll on Molly. Her back and shoulders ache with leaning over the bed trying to keep a flow of mindless chit chat going, her head's thumping and she's indescribably relieved to see Hattie, Max and Sam piling in with arms full of magazines, CDs, computer games and chocolate, ready for their stint at the bedside, and their big attempt to wake Daisy. Sarah Slater is with them and she nods encouragingly at Molly.

'You must be more than ready for a break and a shower,' Sarah says. 'I bet you've not had any proper food today either. You can have a bit of time at home if you like. Sam and I can manage here.'

The thought of a hot shower is very tempting. Molly's had a brief text from Kate to say where Theo is and that she's safe – she doesn't understand what's been going on there but she's definitely not grovelling to Kate for any more information, and at least Theo'll be with her dad and grandpa soon enough. Maybe she *can* pop home for a little while.

Molly will just have to hope Theo will be in touch herself

soon. There are only so many worries she can handle right now, and with her eldest daughter traced, that one can wait till tomorrow. She collects more chairs and they make a sort of camp around the bed with the silent figure at its centre. Daisy looks peaceful – Molly has tried to do her hair and the nurses have washed her and given her a clean nightie but it's very strange to see her sleeping – Molly knows she'd hate them to see her so vulnerable. Molly once walked in on her when she was sneaking a crafty nap one afternoon and she bit her head off.

Even better news is that the kids and Sarah are followed by Rob, clutching a huge bunch of freesias. 'I thought she might be able to smell the flowers in her sleep,' Rob explains. 'They're her favourites.'

'I'm so sorry, dear, we don't allow flowers here any more,' says one of the ward staff, on her way in with a fresh jug of water. Rob's face falls, but he rallies and presents the flowers to Molly with a flourish instead. She blushes, and instantly wonders if Jake would have had such a sweet thought, or if he would have even remembered that his mum loved the scent of freesias. She had them in her wedding bouquet, and even up to the last year, Reginald would always make sure she had a bunch delivered on their anniversary. He was never a bloke for romantic gestures, apart from that one.

Rob hears Sarah once again offering Molly a temporary respite and asks if he can give her a lift home and back to save her driving and maybe call for something to eat on the way home. She's got to eat at some time, hasn't she? There's no harm in a quick bag of chips. No point in risking an energy crisis.

Soon, the kids are well settled, sweet wrappers already starting to pile up and Daisy's bed being used as a general dumping ground. The family unit seems strange without Theo, and Molly can hardly bear to leave them, but she can see that

Daisy is sleeping peacefully now, and the rest of the gang seem happy enough to take over for a while. She picks up her jacket and gets ready to follow Rob from the ward, dropping a kiss on Daisy's forehead on the way out and giving Sarah a hug and her brood a final warning to behave.

'I've got my mobile with me so ring if you need *anything*; I'll be back as soon as I've eaten. Sarah will take you back home whenever you're ready and Sam can cook supper,' she says, trying to sound as if all this is an everyday occurrence.

'What will he make? I might not like it,' says Max, suddenly realising he's being abandoned to the tender mercies of his brother and Sarah, who both have quite strict rules about the behaviour of small boys in public.

'I've got three different sorts of pizza, garlic bread and chocolate ice cream in the freezer – there should be something for everyone there.'

Max looks mollified and Hattie gets up to give Molly a final squeeze round the middle. 'Don't worry, Mum – I bet, by the time you come back, Granny D will be sitting up and eating a Crunchie. I'll save her one just in case.'

Molly blinks away a few tears and waves to them all, then she and Rob set off down the corridor, past groups of beds containing people who are hanging on to life for grim death. She exchanges a few nods and smiles with other fraught-looking visitors – it's like a little exclusive gang in here. They've compared notes at odd times during the day, fetched numerous plastic cups of tea, and generally kept each other sane.

Rob tucks her into the passenger seat, wipes her eyes with a large, soft hankie and says, 'Hang in there, love. I can soon have you back at your house with a chilled glass of wine in your hand if you want a break before we eat? You can even have a shower before we call for chips if you like, there's plenty of time. Lydia's away...'

His voice tails away and Molly can't help but see the flush travelling up his neck. She knows her face must be just as pink. This is new territory, and it's scary.

'I can't be away long,' she says. 'I need to get back to Daisy.'

They look across at each other and Rob reaches out a hand just as Molly does the same. Their fingers link and suddenly they're in each other's arms. This time the kiss isn't spoilt by anything, or at least not until the loud beeping of a car horn interrupts them and they spring apart, looking over their shoulders. A gang of teenagers are piling out of a beaten-up old Land Rover, and the driver is obviously waiting for this parking space.

'Come on, mate – either put her down or get a room!' one of them yells.

'Not a bad idea – the room bit.' Did Molly really say that? She can't believe the words came out. Maybe they should have stayed safely in her head.

'We don't need a room – I've got a whole house,' Rob replies, and then blushes even more. 'Let's go straight there. I reckon my shower's just as good as yours and there's a bottle of very good sauvignon in the fridge. We can have a drink and then – who knows?'

It's hard to tell which of them is the most nervous when they reach Rob's house; Molly's so keyed up that she can hardly sit still. They go into the living room and Rob switches on the harsh overhead light, winces, and clicks a few buttons. Gradually, everywhere is flooded with a gentle glow and soft music plays in the background.

Molly slips her shoes off and curls up in the comfiest chair, avoiding the leather sofa. Soon, a glass of wine is in her hand, cool and smelling of gooseberries and sunshine. Rob has disappeared, but calls from upstairs, 'Your bath's ready when you are. I thought it'd be more relaxing than a shower.'

Molly takes her glass and goes upstairs – when did someone last run her a bath? This is luxury. In the warm bathroom there are candles flickering, more soft music playing and fluffy bath towels waiting on the radiator. Has she died and gone to heaven? Rob smiles at her obvious pleasure and leaves the room.

In the bath, Molly listens to the music coming from the CD player just outside the door. It's a copy of the compilation one that Rob made for her; she knows it by heart, and she sings along to the song with those very words in it – all about knowing someone by heart. It takes years to get to that place. Will she ever know Rob in that intimate, warts-and-all way? Surely it's impossible?

The sounds of Rob moving around in the next room are both comforting and unnerving. Perhaps he's expecting her to burst out naked, doing the dance of the seven veils? She has absolutely no desire to leave this wonderful room. She suspects he's bought the candles with her in mind – Lydia doesn't strike Molly as a woman who likes melted wax on her surfaces.

The scent of lemons is everywhere. After she's soaked for five minutes, conscious of time passing when she should be with Daisy, Molly finishes her wine, pulls out the plug and tries to let all her anxieties seep away with the bath water. The fluffy towel is blissful and she wanders out onto the landing, empty glass in hand, to find Rob right outside the door holding the remains of the wine. He raises the bottle and an eyebrow, fills up Molly's glass and then leads her to the nearest bedroom.

More candles glow in the darkness and – wonder of wonders – he's put tiny white fairy lights all around the bed head! Now all she's got to do is forget her cellulite, her love handles and her habit of hiccupping when she gets nervous. Oh, no – there goes the first one. Rob starts to laugh, and they meet in the middle of the room, both shaking with a crazy mixture of terror and excitement.

Molly hears the distant sound of wailing sirens, and has her usual moment of panic – the roll call of family. Where are they? Who is safe and who is out on the loose? But it's time to get a grip. She's taking time off from worrying tonight and she knows where they all are. It's hard to make herself ignore the stomach-churning noise, but it's someone else's problem for a change this time. She sends whoever it is a quick burst of sympathy and turns back to Rob.

'I can't be long,' she says.

'Don't worry,' he answers, pulling her into his arms. 'I've got a feeling we won't be... I mean, I've wanted this so badly... and me and Lydia... we don't...'

'Shhh,' says Molly, putting a hand over his mouth. 'Don't spoil it.'

50

Well, Poppy's finally done it. She's found the nasty, sadistic git that she married all those years ago. He's living in a seedy cottage in that tiny village only ten miles down the road where everyone seems to be verging on the insane and with an eye in the middle of the forehead. And now Poppy knows what they mean when they talk about a red mist descending. It's getting late and she knows she should really keep her promise to Molly and go to the hospital, but tonight's events have upset her badly and she still can't stop shaking. At least Roger's kids are back with him now, so she's not in loco parentis any more. That would've been one responsibility too many under the circumstances.

Her ex-husband certainly took some finding; he's covered his tracks well after he left their marital home. Her mind flinches from the thought of sweet pink and white baby Oliver. For years she had managed to convince herself that her children were far better off without her. One day, when they were old enough to make their own decisions, they would come looking for their mum and she would make it up to them... somehow.

Why did she ever marry Kenneth Slater? She's prepared to acknowledge that she loved being the scarlet woman in their story to begin with, but what possessed her to carry it on? She should have just run for the hills after the first baby was born – scooped her up and left the bastard. But if you start having a family when you're so young, you seem to lose your confidence in the outside world – well, Poppy did anyway.

Her mum and dad had just been killed in that hideous accident, driving down in the pouring rain from their home in the border country, still furious with their only daughter for having fallen pregnant by a married headteacher. They were coming to fetch her home, so they said, in that last, terrible phone call, when she had screamed that she wouldn't go, they couldn't make her. Poppy still feels as if her heart is being squeezed in a vice whenever she remembers those dark days.

Wading through a deeper sadness than she had ever imagined possible, she reached the eighth month of her pregnancy, and then gave birth to a squealing, puking little creature who seemed to detest her on sight, and was so small that the few baby clothes they'd bought hung from her tiny frame. After that it was just one long round of nappies, feeds, playgroup, school, and so on until it started again the next day.

The tears had to be swallowed, there was no time for grieving for her parents, or to come to terms with the complicated, stomach-wrenching guilt Poppy felt whenever she remembered their last days.

So she stayed with Kenneth, until leaving wasn't an option, because so many babies can't help but tie you down. And where would she have gone anyway? Her parents' legacy had just about covered their funerals and cleared Kenneth's gambling debts. Poppy hadn't known about his little problem when he sweet talked her into his bed on Tuesday nights whilst Sarah was at her ladies' fellowship meetings. Poppy never did see the wonderful Sarah. Well, not until so many years had passed that even Poppy's own mother wouldn't have recognised her.

Poppy had loved them though – all the babies. Well, she thinks she must have done. Ken said she was a lousy mother – drank too much, forgot clinic appointments, argued with the neighbours when they moaned about the kids' crying, and never did any ironing all the time she was with him. Why should she? He never did anything at all to help. He drank even more than Poppy did, and he was forever harping on about Sarah this, Sarah that. If the woman was so bloody great, why did he leave her?

Poppy asked him that once, when she was really angry – normally she wouldn't have risked it – and he said he wished he never had left Sarah, that she was a perfect wife. And that he'd never been happy since he left his job. Then he cried. It was the only time Poppy ever managed to make him cry.

Anyway, this evening she finally knocked on Ken's door, knees shaking and ready for anything. When he answered, he almost slammed the door in her face. Mind you, she did have her long cream trench coat on, he probably thought she was one of those Jehovah's Witness people come to save his soul.

When he finally realised who she was, he tried to shut the door again, but Poppy got her foot in it and let herself in – she was way wider than that weedy specimen now. He looked quite pathetic really; she doesn't know why she was ever scared of him.

They started to argue as if they had never stopped, and it was hideous and brutal – very much like old times, but now Poppy didn't hold back like she would have done before. After a bit, when the insults were really flying, he blurted out that if Poppy was wondering why none of her kids had ever tried to get in touch, it was because he'd told them that their mother was dead, and all her family too. And Oliver had been adopted almost as soon as she'd left, with a family who were planning to emigrate to Australia.

Then he laughed – that wheezing, asthmatic chuckle that Poppy had come to hate so much during her married life. That was when the red mist thing happened. All the years she'd hung onto the forlorn hope that one day her children would forgive her and come and find her were a sham. They were never going to do that. She was dead, as far as her kids were concerned.

Poppy remembers noticing that awful brass table lamp that Ken's mother had given them for a wedding present, but she can't remember how it came to be in her hand. The blood flew right across the room – that coat's probably ruined. Poppy left after that. She's at home now having a large brandy. She's not really sure what to do next but expects the police will be here sooner or later. She's got one or two things to do before they come.

51

So, what now? It's getting late and Nick needs to see Theo; to get his wallet back for one thing, but to see if she's okay too. She must be feeling lousy. He could've stopped her if he'd been quick enough when she made a grab for his trousers, but it's too late to worry about that now.

As he crunches up the gravel drive to the front door, he can hear loud music and shouting. A party? He rings the bell and its jangle is lost in the thumping bass beat. The old teacher-bird next door isn't going to like this. Mind you, her house is in darkness, so maybe they're taking the chance of letting their hair down. As Nick rings again, the door swings open and Sam's there, hair standing on end.

'Okay, mate?' Nick asks, looking past Sam to the kitchen, where a plume of black smoke is coming from the oven. 'Need any help?' Sam seems to be thinking that one over, but eventually shrugs and gestures towards the kitchen.

'I hate to say this, but I'm not doing so well without you and Theo to help, Nick.'

'Well, that's no big deal. I'm here now. What's the problem?'

'I think it's this multi-tasking bit that I'm not so good at. The kids are running riot, the pizzas burnt while I was trying to get Max into his PJs, Theo's disappeared and Mum's gone back to the hospital. Sarah from next door was here but I told her I could cope so she went home. Apart from that, everything's great!'

He's still scowling, but at least Nick's in. It must have been hard for Sam to admit he can't cope. Nick thinks for a moment. 'Got any beer?'

Sam looks surprised, but nods. Nick presses on.

'Okay then, you open the cans, and the windows and the oven door, I'll sort the kids out, then you can tell me about the other stuff.'

He heads off up the stairs, half expecting Sam to call him back or come after him, but instead, Nick hears Sam snort to himself and set off on his part of the mission.

Upstairs, Hattie is trying on her mum's highest shoes and shortest dress, in front of a long mirror. The music from Max's room is mind-blowingly loud, but she's humming a different tune to herself as she slaps on some lipstick. She jumps when she sees Nick, then strikes a pose that's way too old for a kid her age – even he can tell that, and he's no expert.

'Am I gorgeous, Nick?' she asks, wiggling and pouting. What is it with the women in this family? They all need a dose of something on their cornflakes to slow them down, if you ask Nick.

'You look great, Hat, but maybe your mum might not appreciate her stuff being used when she's out?' She pouts some more, but her bottom lip wobbles alarmingly. He carries on before she really gets stroppy. 'Anyway, it's dinner time, and I need some help to rescue Sam in the kitchen. I think the pizzas are off, tonight.'

'What, like, mouldy?'

'No, like, off the menu – didn't you smell smoke?'

'Don't think so. I'm hungry though. Max always gets dead crabby when his dinner's late and tonight it's *very, very* late.' She starts to get back into her own clothes and scruffy sneakers, and Nick turns his head away, feeling uncomfortable, even though she's only ten. At last, Hattie looks like a school kid again.

'Come on then, let's go and find some pasta.'

She grins, hopefully. 'Can we have tuna in it?'

'You what? Pasta and tuna is my speciality, remember? With cheesy topping, and a few peppers and maybe the odd mushroom. And a sprinkle of those fresh herbs your mum grows on the windowsill.'

'You like cooking, don't you, Nick? Can you teach me, do you think? Only, Theo and Sam aren't very good at it, and if everyone keeps going away... and I don't really like mushrooms...' Hattie blinks hard. She looks very young, all of a sudden.

'No sweat, let's start tonight. Just need to sort that maniac out in the next bedroom, and we'll get going. What the f... I mean, what can he be doing in there?'

They set off to investigate, and she slips her hand into his. Nick begins to relax; he feels a bit safer now she looks like a little girl again. In the next room, Max is bouncing from one single bed to the next, and with each jump, the floor shakes, the bed hits the wall, and the light fitting bashes alarmingly on the ceiling. He is shouting along with the music, and doesn't notice the others until Nick switches it off.

'Hey! Who did that? Put it back on!' Max bellows. Nick puts his hands on his hips and goes for a stern look.

'You've got five minutes to tidy up in here, Max, and then

another ten to feed the pets, and then your dinner will be on the table. Come on, get a move on.'

Nick holds his breath; if Max refuses point blank to cooperate, they're done for. After a moment, Max climbs down.

'Hattie can feed the animals, I'm too little,' he says.

'Sorry, mate, Hattie's having a cooking lesson. She wants to make sure you lot don't starve, and you need to help her out. It's a really hard job, feeding a family. Pasta bake with tuna, crispy cheese on top, ready very soon if you get your finger out?'

Max heaves a huge sigh, and sets off at a gallop down the stairs, and Hattie and Nick high-five each other in relief.

'You were brilliant, Nick,' she says admiringly. 'He can be a right little shit when he wants to.'

'Hattie White! That's no way for a lady to speak!' Bloody hell, Nick's starting to sound like that Super-Nanny woman. She smiles, and takes his hand again.

'Sorry, Nick. Come on, I'm starving.' They head off to the kitchen at last. Nick's knackered already; this parenting business is no joke.

* * *

Supper is eventually served up in the kitchen; an enormous, cheesy, bubbling concoction, and then between them, Sam and Nick manage to get Max and Hattie into bed, and – unbelievably – asleep. At last, there's time for Sam to bring Nick up to date with the latest family crisis.

'So, Mum's friend Kate's gone off to try and get hold of my dad… and nobody's got any idea what happened to Gran – why she just keeled over like that – and nobody seems to know where Theo is, and while you were in with Max I had a call from the hospital. Mum reckons Gran's taken a turn for the worse, and I don't know what to do next. I can't go over there and leave the kids but I don't want Mum to be on her own.'

Sam's voice shakes a bit; he's only sixteen and Nick knows he's never been anywhere or done anything yet. He feels like smacking the younger boy in the teeth for a minute. How come he's had such a bloody easy life? Why should Nick do anything for the spoilt kid? But then he remembers why he's here and takes a deep breath.

'Right then, first things first. You need to go to the hospital. I can stay here. Have you got any money for a cab?'

Sam nods, still looking a bit pathetic, but as he gets to his feet, there's the sound of a car engine revving, dying and then doors slamming outside in the drive. Sam's face brightens and he dashes to the front door, flinging it wide.

'Dad! Oh, and... Kate?' He hesitates at the sight of the skinny woman with the sparkling eyes, standing beside his wandering parent.

'Yes, I found him and brought him home as fast as I could.'

Sam's dad and the woman exchange a glance. Nick is immediately suspicious. Their body language shows a lot more than they realise. Nick's good at that stuff. He watches people. He sees things they don't want anyone to see.

Sam seems to sense something too, but the beer takes the edge off his instinct and he's unsure what to do next. As they stand in the hallway, like a group of waxworks, there's the sound of another car approaching, and another set of wheels spins over the gravel, sending chippings flying over Kate's glossy paintwork. She frowns, but then recognises the driver.

'Poppy! I've been ringing you – where have you been?'

Nick's interest's really roused now. He's not come across this elusive fourth friend yet. She is the missing piece of Molly's jigsaw. He's met the churchy one – the one in hospital – she's a bit wet, but by all accounts this new one is the feistiest of them all.

Kate and Poppy hug, and Poppy smiles at Jake, showing two perfectly symmetrical dimples, one in each cheek. They are the sort of dimples that make you want to put a fingertip in each. Nick knows what that would feel like. His hands are in his pockets, waiting to remember those dimples.

'The wanderer returns, Jake?' Poppy says, wryly. 'Well done, Kate – mission accomplished.' Her voice is unusual, husky and with a weird sort of lilt. Nick feels sick, as if he's lost his balance. Poppy turns to him.

'So, you must be Nick? I don't know why we've not met before; have you been avoiding me?' She flutters her eyelashes as if she's trying to flirt, but then stops and stares. She moves closer. Nick flinches and looks at his feet. The off-balance feeling is getting worse. He wishes this woman would just go away.

'That's funny...' Poppy murmurs.

'What's funny?' asks Sam, touchy as a cat.

'Nick's got one green eye and one blue. I've seen that before. I've seen it four times.' She's very pale now.

'What are you talking about, Poppy? Whose eyes?' Kate obviously wants to get inside the house – her hand is just touching Jake's back, trying to move him forwards, but secretly stroking too.

'Those eyes. David Bowie, for one. My dad, for two,' says Poppy, in a small voice.

'Have you lost your marbles, Poppy?' says Jake. 'Look, my mum's in hospital, I need to get organised here and get going to see her. I finally got hold of our Matt, and he's on his way back from Portugal at last.'

'Uncle Matt's coming? Brilliant!' says Sam.

'Yeah, he'll be here soon. Get yourselves inside everyone, come on. Where's Molly? Is she already with Mum?'

Jake chivvies everyone towards the door, still looking for his wife. Poppy doesn't move, and soon there are just the two people left on the drive. Nick takes a deep breath and waits. He's been waiting for this moment for a long time, but he didn't know it was possible. Why isn't she dead? Poppy steps forward.

'And the other two with the strange eyes were twin boys. Kris and Will, they were called. Do those names ring any bells with you at all, Nick?'

The night air is chilly now but Nick feels warm all over.

'Mum?'

'Will?'

52

The house seems very empty after Jake leaves for the hospital. In all the emotional upheaval, Poppy can't quite remember who is where at the moment, but Sam must have gone with his dad, and Kate disappeared at the same time.

When Molly finally calls to say Daisy's passed away peacefully, Will and Poppy are halfway through their second bottle of Merlot, and have emptied the box of man-sized tissues. They've also made a fire, which has been useful for burning tissues and has stopped their teeth from chattering, but Poppy is a complete wreck.

They've talked about some of the reasons why she left them all, and about Poppy's time in hospital on the psychiatric ward, and a bit about Kris, but there are still grey areas that Poppy's afraid to mention yet. They're just beginning to discuss the other children when Molly rings. As she sobs out the news about Daisy, Poppy tries to be supportive but all she can think about is her own four children.

She hasn't allowed herself to give them this much thought for years, but the pain of leaving them has never really gone away. She doesn't know how to explain to this thin, angry boy in front of her that she did love them all – she *does* love them all. She'll never stop loving them.

Will is chain-smoking now, lying on the hearth rug. Molly will hate the smell in her best room but Poppy can't tell him not to smoke indoors. She can't tell him to do or not to do anything; she forfeited that right long ago.

Poppy grabs a pen, and scribbles a list of people that Molly wants her to ring with the news about Daisy; near the top of the list is Sarah Slater, who she has managed quite successfully to avoid since she stole the older woman's husband. Poppy was a different person then – thin as a supermodel with bleached white-blonde hair, very short and soft, like a brush. She used to pencil kohl all around her eyes and she had so many ear-piercings that it was a job to hold her head up some days.

She'd thought she was so cool then. Maybe she was? Now Poppy's hair is long, wild and auburn. The weight she put on so quickly in the hospital never went away after she stopped smoking and started eating instead, and she rather likes it, it's part of the new image. More normal; less edgy.

Poppy's curvy and comfortable these days, and she could never deprive herself of good food and wine now. The doctors say she's unusual because she drank like a fish, stopped for a year or two, and then started again in a less manic way without going completely over the top. She can't help wondering if this new medical crisis she's having is because of the drink. Still, life without wine would be depressing, and she's quite civilised these days, on the whole. The piercings have all but healed up and her make-up is a lot more subtle.

Sarah couldn't possibly recognise Poppy now, but she might twig if she hears her voice. It's supposed to be quite memorable.

Molly gives instructions for Poppy to speak to Theo (when

she reappears), Geoff, Rob Jennings, the Methodist minister and one or two other friends and relations, who will then activate the bush telegraph. By the time Molly returns, the world will know that Daisy is no longer in it. Poppy wonders how long it will take for all the travellers to return. The thought makes her catch her breath – Will has told her about Kris and their bet. Perhaps he'll ring his brother and tell him to come home too, wherever he is. Could it be that two of Poppy's sons might soon have forgiven her?

Will gets to his feet and comes over as she puts the phone down. They look at each other for a long time. He clears his throat – the recent tears have made his voice husky, just like his mother's.

'Do you want me to do some of these calls for you?' Poppy wishes he would call her Mum again, as he did when they met. She probably needs to earn it, though.

'We could maybe do them between us? I could really do with some help, Will.' He blinks at the unfamiliar name, but Poppy's not about to start calling him Nick – it took her ages to think of the boys' names, days of poring over a little book, rejecting Conrad, Marcus, Reuben and Barnabas, to list but a few. 'Sweet William' and 'Charismatic Kris' were just right for them, and they grew into their names beautifully.

Will was always smiling and keeping the peace and Kris was full of charm. They seemed joined at the hip in those days, even when they fought, which wasn't often. Shelley used to do a lot of my mothering as she got older, Poppy realises, guiltily. She was drinking seriously by then. Shelley became bossier and crosser the more Poppy drank. No wonder she got on everyone's nerves, but none of them could have coped without Shelley.

With hindsight, Poppy knows it was Oliver's birth that really tipped her over the edge. She had told Ken that there would definitely be no more, and she was giving the pill another try, while she waited to be sterilised. She doesn't know what went wrong.

Oliver was another screamer like his sister, never quiet for more than a few minutes at a time. He had colic all the time, drawing his little knees up in agony. Poppy stopped trying to feed him herself in desperation, but powdered milk made him even worse. Then the doctors said there was something wrong with him. Well, Poppy could have told them that from the first moment she saw him.

When Oliver was six weeks old Poppy had taken the car keys, walked out of the house and never returned. Even now, she has only a vague idea of where she went. She can't remember anything clearly until she woke up in a cell.

Eventually, she was released with a caution. She doesn't tell Will what the caution was for, there are some things that no one needs to know. After that, it was the psychiatric hospital, locked into a secure ward. It was a long time before she even remembered she had been married, let alone had four children.

To this day, Poppy doesn't understand why she eventually came back to this area, but being so much rounder in shape, and having such a different image made her feel invisible and safe. She secretly hoped that Sarah would still be living in the house that she had shared with Ken, because she wanted to know if Sarah had taken Ken back.

In her darkest times, Poppy had a mad hope that Sarah could have still loved Ken enough to give him another chance and might have taken over looking after the four children. A teacher would be ideal for that job – the thought had kept her going through many long nights. It was a ridiculous, bitter-sweet dream.

Anyway, of course that hadn't happened. Poppy had tried to

track Ken down; tried all sorts of ways of finding her kids, but every trail was cold. Will says it was because they were constantly on the move. Ken went from job to job, and county to county. Somehow it seemed to Poppy that the more time went by, the less she deserved to see them.

Her lowest ebb was on the twins' birthday when they were going to be thirteen. She doesn't know why that seemed so dreadful. Shelley would have been sixteen by then. She and Poppy never got on, even when she was small. Poppy hopes Shelley's not having to look after anyone but herself any more though. She was very much like her father – thought life wasn't fair and that everyone was having a better time than her. Poppy hopes she's found out that she was wrong.

Will begins to work through the phone calls, and Poppy makes sure to ask him to get Sarah's call out of the way first. Daisy's death really seems to have shaken him. He's pale and jittery as he speaks to one person after another, but he knows how to handle himself, and Poppy feels the first stirrings of pride in her son. It's amazing to be able to think that word without wanting to die.

After the calls, they give each other a smile of sheer relief, and then, realising how hungry they are, quickly rustle up beans on toast. They find that they both hate tomato ketchup but love brown sauce on beans. They also prefer lightly done and lavishly buttered toast, and strong, sweet tea. Is that a strange coincidence or did Poppy just feed him too much of this comfort food when he was small?

Somewhere in the course of the evening, the very beginning of a relationship is being born, but Poppy can feel how angry Will still is, and she almost welcomes it. She needs all of his anger, and more.

'Will, how did you recognise me?' Poppy finally finds the courage to ask.

'It was your dimples.'

'You used to...'

'Yes, I know.'

And slowly, as they sit opposite each other at the kitchen table, Will raises his two index fingers, and places one in each of the dips in Poppy's cheeks. She puts her hands over his, and time seems to stand still.

After a while, Poppy shakes herself and gently moves away. Will has been crying again, and she reaches for the kitchen roll to dry his tears. It's time to face the music.

'Will?'

'Mmm?'

'I've got to go home now; there are a few things I need to sort out.'

'Oh.' His shoulders droop. 'Is there anything else you want me to do for you?'

'How long is it since you saw your dad?'

'Um... I don't know – years and years. Why do you want to know that? He's nothing. He's even less than nothing, really.'

'I just wondered. I thought he'd see you right, that's all.'

'You're joking, aren't you? Dad said it was time we started looking after ourselves. He was retiring early, fed up with teaching, and he wanted a fresh start, apparently, without us kids holding him back.' Will laughs sarcastically. 'As if he ever let us stop him doing anything he wanted to do.'

Poppy shudders, remembering Ken's knack of going his own way. She should have known he'd never let a small thing like a dependent family tie him down. Well, as parents went, Will had been dealt a rubbish hand.

'Did he tell you where he was going?'

'Nah, he didn't want any of us following him and ruining his precious retirement. He reckoned he'd done his bit for us... been both father and m...' Will's voice tails off, and the anger is back. He begins to clear the table, crashing the dishes around until Poppy fears for Molly's kitchen.

'So you didn't know that he lived ten miles up the road from here?'

The clattering of pots stops suddenly. 'He doesn't, does he? Bloody hell.'

'Yes, it's true, unfortunately. I went to see him today.'

They look at each other, and the silence becomes uncomfortable. Will clears his throat.

'So, what happened? Is he still a sadistic, ignorant tosser?'

'Was.'

'What?'

'Was still all those things. He isn't anything now. I hit him with his mother's lamp.'

'You... you... killed him? W... why did you do that?' Will gazes at Poppy in disbelief. 'You'll never get away with it.'

'Well, he said he'd told you all that I was dead, and then he said that Oliver had gone to Australia with his new foster family. I didn't mean to do it, but I'm not sorry. I should have killed him years ago.'

'But you'll go to prison. You'll get life. They'll find you, for sure.'

'I know. So that's why I need to get back home. I guess the police will be there by now; I'm still his next of kin, and it won't take them long to put the pieces of the jigsaw together.'

'But Mum.' Poppy is breathless from the wave of happiness that the simple word sets in motion. 'You can't just go and walk straight into the trap. We've got to get you away from here!'

Oh, the bliss. Her son wants to save her. 'There's no point,

Will. I can't just run away. I'd have to hide forever, change my name, cut my hair, even go on a diet. No, I've got to get it over with.'

Poppy fumbles for her bloodstained coat and rolls it up tightly, shivering at the thought of the coming hours. Another cell. Well, it will have been worth it. The ecstasy of Will's support and the sheer vindictive triumph of having had the final word in an argument with Ken Slater are enough to get her through. And who knows how much longer she'd have had anyway?

'I'm coming with you, then.'

'You can't, my love. We promised to listen out for the kids.'

'I should be with you, Mum.'

'You're very sweet, but you should stay here to help Molly cope when she gets back.'

'I don't need to impress Molly now...' He stops, and looks horrified.

'What do you mean?'

There's a brief pause, and then the plan comes pouring out. How Will and Kris need a mum so badly they're prepared to make themselves homeless and go out on the road to find one. Poppy feels so battered she can hardly bear to look at her boy, but all this will have to wait.

'I must go, Will. Give me your mobile number. I'll let you know where they take me. They might not even be there yet.'

Bu Poppy knows better than that. And sure enough, she has a reception committee back at the flat.

53

Molly feels as if her heart is breaking. She's gone; lovely, funny, motherly Daisy, Molly's best friend, and the one who holds everything together when no one else understands.

Molly is holding Daisy's hand in both of her own, and looking at Jake and his brother Matt, who have their arms around each other and are weeping great gulping sobs. Daisy's hand is still faintly warm and Molly realises she's rubbing it gently, as if it's a cold day. The nurse pats Molly on the shoulder, and asks if they're all ready to move into a side room for a cup of tea.

'No rush, love... just when you feel you'd like to.' But Molly can tell the nurse wants them to go, so she can get the next stage under way. Molly can't cry yet, but she strokes her beloved mum-in-law's hair, squeezes her hand for the last time and gets up stiffly.

'Come on, guys – we'll go and have a nice cup of tea; we all need one.' Molly grins faintly even in the midst of her sadness – she sounds like Daisy already. Is she going to have to do all the mothering around here now? Suddenly it's all too much, and she ushers the others out of the room before the tears start in earnest.

As they sit in the visitors' room with some weak tea and broken digestives, Molly thinks about the evening that's nearly over. Rob had been right, their flash-in-the-pan bedroom experience had been just that, and she'd had no appetite for chips afterwards so he'd taken her back to the hospital and reluctantly left her there. Molly had needed to be alone with Daisy and to have time to process what had just happened.

Somehow, the brief time she and Rob had spent together receded in the teeth of the crisis with Daisy, who when she'd rung the hospital appeared to be going downhill quite fast, so that they were at least able to function like responsible adults, although by the time they reached the hospital car park, Molly was trembling so much that she wasn't sure how to get inside. She left Rob so hurriedly in the end that he looked like the last puppy in the shop, but all she could think about was Daisy.

When Molly got to Daisy's ward and saw the empty bed, she must have cried out, because a nurse came bustling over making soothing noises, and led her to the side room, where Jake sat watching his mum's chest rise and fall unevenly. He turned to face her, eyes lighting up.

'Molly – where the hell have you been? I needed you,' he blurted out and started to cry quietly, snuffling, and rubbing his eyes like Max after a telling off. 'Sam's here with me, but he went to ask them for an update – he'll be back soon. I missed you, Moll.'

Molly stood behind Jake with her hands on his shoulders, and looked at her beloved Daisy as she slept. She'd always been so much more than a mother-in-law. Surely she wouldn't leave them, especially now, when they needed her more than ever?

How could this precious friend be lying here in this silent room, struggling to breathe?

Listening to Daisy's laboured breaths was making Molly tight-chested in sympathy and she found it impossible to answer Jake's question, but just then, the door opened, and in came dapper, elegant Matthew, closely followed by Sam, and also another man so like Matt that they could have passed for brothers. The men wore matching, elegant black-framed glasses and both had closely cropped black curls.

Jake leapt to his feet and hugged his brother fiercely. The two of them looked down at Daisy with their arms still wrapped round each other. He moved forward instinctively – the other man was hesitating, unsure of what to do next. He looked as if his natural expression would be much jollier than this; the laughter lines around his eyes and mouth were deep and attractive and he had the beginnings of a paunch. His stubble was just obvious enough to be sexy without being contrived, and, like Matt, he wore a camel overcoat, long and flowing. Matt seemed to remember who he was with, and turned from the bed with a shy smile.

'Jake, Molly, Sam – this is Gordon. We're business partners, or we soon will be. We've bought a bed and breakfast place back in Brighton and I'm coming home. Gordon offered to come with me today... to...' He floundered as he saw Gordon's face fall, and tried again.

'Okay, I'm sorry – let's do it properly. We're not just business partners; we're life partners too. We're hoping to get married at Christmas. I was going to write...'

Sam opened his mouth wide, and Molly could see how desperately he was trying to find the right words. She stepped in to rescue the situation.

'Welcome, Gordon – this is great news!' No, too gushing.

Start again. 'I mean, we're really pleased to finally meet you – we wondered when Matt kept mentioning you in his emails... I mean we thought maybe... oh, I'm making a right balls-up of this.'

Matt and Gordon both laughed, then looked at each other guiltily and down at Daisy, who had finally opened her eyes and was watching the scene with interest.

'Matt?' she whispered, smiling her broadest smile.

He fell to his knees next to the bed, and Jake moved quickly over to the other side. Gordon and Molly stayed at the foot of the bed as Daisy's tired old eyes flicked from one to the other. She cleared her throat painfully and tried again.

'So... like Shaun then, in the end?' She was still smiling. Molly suddenly, urgently wishes Shaun was here to give them all one of his fantastic, lime-cologne-smelling hugs and make everything normal again. If anyone was needed here, it was their lovely friend, who always knew the right thing to say.

Matt smiled back and nodded at his mum, beckoning Gordon to come closer. Gordon approached the bed and bowed respectfully to his almost-mother-in-law, and she nodded back, approvingly.

'Happy, Matt?' Her voice was fading now. Matt leaned closer.

'Yes, Mum. More than happy. Oh, Mum, I've missed you so much.'

'Good boy. You'll be all right now.' She gave Gordon another look, part threat and part challenge, then gave a slow wink.

Matthew put his head down on his mother's shoulder at this, and she stroked his curls as he wept. She glanced over at Jake, who was trying to blink his own tears away.

'Happy, Sam?' Sam nodded, lost for words.

'And my Jake?' Daisy looked at Molly then, a long,

measuring stare that made her toes curl and her stomach clench.

'Yes, Mum,' Jake replied.

'Ha!' The explosive noise was shocking, and the nurse who had just entered the room came to Daisy's side, moving the men gently out of the way and checking her patient's pulse. Daisy closed her eyes and began to breathe more slowly.

'Not long now,' said the nurse.

'What? You don't mean she's going to... but I've only just got here!' spluttered Matt. At this, Gordon spoke for the first time, in the most seductive Scottish accent she had ever heard, with a low tone that matched his elegance perfectly.

'I don't think you can really argue with this one, Matt. Speak to your mum again and tell her you love her, while you still can.'

Matt, after a startled look, touched Daisy's face and said obediently, but with deep feeling, 'I love you, my wonderful, wonderful mum.'

Jake, crying openly now, said, 'Me too. Mum, please don't go?'

Daisy sighed raggedly and the room fell silent, but for the strange noises of four adults managing their tears as best they could; for the moment, both joined and separated by their pain.

54

This is all very confusing. Who is he now – Will or Nick? He supposes he's going to go back to being his real self. But why has he let that woman into his nice, organised life? Everything was going to plan. The scabs were healing, Molly was going to become his proper mother very soon, he was going to move into the spare room, and then, after a decent waiting period, into Theo's bed, by which time he'd be such a permanent fixture that even Sam wouldn't mind too much.

Now look at the state of him. Bleeding again, and his nails are in shreds. After all these years of not giving a stuff about the woman who left them all, Will's even let himself call her Mum. He must be raving mad. But it was the dimples that did it.

He'll never be able to forget sitting on her knee as a little boy and poking his fingers into them, making her laugh even when she was... no, don't go there. She looks so different though. Her hair used to be all soft and pale, and she was so skinny, like a bag of chisels, Nan used to say. These days she's round and cuddly, but the dimples are the same.

On top of this crazy reunion thing, there's the thought of

Daisy that keeps coming back to bug him. What if it was seeing Theo and Will that made her go and die like that? What if Molly finds out? How's Theo going to feel about having frightened her grandma to death? It's really freaking him out. There's only one thing for it now; he's going to have to ring Kris. There's no way he's up for doing all this emotional stuff on his own. It's time Kris came home anyway, wherever home is. Their mum needs them. She doesn't deserve them though.

55

Molly's sitting at the top of the hill by the statue, thinking how beautiful late September can be, and how painful the sunshine is when you feel so desperately sad all the time. There's something about the hint of a chill in the air, and the smell of wood smoke coming from the narrowboats chugging along the canal that makes her more melancholy than she's ever felt in her life, even without the obvious reasons.

The trees are swaying gently and there are dragonflies everywhere today, whizzing around Molly's head as she watches the boats, wishing she was on board, off on an adventure. Where would she go? Anywhere that's not here, really. It's all so difficult. She misses Daisy more every day.

It's easy to forget she's gone for a moment or two and reach for the phone to ring Daisy and update her on all the mad things that are happening in the family. Molly even got as far as picking up the phone and pressing Daisy's number this morning before she remembered, and the remembering is the worst part.

It's like straying into some parallel world of madness; in

some ways it's as if the disappearances never happened. Her mum and dad are back at the shop but Molly's got the feeling that Mum has her own agenda. She's just biding her time before she makes her next move. Dad is tiptoeing around her, making cups of tea, minding the shop without sloping off for a crafty smoke, and yesterday Molly even caught him washing up, but he doesn't look at all happy.

Back at home, Theo has settled back into her old routine, and so has Jake, although he's sleeping in the spare room at the moment. He didn't ask Molly, just picked up his memory foam pillow and his dressing gown and slunk off at bedtime. They were all so shattered by then that Molly would have happily slept in the garden.

Kate and Molly are avoiding each other for now. The funeral is tomorrow, and after that, there will be some reckoning to do. Rob has texted once or twice, but Molly hasn't answered – she doesn't know what to say to him yet.

The most earth-shattering of the new developments have been centred around Poppy – or Pamela, as she seems to be called. Pamela? That makes her sound like a sensible twin-set-and-pearls lady or a clerk in a solicitor's office, with low-heeled court shoes and tidy hair in a ponytail. Not mad ginger curls and a naughty laugh.

Apparently, when Poppy-Pamela left here, on the night Daisy died, she was arrested as soon as she reached her flat for what she did to Kenneth Slater. She was taken to the police station in Hopton where she collapsed in terrible pain and was rushed to the county hospital thirty miles away. Molly tried to get in to see her yesterday to get to the bottom of what's happened, but she was all woozy from an emergency operation, and the nurses wouldn't let anyone in.

If she'd thought quickly enough, Molly could have lied and

said she was her sister, but she didn't think of that until it was too late. She's going to try again today, and she'll think of some way of getting round the staff. No one around here seems to know the full story, but Nick has been allowed to see Poppy every day, with his brother, who suddenly appeared in the wake of Theo, the prodigal daughter.

It's like one of those daytime soaps, where, if you miss an episode, it takes weeks to catch up. What's happening to them all? And why would Poppy have brutally attacked Sarah Slater's ex-husband? Normally Molly would probably be able to think of a way of finding out in no time, but she can't seem to think about anything but Daisy.

The funeral director came round with his catalogues yesterday. He asked the family what colour shroud they'd like for the deceased. Molly couldn't believe what she was hearing, and laughed for quite a while before she realised he was serious. Apparently, people have strong preferences about this.

They chose apple green, for what it's worth. Daisy wasn't a pink shroud type of lady really. It was a difficult meeting. Jake and Matt were no use at all, but Gordon was brilliant. He kept Molly sane with his ironically raised eyebrows, and he chose the beautiful atmospheric music for the committal, even though the hymns were as traditional as they could manage.

Jake asked if the kids could be involved in the service but it was very hard to decide if they really wanted to, or if they felt obliged. In the end, Sam said he'd do a reading and Theo found a poem she thought Daisy would have appreciated. The little ones are not sure if they want to be at the funeral at all yet. Molly knows how they feel, but surely they should be there?

The minister was kind about it though, and said to explain really carefully to Max and Hattie what a funeral's really like, including the coffin, where it goes during the service, where it ends up, and so on. Molly thought they would know all that sort of thing somehow, but why would they? Max asked what's going to happen to his gran after the funeral, and Molly tried for quite a while to think of a nice way to say that someone's going to set fire to her. In the end she left the explaining to Jake; it's time he did some of that, one way or another.

Sighing, Molly picks up her phone, snuggles further into her coat and wanders back down the hill. All the boats have gone now, but she can see a man on his own trudging along the tow path. He's got a scarf pulled up around his ears and she can't see his face, but she knows it's Rob. He looks completely dejected.

Molly wonders if he'd wanted to use her as an excuse to leave Lydia. Maybe he just saw her as an escape route right from the start and that's all he cared about. When Jill comes back she's going to ask her why she's so anti-Lydia. Jill should be home soon, she's doing really well now.

She turns her face towards home, hoping Rob won't see her. Part of her is dying to run after him and let him wrap her in one of his enormous, loving hugs, but in her heart, Molly knows she can't deal with that at the moment. She needs to sort her own life out before she sees Rob again, and that's going to be difficult, because she can't help wanting to smother Jake with his special pillow every time she sees him.

Surely she must still love him if she's feeling so painfully jealous of Kate? But then why does she hate him so much when she's just as guilty as he is? She picks up speed; home is calling. The comfy sofa and chilled glass of wine will have to wait until she's been to the hospital to see Poppy. Only one glass though – tomorrow they'll say goodbye to Daisy and a hangover would be the last straw.

56

It's terrifying to be in hospital again after so long, but the nurses and doctors are amazing. Poppy is getting used to various new feelings; the first and most urgent one is that she might actually die much sooner than she'd expected, and the second is that she doesn't want to.

Next comes the fact that her boys are adorable, and they seem to be starting to thaw a bit. She can see her younger self in their sharp cheekbones and their individual hairstyles. They're kinder than she would have expected, given their upbringing.

It's strangely peaceful here; a limbo time. Poppy even likes the hospital food. It's all a bit of a dream world really, she can close her eyes and drift off to sleep any time she likes, and sooner or later some kind soul will come along and either tuck her in, administer some great drugs or bring a cup of tea.

The only thing they won't give her is a great big drink, but to be honest, she doesn't feel like alcohol just now; she has felt quite rough one way or another. Dr Crispin says Poppy has a fighting chance of getting over this stupid illness, maybe 60–65 per cent, and the operation she had was successful, so who knows? Poppy considered flashing some cleavage and giving him her address but then remembers she's trying to turn over a new leaf. She doesn't want her boys to think any more badly of her than they have done already.

Poppy gets the impression that everyone here expects her to be more worried about her health and the future, but it's really hard to think about anything else but the twins. They turn up every day, bringing whatever they can scrounge or buy with their benefit cheques; tatty flowers from the park, battered cakes from the reduced rack, and every day they become more precious to her. Will is still trying to be cool, when he remembers, and the sight of his poor ravaged arms makes his mother feel sicker than even the nastier drugs.

Kris is easier to hug, but both of them must still bitterly resent Poppy much of the time. Every now and then though, another possibility peeps out, and she desperately hopes that one day they'll see that they can love her again without losing face.

Poppy's building up to her big suggestion but it's too soon yet even to try to persuade the boys to move somewhere new with her. She doesn't care where it is – the only conditions are that it must be a place where none of them have ever been before, and it needs to be as far away as possible from Mayfield. France would be perfect, she thinks, but they will have to take it a step at a time. There are still issues to deal with here, and not only health ones.

The police interview keeps running through Poppy's head; she can't remember all the proper CSI-type language, but she gets the gist of it:

Bad Cop: 'So, Mrs Slater...'

Poppy: 'Oh no, I haven't been that for years, and I wish I never had been. Should never have married him, he should have stayed with that smug tidy wife of his – do you know Sarah Slater, by the way? Wish I'd have let her keep him.'

Good Cop: 'Of course you're not Mrs Slater, my colleague meant to give you your current name, which is, I believe, Ms Take.'

Poppy (still woozy from anaesthetic): 'Yes, it definitely was, ha ha ha ha…'

Bad Cop: 'I beg your pardon?'

Poppy: 'A mistake! Worst one of my life, as it happens.'

Good Cop: 'Let's start again from the beginning.'

Bad Cop (clearing his throat officiously): 'You are Ms Pamela Anne Take, I believe?'

Poppy: 'Ha ha ha, Pam-a-Take, or sometimes Pamcake, that's what they used to call me at school, ha ha ha…' (What can she say? That stuff they gave her was mind-blowing.)

Bad Cop: 'Did you visit Mr Kenneth Slater on the night before last, and during that visit cause him grievous bodily harm?'

Poppy: 'You what?'

Good Cop: 'Did you visit your ex-husband and do him some damage? Think very carefully before you answer. Your solicitor is here to support you.'

Poppy (proudly, with a beaming smile for the pallid little man sitting on the edge of his seat in the corner): 'Oh, yes, I certainly did. I hit him with the hideous lamp. I'm very glad he's dead, too.'

This could have been a really bad moment, but it turns out that she didn't bash the slimy little git quite hard enough and Kenneth Slater is actually in the next ward, well on the way to recovery. Bastard!

57

Home at last, Molly is lying on the sofa with a mug of tea and Jake's sitting on the hearth rug in front of the fire with the cats curled up nearby. It looks like the perfect domestic scene – cosy lamplight, peaceful music playing. It's a shame life isn't quite as it seems.

At least the children are in bed, or safely in their bedrooms at any rate. Molly feels a surge of relief that they're all where they should be for once, and is sad to think that these days of knowing where they all are at bedtime will soon be at an end. How will she cope with the university years, if that's what they choose to do? What will the empty nest syndrome be like? She sighs, and Jake glances at her warily.

'Okay, Moll?'

'Nope – you?' He grins, and gives their standard reply.

'Nope.'

How will it be if they separate, and Molly can't share these silly traditions with Jake any more? Who will rub her legs when she gets cramp in the night? Who will she cuddle when everything gets too much? Who will understand her jokes? Who will talk her private language? Against her will, she starts to sniffle. Jake looks up again, alarmed now. He takes a deep breath.

'Moll, I need to talk to you.' She nods encouragingly, and he carries on.

'Do you really want us to split up? Because, even though everything is bloody awful at the moment, I really don't want to lose you. I know I've been stupid... and I think maybe I'm not the only one?' Molly can't look at him now, but he keeps talking, regardless.

'Yes, well... never mind all that. I've been thinking. Do you remember when we first got married, and I used to do all the cooking?'

Does she remember? Is he mad? Of course she does – it was wonderful. Molly used to come home to all sorts of delicious smells coming from their tiny kitchen. They lived in a terraced cottage in those days and the gas cooker only had two burners working, but Jake used to make the most amazing concoctions. They were so broke that he would only shop at the end of the day to pick up all the bargains so there were some strange combinations of food in those days, but everything was delicious, or if it wasn't, she's blanked it out.

'Yes, you were a brilliant cook in those days, Jake – why did you stop?'

'I think it was when I went over to working shifts; I never seemed to be at home when you were, and then the kids started arriving and you were at home anyway so you just took over.' They look at each other, remembering those days. 'Anyway, I've been thinking. My redundancy letter was waiting for me when I got back from Norfolk, but what with Mum and everything, I didn't get round to opening it till today. I finish at the end of the month.'

Molly catches her breath – poor Jake; all those years of

faithful service to the company and they just send a crumby letter. She's outraged for him.

'The buggers! Can't you contest it? Why should *you* be chosen?'

'Why shouldn't I? And I don't want to appeal against the decision; I can't wait to go.'

'Really? But what will you do?'

'Ah, now that really depends on you, Moll. I think if we're going to stay together, there's only one way we can do it. That's if you do want to hear my plan?' He looks at Molly properly now, and she looks back, suddenly sure that she doesn't want to be without him, even if it's going to be very hard to rebuild what they had before. She nods again, and he sighs with relief.

'Well, that's the first part of the battle... now the hard bit...'

Jake outlines his scheme to sell up their home and move to the Norfolk coast. He explains the idea well – he must have been practising – and by the time he runs out of steam, Molly's almost convinced.

'It does sound like the best thing for you and me, away from the... erm... distractions... but will the kids settle? And what about my mum and dad? And what about money? Won't it be more expensive to live near the sea? And we might take ages to get jobs.'

'Well, that was why I was talking to you about the cooking – I want to buy a little café or a bistro and start up on my own. I've been experimenting with all sorts of different recipes while I've been with Geoff.'

'Wow – what a great idea!' Molly thought Geoff had put on a few pounds, for saying he was supposed to have been worrying about finding her mum. 'Have you got anywhere in mind?' She surprises herself with her enthusiasm, and Jake grabs both her hands.

'Yes, I have; I've seen somewhere to let, and it's right on the sea front. It needs a lot of work doing to it, but it's got loads of potential. It could be a goldmine. And you know, there'll be quite a bit of Mum's money too when everything's sorted.'

'You're kidding? I thought she only just had enough to live on?'

'Yes, so did I, but apparently she got quite a good lump sum from the insurance when Dad died, and Matt's been secretly investing it for her, so we'll have enough to move, and to rent the café for a few months, if we're careful. Matt says she didn't want to tell us in case the stock market went pear-shaped again and we were cross with her.' It takes a while for this to sink in. Is Molly really ready to uproot the family?

'Would my mum and dad be welcome to come and stay whenever they liked?'

'Better than that – they'll probably come with us. Your dad loves it there. He had a hard time tearing himself away from the folk club and he can have a part-time job at the pub any time he likes, apparently. He thinks it's time they got rid of the shop and your mum had a chance to enjoy herself for a change. I don't think she'll put up too much of a fight.'

'What about my friends? Poppy and Jill will need some-where to go while they recuperate.' She doesn't mention Kate. No need to rock the boat just now. That can wait.

'No problem – we'll make sure we have space for visitors, and we can always have the caravan moved into the garden for the overflow if they all want to see us at once. We can take them sailing, or windsurfing, or anything they like.'

Molly gazes at her previously unsociable husband. Has he really changed as much as all that? It doesn't seem possible, somehow.

'Jake, are you sure? You're not just saying all this to get me to agree to the move?'

'No, I mean it, Moll. I'll do anything to keep us together but we can't do it here. The kids will adjust. I even checked online if the schools were good. We can rent a house for a while, till we see where we want to live. Things will change.'

The idea is definitely taking shape. A whole new life, away from the temptations and memories of Mayfield. The sea on her doorstep. Maybe the chance to take up her music again? She could get a job in a school; long-suffering people to teach the clarinet and the keyboard and so on are always in short supply.

Things will change. The words echo round Molly's head. It will be hard work, rebuilding their marriage and even if it's fixed, it might not be wonderful. But for now, just enough will do. It will do very well.

She gets up and stretches luxuriously in the firelight. Outside, the moon is shining down. Molly turns up the music. She's been listening to some of Poppy's CD collection. 'The Prettiest Star' is just beginning.

'Will you dance with me, Jake?' she asks, holding out her hand.

'Huh?'

'You said things will change. Well, this is the first one. I want to dance in the moonlight.'

'Don't let me stop you.'

'With my husband.'

He raises his eyebrows but gets to his feet and takes her hand. 'You know I don't do dancing, Moll.'

'And I can't windsurf, but I don't mind having a go sometime.'

He grins and opens the patio door to the garden. As the music builds up its pace, they step out onto the lawn. At first, Jake treads on Molly's toes and can't quite decide where his hands should go, but soon they settle into the rhythm, arms around each other's waists.

'Molly?' Jake's voice isn't much more than a whisper.

'Yes?'

'Can I move back into our bed again tonight?'

She hesitates before she nods, but only for a second or two. Jake's breath is warm on her face as he bends to kiss her. The song ends but Molly doesn't notice. This new start is definitely not going to be *just enough*. It shows all the signs of doing very well. Very well indeed. Molly and Jake carry on dancing in the silence of the night as the moon shines down on them. Their arms tighten around each other and, just for now, the world slips away. Tomorrow can take care of itself. Tonight is for loving, and for dancing under the moon.

* * *

MORE FROM CELIA ANDERSON

Another book from Celia Anderson, *A New Lease of Life*, is available to order now here:

www.mybook.to/NewLeaseBackAd

ACKNOWLEDGEMENTS

It's been a very strange experience revisiting a book I began writing way back in 1996. I was on the brink of a new career as a teacher, but at almost forty years old, it soon became clear that before I could begin training, a year's refresher course in studying was desperately needed. The Access course was a steep learning curve, but the best part was the creative writing module. A wonderful tutor called Pat Free (who I've tried to find to thank since then but had no success) inspired me to try writing in various different genres, but the one that stuck, contemporary fiction, was sparked by an assignment to write the first chapter of a novel.

The story quickly came to life, originally called 'Something for Molly', but over the next few years, my life as a busy teacher didn't leave much headspace for my own writing. I wrote numerous plays with the children and, in the odd hours left, plugged away at the book, sometimes forging ahead, other times neglecting it for months. Eventually, in 2006, life took a very sudden, sad turn when I was widowed for the first time. In the following months, I went back to the computer keyboard as a kind of therapy, and eventually Molly's story was published in... I think... 2012.

So, the thanks for this one go way back. To Pat Free, wherever she may now be, for the kick-start to a life I can't now imagine being without. To the brilliant Francesca Best and everyone at Boldwood for giving Molly a second chance to be out there in the world. To the book's first editor back then, the very lovely Christine McPherson, still an online friend and a great supporter of every book since that time.

To Cecily Blench for her copyediting and Rachel Lawston for the beautiful cover.

And a message to anyone who's read this before and fancied a re-run – who knew Friends Reunited would disappear without trace and giant yellow phone books would be no more? It's a different world in quite a few ways!

Finally, thanks to my lovely agent, Laura Macdougall, who bravely ploughed through my backlist and as always, has my back, and to my amazing family who have recently had to listen to me ramble on about how weird it is to work on a book that feels like stepping back into another life. Weird, but kind of cathartic. It's good to see Molly enjoying a whole new moondance. And if you get the chance, please do join her.

ABOUT THE AUTHOR

Celia Anderson is a top ten bestselling author of women's fiction. She writes uplifting golden years fiction for Boldwood.

Sign up to Celia Anderson's newsletter and get a FREE short story!

Follow Celia on social media:

facebook.com/CeliaAndersonAuthor
instagram.com/cejanderson
x.com/CeliaAnderson1
goodreads.com/CeliaAnderson

ALSO BY CELIA ANDERSON

Life Begins at 50!

A New Lease of Life

Dancing Under the Moon

BECOME A MEMBER OF

THE SHELF CARE CLUB

The home of Boldwood's
book club reads.

Find uplifting reads,
sunny escapes, cosy romances,
family dramas and more!

Sign up to the newsletter
https://bit.ly/theshelfcareclub